Wit... ...pped forward to greet the sexy siren before him. He brought Jessica Harrington to him for what he'd planned to be a quick, brotherly hug. But her warmth seared him—and he ended up holding her close. His mouth felt bone-dry as he pecked her cheek. Weston couldn't believe this was the same person he'd once taunted and ribbed unmercifully. Weston cringed when he thought of how he had nearly torn off her pigtail.

It had shocked Weston to see that Jessica was no longer the pudgy, clumsy, tomboyish teenager he'd remembered. The ugly duckling had turned into a magnificent, graceful swan!

Knowing the way they *hadn't* gotten along as kids, Weston wasn't so sure they could be amicable as adults. But one thing he knew for sure. If they were going to be thrown together every single day and night for a week, he had better find a way to hide his newfound attraction to her....

LINDA HUDSON-SMITH

was born in Canonsburg, Pennsylvania, and raised in Washington, PA. She furthered her educational goals by attending Duff's Business Institute in Pittsburgh, PA.

In 2000, after illness forced her to leave a successful marketing and public relations career, national bestselling author Linda Hudson-Smith turned to writing as a healing and creative outlet.

Linda has won several awards: a Gold Pen award, numerous *Shades of Romance Magazine* awards, and an African-American Literary Show award. She is an *Essence* bestselling author. Linda was nominated for two Emma awards and a Career Achievement award by *Romantic Times BOOKreviews*. She is a member of Romance Writers of America and the Black Writers Alliance.

For the past seven years Hudson-Smith has served as the national spokesperson for the Lupus Foundation of America, making Lupus awareness one of her top priorities. She travels around the country delivering inspirational messages of hope. Linda was awarded the key to the city of Crestview, Florida, for her contributions.

The mother of two sons, Linda shares a residence with her husband, Rudy, in League City, Texas. To find out more about this extraordinary author go to her Web site at www.lindahudsonsmith.com.

FORSAKING ALL OTHERS

LINDA HUDSON-SMITH

 **KIMANI PRESS™**

ISBN-13: 978-0-373-86045-6
ISBN-10:   0-373-86045-5

FORSAKING ALL OTHERS

Copyright © 2007 by Linda Hudson-Smith

www.kimanipress.com

Printed in U.S.A.

Dear Reader,

I sincerely hope that you enjoy reading *Forsaking All Others* from cover to cover. I'm very interested in hearing your comments and thoughts on the romantic story featuring Jessica Harrington and Weston Chamberlain, who find love despite their attempts to thwart their parents' lifelong hopes and dreams of their children marrying each other one day.

Please enclose a self-addressed, stamped envelope with all your correspondence and mail to: Linda Hudson-Smith, 16516 El Camino Real, Box 174, Houston, TX 77062. Or you can e-mail your comments to LHS4romance@yahoo.com. Please also visit my Web site and sign my guest book at www.lindahudsonsmith.com.

Dedication

This novel is dedicated to the loving memory of
Michael Bruce Randolph, my friend of 40 years.

Michael, your warm and loving presence will be forever
missed by all of us who love you. May you rest in peace,
safe in the hull of God's unchanging hands.

Sunrise: August 28, 1951
Sunset: March 18, 2007

This novel is dedicated to the latest addition to
the Smith family; a sweet little bundle of joy.

Our 6th grandchild and 2nd granddaughter.

Synia Justice Smith
Born: May 1, 2006

Chapter 1

Stunning twenty-five-year-old Jessica Harrington couldn't believe the beauty of the Aspen, Colorado, resort areas. She and her parents, Roman and Sahara, and her older sister, Jennifer, and her husband, Samuel Ellington, were actually spending the Christmas and New Year holidays in this wonderland. The other family members had been to Aspen several times, during different seasons of the year, but Jessica's acrophobia, her fear of heights, had kept her away.

Jessica had finally learned to conquer her fear of heights and close spaces. There was no place or tight space on earth she wouldn't now dare to venture to. Flying in an airplane had never been a problem for her. Driving up into the mountains and dealing with heights had been a major one, though, for as far back as she could remember. Just getting up on a six-foot ladder had once scared her silly.

The plush condominium/town house resort of Snowmass was located in the heart of Snowmass Village at Aspen. Base elevation of Snowmass Mountain was 7,870 feet, with a vertical rise of 2,030 feet.

Not so long ago those were heights Jessica wouldn't have even considered taking on. Now, she couldn't be happier to have made the trip to this winter paradise. She could hardly wait for all the festive holiday events to begin.

The Harrington family was joining up with Roman's lifelong best friend, Jacque Chamberlain, his wife, Sandra, and their only son, twenty-six-year-old Weston. The two families would share separate three-bedroom town houses across the corridor from each other.

Jennifer and Samuel had leased a two-bedroom condo in the same resort, in the opposite building. A couple of other families were also joining the small group, good friends of the Chamberlains, who were not due to arrive in Aspen until the day after Christmas. The Carlyle and Holloway families and their two teenagers, a boy and girl, had also leased town houses at Snowmass.

Sahara stepped out on the balcony and lowered her arm around Jessica's shoulder. "Isn't it breathtaking way up here? Are you okay with the heights?"

Jessica reached up and patted her mother's hand. "I'm fine. It's a wonderful vision to behold. The stark whiteness is near blinding. Haven't decided to try skiing, though. That may be a little too much bravery for my first trip up such a high mountain. Sledding sounds more interesting to me as an alternative to skiing. I think it'll be fun."

"Everything we do will be fun. The Chamberlains should be here any minute. Are you nervous about seeing Weston? You guys haven't been together since your teens."

Jessica shrugged with nonchalance. "Nothing to be nervous about. He's probably the same nerdy guy he was back then. We never did see eye to eye. I don't expect a different outcome this trip."

"Oh, Jess, I hope you don't act nasty with him. Pulling hair is what most boys do at that age. Are you still holding the pigtail incident against him?"

"Incident, my foot! He nearly scalped me, pulling my hair so hard. But I don't hold it against him." Jessica sighed. "Hope I meet an interesting guy up here, but there won't be anything happening between Wes and me. That's Dad and Mr. Jacque's dream. Not ours. I'm only here out of all the guilt you guys made me feel about going away with my girlfriends for Christmas."

"Guilt was not our intent. That's nonsense. We've never been apart for Christmas. We're not starting now. Just concentrate on having a good time. Don't put restrictions on yourself. I'm going in to wake up Dad. He wants to be up and dressed when Jacque and Sandra arrive. Jenny and Sam will be over any minute. We'll all go to dinner once everyone gets here. Besides, you and Wes might find something in common. Who knows?" Sahara kissed her daughter's cheek before stepping back indoors.

"Fat chance," Jessica mumbled under her breath. The only thing she and Weston had in common was their intense dislike for each other. She hoped he had at least grown up some. His immaturity had gotten on her nerves the last time they'd seen each other in Ocho Rios, Jamaica.

Jessica shivered as a blast of cold air hit her head-on, her hazel eyes watering at the shock. "Wow!" She didn't waste another minute getting back inside where a warm fire roared in the stone fireplace. She hadn't been used to this type of cold weather where she grew up, although California did get lots of snow up in the mountainous areas.

The Christmas music playing on the CD player was so nice. Jessica loved Nat King Cole's mesmerizing voice. Her parents always played songs by him, Johnny Mathis and other singing greats during the holidays. This was the season her family practically lived for all year long. They had never visited a ski resort area at Christmastime because Jessica had only recently conquered her fear of heights. Seeing the beauty of the mountains had her repeatedly thanking God for what He had helped her accomplish.

While Jessica warmed her hands by the fire, rubbing them together vigorously, she enjoyed the blazing show of colors. The oranges, yellows, reds and warm blues helped to further light up the romance of the candlelit room. Her mother had set out most of the candles she'd brought along from home soon after they had checked into the resort. Sunset had occurred over thirty minutes ago.

The sound of a key being inserted into the door caused Jessica to jump involuntarily. She figured it had to be Jennifer and Sam. Sahara must have heard the key, too, because she had just come running into the room.

It always gave Jessica a warm feeling when her mother was affectionate with her and Jennifer. Neither of their parents had ever failed to show unconditional love for the girls. Sahara and Roman also thought of Samuel as a son, not just a son-in-law. They had wanted at least one male child, but they still felt incredibly blessed to have had such beautiful, healthy daughters.

Jessica had light hair and was fair-complexioned like her father. Jennifer had the same olive skin color and dark hair as her mother. Everyone knew they were sisters despite their hair and skin coloring. Two years apart in age, both Jessica and Jennifer had sparkling hazel eyes and full-dimpled smiles.

"Hey, Jess," Jennifer sang out, "how you doing with the heights so far?"

"So far so good. It hasn't bothered me yet."

"Then it probably won't." Samuel crossed the room and gave Jessica a warm hug. "Proud of you, sis."

"Thanks, Sam. I'm proud of me, too."

"We're all proud of you," Sahara said, smiling brightly at Jessica.

The hard knock on the door caused Jessica to speed from the room. This time she was sure it was the Chamberlains. She had intended to comb her hair and put on fresh makeup long before they had arrived. Her face felt naked and a tad raw. For sure, she would have to keep her face moisturized against the cold weather. Sunblock protection was also a must. The cold air outside had done more than freeze her tail off.

All the animated greetings could be heard from the bedroom where Jessica repaired her makeup. The love between her father and Jacque Chamberlain was amazing. The men had grown up on the same street in southern Cali-

fornia and had been as close as brothers. Amos and
Gardenia Harrington, Roman's parents, had treated Jacque
like a son, making him very welcome in their home.
Jacque's mother had been ill a good bit of his youth so he
had spent a lot of time with the Harringtons. After she'd
died when he was seventeen, they had taken him in. His
father was a long-distance trucker and had lived on the
road a good bit of the time, even more after his wife had
died.

Roman and Jacque had also attended the same college
and had ended up working in the same profession. The two
men had made their fortunes in real estate and had high
hopes of merging their two companies in the near future.
They also still hoped that Jessica and Weston would one
day merge their families in holy matrimony.

Jacque planned to move back to California from New
York City within the next year or so. He had grown tired of
the harsh winter weather and longed to be back under the
extremely agreeable Southern California sun. He had only
moved to New York because his wife had wanted to be near
her parents. Sandra's wishes were his commands. Jacque had
often said he lived to please his wife and only son, Weston.

After taking one last glance in the mirror, Jessica headed
for the bedroom door. She couldn't wait to get through the
trauma of seeing Weston. She hated that she had to be
around him for the next ten days, but she'd do anything to
make her parents happy. Anything but marry the man her
father and his best friend had in mind for her. The two
friends had always said their kids would marry. Jessica
didn't even think Weston was marriage material, sure that
he had grown up only to become all into himself.

Jessica was pulled into the warm embrace of Jacque and then Sandra before she had barely stepped into the room. She had seen them a couple of years ago, when they had visited in California. They were really nice people. Like her parents, they were big on doling out loads of love and affection.

Weston had the most stunned looked on his face as he stepped forward and brought Jessica to him for what he had planned on as a quick hug. Her warmth went straight through him—and he ended up holding her longer than anticipated. His mouth felt bone-dry as he affectionately pecked her on the cheek. He couldn't believe this was the same person he used to taunt and rib unmercifully. Weston cringed when he thought of how he had nearly torn off her pigtail.

It had shocked Weston to see that Jessica was no longer the pudgy, clumsy, tomboyish teenager he remembered. The ugly duckling had turned into a magnificent swan, beautiful and graceful. He was so taken with her, but he had to hide it for fear of her shooting him down.

It wasn't as though Jessica and Weston had gotten along famously as children; he wasn't so sure they could be amicable as adults. The two of them thrown together every single day and evening for the next ten days would make it doubly hard for him to hide his wild attraction to her. Weston could only hope Jessica was as sweet as she was beautiful. Would wonders never cease!

Jessica clearly remembered Weston as a gangly, acne-faced, nerdy teenager, one who had possessed very little personality, if any at all. She nearly fainted when she first laid eyes on the drop-dead gorgeous, magnificent specimen he had turned into. It was then Jessica admitted that deep down inside she had always had a serious crush on Weston, though the feelings on his part had never been mutual.

Oh, how beautiful are those long lashes and dreamy eyes? She tried hard not to stare at him. It was obvious to her that the boy was in the gym on a regular basis. Muscles were bulging in all the right places on his rock-hard anatomy. When had he been blessed with such dark, softly piercing eyes and full, pouting lips? Her new attraction to him was as instant as his had been to her. His curly hair looked soft and silky, making her desperately want to drag her fingers recklessly through the strands.

Jessica tried hard to hide the tumultuous feelings inside her. She knew she would have constant thoughts of him whether they were together or apart. She knew for a fact she'd find it pretty hard to sleep at night with him right across the corridor. Thank goodness they weren't sleeping in the same town house. That had been suggested initially. Jessica had been the one to protest the arrangement vehemently, vowing not to make the trip to Aspen if she had to sleep in the same space with the nuisance of a boy she recalled all too well. Now she had to wonder.

As if Jessica and Weston were the only two people in the room, they had become oblivious of the other family members, until Roman had asked if everyone was ready to go to dinner. She was happy for the timely interruption. Her uncontrollable thoughts had taken her to places she had once dreamed of on a daily basis, pining away for one

Weston Chamberlain. Her thoughts about him had been torrid ones. That hadn't changed.

In the car with her parents, Jessica suddenly felt so darn empty. It was as if someone had suddenly snatched away from her the warmth of intense sunlight that had nearly blinded her earlier. Her reaction to Weston was impossible. How could she feel like this about someone she didn't even like? Oh, she liked him, all right. Jessica hated admitting how strong her liking was for him. Jessica couldn't believe how silly she felt. The passage of time hadn't changed a thing.

At the restaurant, it really surprised Jessica when Weston sat down in the wingback chair next to hers at the long table. There were so many empty chairs he could have sat in, but he had opted for the one closest to her.

The others in the Harrington party were all milling about, pointing out their favorite points of interest. The restaurant had high, vaulted ceilings and a massive wood-burning stone and marble fireplace, a definite focal point from nearly every seat in the house. A large rustic bar also made an interesting topic of conversation. The latest tunes were piped in over a state-of-the-art audio system.

"So, Jessica, how've you been? Long time no see for us."

Too long, she thought, wishing she had some kind of control on her wretched emotions. She found it so hard to believe her heart was still going gaga over this man. "I know. Busy with work and all. Since we're both in real estate, you know how long the hours can be. Sometimes I overdo it. I always find one more thing to do before I go home. What's up with you?"

"Pretty much the same as it is with you. I stay busy at the job. Guess that's why I don't have much of a social life."

What was Weston trying to tell her, if anything? Did very little social life mean no steady girl? Jessica had to wonder. She didn't know how to respond to what he had said, so she said nothing. She wouldn't be surprised if women were lined up to go out with him. Weston was really *that* good-looking and he hadn't annoyed her once thus far.

As the rest of the party came and took seats at the table, Jessica and Weston's conversation was abruptly interrupted. This time she wasn't too relieved about the disruption, but she then figured they had lots of time to catch up on each other's lives. She was certainly eager to find out everything she could about the new and improved Weston.

A waiter and waitress came up as soon as everyone was settled down at the table. Menus were quickly passed around to each of the patrons. The waitress took the drink orders and then left the food orders up to the waiter. Teamwork was the obvious intent.

In a matter of minutes everyone at the table had ordered their meals.

Jessica was impressed by the quick service. She had been to restaurants with large groups of people, where it had seemed to take forever to get the orders taken. When she had looked around the place a moment ago, she saw there was no shortage of waiters and waitresses. Understaffing was a big problem in a lot of restaurants, even the extremely popular ones. It was not a problem here at the illustrious Rustic House Restaurant.

Conversations flowed with relaxed ease as the diners sipped on hot or cold drinks while waiting for the meals to be served. Roman and Jacque were chatting and laughing to beat the band. Sahara and Sandra were also catching up, talking up a storm.

Jessica loved seeing her parents so happy. She knew for a fact her father had never been as involved with a male friend as he was with Jacque. He had a few good golf buddies, as well as his bowling-league friends, but his relationship with Jacque was unrivaled. The two men and their wives saw each other three or four times a year at realty conferences or while vacationing in exotic locales. Each couple was often a guest in the other's home. Her parents loved to visit the Chamberlains in New York City.

Weston had a hard time keeping his eyes off Jessica. The changes in her were remarkable. Perhaps she had always been pretty. In his adolescence he might not have been able to see it. It had taken him a long time to get interested in girls, period. Most guys had had several different personal relationships by age seventeen, which was the age at which Weston had had his first date. A young lady had asked him to take her to her senior prom. That evening had been one disaster after another. Weston hadn't bothered to learn to dance, and his date had been furious with him when she had figured it out.

Weston had tried hard to get it going, though, but his soulful coordination hadn't come together quite yet. Rhythm didn't move into his body until a couple of years later. Now Weston could hold up against the best on the dance floor.

The variety of great music made Weston think about the possibility of dancing with Jessica. There should be plenty of opportunities. The formal New Year's Eve gala sponsored by their parents was to be held in one of the resort ballrooms. A slow tune worked best for him, though he also loved to dance to faster-paced music.

Holding Jessica close to his body was right up there on the top of Weston's list of desires. She had fitted perfectly into his arms when he'd hugged her earlier. His limbs seemed to have wrapped around her of their own accord, holding her much longer than he had anticipated. It had felt good, too. The feelings surging through him had been wild.

The delicious scents from the food caused Jessica's mouth to water. She hadn't realized how hungry she was until now. The family had had lunch right after they had arrived at the resort, eons ago.

Jessica was a perfect size-six petite, but the girl had a ravenous appetite. However, the only fried foods she ever ate were French fries and the occasional fish sandwich. The weight problems she had had in her youth had one day up and disappeared, without her resorting to dieting.

Weston gently nudged Jessica. "Pass the salt, please."

That little insignificant touch from Weston had Jessica's heart doing flip-flops. But it was those dark, dreamy eyes that made crazy things happen inside her body. "Sure." She picked up the saltshaker closest to her and handed it to Mr. McHunk. In her mind she had already referred to him as such a few times.

As Jessica looked over at Jennifer and Samuel, she had

to smile. The two sweethearts had been in love since junior high school. They were the same exact age, twenty-seven. She had often prayed to find the kind of relationship they had, with no immediate interest in forever after. She thought thirty was the perfect age for women to marry and thirty-three or even a bit older for men. That gave her five years to find her Mr. Right. Jessica wasn't sure she wanted kids, but she hadn't ruled them out, either.

The grilled Chilean sea bass Jessica had ordered tasted so scrumptious she closed her eyes to savor the expertly prepared seafood. Her salad greens were fresh and crisp; the tomatoes had to have been grown in the Garden of Eden. They were the most flavorful ones she had ever tasted. The others also seemed pleased with their meals, Jessica noted. Her family were huge seafood lovers, evident by what each one had ordered. Roman and Samuel's favorite was grilled salmon. Sahara and Jennifer were into the different varieties of shellfish.

Weston had ordered a huge porterhouse steak that looked grilled to perfection. He had also ordered a Caesar salad, loving the tangy taste of the dressing. His baked potato was stuffed with everything imaginable. He had dug right into his meal as soon as Roman had passed the blessing.

Jessica would love to eat steak, but she had a hard time digesting beef. The only ingredients she liked on her baked potatoes were butter and sour cream, at a minimum. Jessica could tell that Weston was enjoying what he had put on his.

"Mind if I taste your fish, Jess?" Weston asked. "It looks good."

Jessica was once again surprised. She didn't object to giving Weston a bite, but how was she supposed to serve it to him? It was out of the question for her to put some on her fork and feed it to him. Weston handed Jessica a small bread plate and indicated for her to drop it there. She was glad he had solved her dilemma. She didn't have to look up to know all eyes had been on her, anticipating how she might respond.

On purpose Jessica refused to make direct eye contact with anyone in her family. The look in her eyes might just be a dead giveaway for how besotted she had become with Weston. No matter what her misguided feelings were for him, they just couldn't happen as a couple. That was like falling right into the trap their parents had set for them as mere babes in arms. No one with any common sense ever walked into a visible trap.

The small group had moved over into the lounge, where several tables for two had been put together. There was no odd man out.

Jessica was highly aware that she and Weston were the only two single people in their party. She was sure it had been by design, that both sets of parents were still hopeful they would become an item.

Jessica had thought about asking her best friend Jarred Wilkerson, to come on the trip with her. Her parents would've done their level best to talk her out of it. She and Jarred enjoyed each other's company tremendously. Each valued their special friendship. He was happily single now after recently breaking off his two-year relationship with Melanie Holt. However, he and Jessica weren't remotely interested in each other in a romantic way. They just hung out together a lot.

On the other side of the coin, Jessica had hoped and prayed Weston would bring along a lady friend. That hope had vanished in the same moment her mother had informed her he was coming to Aspen alone. Now she was glad he hadn't brought along a date and that she hadn't invited Jarred. She liked having Weston's undivided attention. Of course, he hadn't paid her an ounce of attention since his plate had first arrived, other than to ask her for a bite of her fish. It looked as if she had a meaty rival.

Jessica chuckled inwardly at her last thought.

Swallowing the lump in her throat came hard for Jessica after Weston had asked her to dance. Jennifer and Samuel were already on the floor gyrating to the funky beats. The four parents hadn't stopped talking since sitting down in the lounge.

What was a girl to do? *Accept his invitation.* She tried to hush the little voice inside her head. Still finding it difficult to speak, Jessica simply got out of her seat. That move should be evidence enough that she wanted to dance with him. She *had* wondered if he would ever ask her. Now that he had, she was ecstatic about it.

Four songs later Jessica and Weston were still on the dance floor. A couple of times they had changed partners with Jennifer and Samuel, but only for short periods. When a step-dance tune came on, Weston didn't miss a beat. He began stepping, glad that Jessica also knew how to. Their laughter rang out as they put on a show.

Many of the patrons gawked at Weston and Jessica's spirited moves.

As Weston's hands spanned Jessica's waist through several of the steps, she continued to keep pace with the music, though his deliciously warm hands had set her body ablaze. He didn't seem to miss the nervous look on her face when the music suddenly turned slow and romantic; before her fears could take her over completely, he tenderly brought her into his arms, pulling her closer in to his body. Perhaps he found it comforting that she was as nervous about him as he was about her.

The urge to lay her head against Weston's chest was overwhelming to Jessica, yet she kept her head raised, her eyes straight ahead. She'd have to look up to peer into his sexy eyes, something she would love to do. Jessica knew she could lose herself there.

The slower set had consisted of three songs. Jessica and Weston stayed on the floor for each one. Each dance had drawn them closer and closer together.

As the smiling couple were about to return to their seats, Róman came up and took a hand of each of his daughters. Jessica and Jennifer often danced with their dad. It was always a highlight of any event for them. One song later Sahara eagerly joined her husband and their two girls for a family dance.

Weston kept his eyes trained on Jessica as she laughed and got down with a line dance she had a ball doing with her family. The girl was as sexy as women came, having gotten him all hot and bothered when he'd held her in his arms. She had a cute little way of twisting her hips and making her upper body wiggle in rhythm to the music. He'd been surprised to learn that she could step, had been pretty darn good at it. He had to admit to the numerous surprises, expecting even more. This was going to be one interesting holiday trip.

Chapter 2

Weston and his parents waited in the parking lot for the Harrington car to make it back. The families had decided to have a nightcap and watch a movie or do something else fun in the Harrington town house. The Harrington family had been right behind the Chamberlains, but when Weston had last looked, they weren't anywhere in sight. That caused worry in the Chamberlain clan. The roads could be treacherous.

Weston sighed with relief when he spotted the van pulling in, glad everyone was safe. He hurried over to the van to open the door for the passengers seated in the rear. Of course, he knew where Jessica was seated, because he had opened the vehicle door for her to get in.

Once Jessica was out of the car, Weston took her by the hand. "How about taking a short walk? It's a beautiful night."

Jessica rolled her hazel eyes, wondering if Weston was kidding. It was freezing outside. "Kind of cold out here, don't you think?"

Weston halfway closed his eyes, slightly tilting his head to the right. "I think I can keep you warm. In fact, I know I can deliver the heat."

Jessica had seen Weston's eye and head gestures as so adorable, his remarks confident. There was no doubt in her mind he could deliver on his word. He had a way of making her hot all over just with a visual connection. "Let's do this, already. Standing in one spot is freezing my feet to the ground."

Weston grinned. "Okay. First things first, though." He lifted the hood of her heavy jacket and pulled it over her head. As he tied the strings snugly under her chin, he wanted to kiss her ripe lips so badly it hurt. Even outdoors where the icy wind blew hard, he smelled her sensuous perfume. He'd asked the name of the scent earlier.

The trek around the resort started out with Weston's arm tightly around Jessica's waist. She silently promised not to fight any of her romantic urges. If she felt like laying her head against his arm, she would. Her mind wasn't so sure about any lip action. Her heart certainly wasn't opposed to it. She couldn't help recalling all the times she had dreamed about kissing him in the past.

Minutes later the numbing cold no longer seemed to matter to Jessica. The couple were now scooping up handfuls of snow and tossing it at each other, seemingly oblivious to the freezing temperatures. When she lost her balance, nearly toppling over, Weston was right there to keep her upright. She rewarded his rescue mission with a warm hug, sending his body temperature right up to the sky. He found her protesting when he had thought they should get indoors funny. Seconds afterward, large snowflakes began to fall.

Back in the town house, Jessica and Weston totally ignored the curious looks from their parents. All they were interested in was something hot to drink. Jessica loved hot cocoa and hot chocolate, and Sahara had packed up both drinks, along with delicious flavored teas and coffees. She was the type of mother who easily anticipated the needs of her family. No matter how old Jessica and Jennifer got, they would always be little girls to Sahara and Roman.

Jessica didn't know what the others were watching on television, but she wasn't interested in viewing anything. She had a television in her bedroom and liked to fall asleep with it on. She planned to do that a little later, but now it was only 10:00 p.m.

Jessica instead pulled out the travel Scrabble board and challenged Weston to a game. He told her he was a terrible speller, but he'd indulge her in one game. He immediately commenced beating her pants off. His ability to spell and come up with words she hadn't even heard of was top-notch.

"Was that a white lie you told about your spelling skills or a bald-faced one?"

Weston had the good grace to look ashamed. "I guess both. If I'd told you I was an excellent speller, you might have backed out. Most men are terrible spellers so I figured I'd just play the part."

"You lied, is what you did! That's okay. Look for a rematch tomorrow."

"You're on! We can play chess, too. Want a refill on the hot chocolate?"

"Please." She wouldn't warn him on how good she was at chess.

Amazed at how well things were going, Weston got up from the kitchen table and refilled both mugs. He had actually expected the fur to fly the entire vacation, just as it had done years ago. This was a pleasant diversion from how they had once acted. As he thought more about it, Weston had to admit that he had treated her badly. There was a time when he'd been stupid enough to believe she had a thing for him. No real proof of that had ever come forth.

Weston carried the mugs of hot chocolate back over to the table. He placed Jessica's down in front of her. "Here you go, sweetie."

Sweetie! Hmm. Jessica liked that term of endearment, especially coming from Weston's pouting lips. Those babies looked so kissable. She closed her eyes just to conjure up an image of him seducing her mouth in the hottest way possible. When his fingers began to slowly trace the underwire of her bra, she quickly popped her eyes open. She couldn't let her mind go there, not in his presence. She wasn't ready for him to leave, even though she was eager to conjure up more erotic images of him in bed later.

"What're you thinking about? You should've seen that sensual look. I hope I was somehow involved in your thoughts."

Jessica had to clear her throat. "Dream on, fellow. Dream on."

"Like that, huh?"

Jessica failed to stifle a giggle. "Uh-huh. Just like that."

Weston got to his feet. "I know when I've worn out my welcome. I'm out of here. Are we on for some serious skiing tomorrow morning?"

Jessica shook her head. "Not sure about that yet."

"Still scared of heights, huh? How'd you manage to get up to this elevation without losing it?"

"Is there nothing sacred with my parents? How much *do* they tell you about me?"

Laughing, Weston shrugged. "I actually got that one from Mom, who got it from yours. But I remember your reaction to getting up on the monkey bars when we were kids. You weren't having any part of it."

"God forbid that you should remember all the bad stuff."

"I do remember the past. But this is now. I'm for making new memories, good ones. What about you?"

"Didn't you say you were leaving?"

"What I said was I know when I've worn my welcome out." He stretched out his hand to her. "Come on and walk me next door. If we're to have a good day tomorrow, we'd better get plenty of rest."

"I agree. Sledding is more appealing to me than skiing. I hope you'll join me. Don't give me an answer right now. Sleep on it."

Weston gave Jessica his brightest, sexiest smile. "You have no idea what I plan to sleep on tonight while sleeping in nothing. Care to star in my wildest fantasies?"

Jessica jumped to her feet. "Let me see you out. You've gotten punchy."

"It happens. I'm overly tired."

"Tell me about it!"

"I'll tell you anything you want to know. All you have to do is ask."

Jessica smiled smugly. "Gee, thanks. I'll keep that in mind."

Jessica lay comfortably in bed. As she thought about all the things that had transpired between her and Weston, she wondered if maybe they'd gotten too friendly too quickly. Many of his remarks to her after the walk and the game of Scrabble had become extremely flirtatious. Maybe so, but she had liked the attention.

Care to star in my wildest fantasies? had flattered the heck right out of her, not to mention that sexy little smile of his. Had there been real sexual connotations in his comments? She sure hoped so.

Deep down inside her heart Jessica hoped that Weston found her as sexy as she did him. She was trying hard not to come up with any reasons she couldn't or shouldn't get romantically involved with him. Surprisingly, she wasn't terrified of her feelings for him. Being attracted to him before, with no favorable outcome, didn't make a good case for compromising her feelings again.

Of course, Jessica had been barely a teenager then. She hadn't known the first thing about true love, yet she had been impressionable. His cruel treatment had hurt her pretty badly. Still, she wanted to give him the benefit of the doubt. He hadn't known any more about love than she had. They had been kids, for goodness' sake.

Weston hadn't shown an ounce of cruelty toward her this evening; quite the contrary. If she had gotten the signals right, he definitely had a romantic interest in her.

The feelings were mutual. It hadn't gotten past Jessica when both had said they wouldn't want to live anyplace other than where they now resided. She couldn't imagine how they'd ever have a long-distance relationship. It wasn't like they'd be living a couple of hours apart; they lived on totally opposite coasts.

This was merely a vacation. Jessica felt foolish entertaining the idea of anything happening beyond the holiday. Enjoy this time and move on, she quietly told herself. Make the best of the next ten days. Then give Weston a warm farewell hug. With her mind made up not to take anything too serious, she closed her eyes, hoping to fall right off to sleep. Tomorrow had already been ushered in. It was well after midnight.

Weston had been tossing and turning for over two hours. Thoughts of Jessica had nearly consumed him. It wasn't a problem to admit being quite intrigued with her. What to do about it was his biggest dilemma. It was hard not to look ahead to when they'd part company. She'd go back to Los Angeles and he back to New York City. Not seeing her again after Aspen troubled him, despite the nine days of vacation they had left.

For a few moments Weston wondered if he could possibly live in Los Angeles after his parents moved there. It didn't take him long to realize he was acting downright ridiculous. It was silly to give the idea any more thought. Nothing assured him that he and Jessica would hit it off so much that either would consider moving to be near the other. He was way ahead of himself and he vowed to stop the mad thinking run before it drove him insane.

Weston quickly decided that he and Jessica would

enjoy each other while in Aspen. That would be the end of it. They might even find other people they were attracted to while on vacation. No one really knew what would happen. They would be meeting a lot of different people at the numerous social functions planned by their parents. After Weston plumped his pillow for the umpteenth time, he settled down in bed, falling asleep minutes after he completely turned off his thoughts.

The sun was high, seeming to shine brighter than Jessica had ever seen before. The resort was covered in a glistening white blanket from the previous night's snowfall. It was like stepping into a fairy-tale village nestled snugly between tall mountain ranges.

The waiter at Café Aspen had already given Jessica and Weston breakfast menus. The café was only a couple of miles down the road from the resort. Weston had taken a quick jaunt to the men's room, leaving Jessica at the table.

The two families had gotten up bright and early to hit the slopes. Sahara had prepared breakfast for the ski group before they'd taken off, excited to get the adventurous day under way.

Jessica reflected on how quiet Weston had been on the drive to the café, wondering what that meant. He hadn't made one flirtatious comment, yet he'd held her hand on the way to the car. The kind gesture might have been to keep her upright. She had been slipping and sliding all over the place. If his attitude changed toward her, she hoped she'd know how to get him back into the fun, flirtatious mode she enjoyed tremendously.

Jessica and Weston planned to go sledding later since

she had chickened out on skiing. She had to take things slow. She had already conquered her fears enough to get up the mountain. *Jumping on a ski lift?* She wasn't there, though proud of what she *had* already accomplished.

Both sets of parents had requested Jessica and Weston's presence when they went into town to pick out the Christmas tree. It was a family tradition in both households to pick out the tree together—and later to trim it.

The warmth on the back of Jessica's neck caused her to look up. Her heart leaped at the beautiful smile on Weston's face.

"I heated my hands by the fire. Did they warm you?"

Jessica smiled and nodded. "Sure did. Where *is* the fireplace?"

"A cozy room in back of the place." Weston took a seat. "Lots of tables for dining, but the room is empty. Want me to ask if we can eat back there?"

"I'd like that. The employees likely fill up the outer rooms first."

"You're probably right, but it won't hurt to ask. I can be pretty persuasive."

Jessica didn't doubt that. "Go for it."

Jessica looked after Weston as he walked away. She could hear his fine body screaming out her name. She loved the beautiful black-and-white Italian knit sweater he wore with a pair of dark wool pants, casual in style. He had earlier complimented Jessica on her navy-blue wool sweater and slacks, and a crisp white shirt. Her thick-soled winter boots were burgundy in color.

Weston had yet another huge smile on his face as he winked at Jessica. "I'm good, girl. You have no idea."

Jessica laughed. "Oh, I think I do. Incredible charm runs in your family."

"Come with me. The hostess said to take any table we want. She also said we might be the only ones dining there. As you can see, they're not busy this morning. Are you okay with that?"

Shrugging, her mouth turned down at the corners, Jessica said, "Fine by me."

Weston picked up the menus off the table and carried them into what appeared to Jessica as a cozy alcove. The space was very intimate and she liked the feel of it.

The waiter showed up within a few minutes of the couple taking seats, bringing along with him a carafe of hot coffee. Jessica wasn't big on coffee, but she did drink it occasionally. She let the waiter know she preferred a small pot of chamomile tea when he took their breakfast orders.

Weston's order indicated to Jessica that he was a hungry man again this morning. She wasn't that surprised by the amount of food he ordered, considering the size of the meal he had practically inhaled last evening.

Jessica's order consisted of two boiled eggs, a turkey sausage patty and a small order of home-fried potatoes. Instead of toast, she ordered a freshly baked blueberry muffin, and then orange juice as an afterthought.

"How did you sleep last night, Jess?"

"Once I managed to get there, I knocked out completely."

"Did you have as hard a time getting to sleep as I did?"

"I wasn't able to fall right off. Had quite a few things on my mind." *Mainly you.*

"Sure you don't want a cup of coffee? It's pretty good stuff."

"No, thanks. I'll wait for the tea." She looked out the window. "It's such a beautiful morning. I can't get over the magnificent view from our town house. I've heard so much about Aspen. I'm glad to actually experience it. It's like another world."

"You haven't seen the half of it. This place *is* amazing. I read somewhere that Mariah Carey's been living here for a couple of years."

"I read that, too. Quite a few celebrities live here in Aspen, either full-time or part-time."

"A wonderful place to visit, but I don't want to live here."

"Yeah, I know. Nowhere for Wes but NYC."

Weston leveled curious eyes on Jessica. Something about the way she had snapped out her last remark had him wondering. She had sounded a bit annoyed. He quickly dismissed the thought since it made no sense at all.

The waiter came and dropped off Jessica's tea and immediately took off again.

The couple got into a conversation about how the real-estate market had boomed in California. It was unbelievable the way it had suddenly shot through the roof.

Jessica mentioned that the folks who had taken out interest-only or arm home loans were in for a rude awakening. Weston figured they could beat the odds if they could refinance at a fixed rate before the bad stuff happened. A lot of people had also opted for balloon payments, all just to own a piece of hot California property. Shanties and fixer-uppers were even selling for indecent amounts. Things were now starting to cool off a bit. Both Jessica and Weston expected a lot of home foreclosures to occur in the very near future.

"New York real estate has been high for a long time. I'm sure you do well."

"Extremely. That's why I don't understand why my parents want to up and move to L.A."

"Maybe because your father was born and raised there."

"I guess. They're financially set, so they don't have to worry about money. Dad *does* complain about the harsh winters in New York."

Jessica faked a believable shiver. "If it's anywhere near as cold in New York as it is here, I can't blame them for wanting to move to California. Don't think I could brave winter weather like this year after year. The roads are frightening. Seeing the snowstorms on television is enough for me."

"If you grew up in winters like this, it'd be just a way of life. People manage it all the time."

The return of the waiter kept Jessica from responding to Weston's comments. Not wanting to get into the subject of living so far apart, she saw the interruption in conversation as a good thing. The very idea of it bothered her to no end, no matter how much she didn't want to make it an issue. Sticking to the plan she had laid out for herself last night was hard to execute. Denying her wild attraction for Weston wasn't happening. Jessica wanted him in the worst way.

There were far too many beautiful Christmas trees to make it easy for the visiting families to choose quickly.

They had been on the tree lot for nearly an hour when Jessica had spotted the perfect tree, its branches full, long and sweeping. After a couple of minutes of deliberation, everyone had agreed it was indeed the one. The men had taken care of the hard work to load the tree onto the top of one of the vans.

Once the ideal tree had been deposited back at the Harrington's town house, Jessica and Weston had promised to return home in time to help with the trimmings. The group had decided to order food to be brought in for the evening meal before the younger generation had left to go snowmobiling. Weston thought Jessica might enjoy riding a snowmobile more than sledding. Samuel also preferred snowmobiling.

Jessica constantly laughed and screamed as Weston expertly maneuvered the snowmobile around the area he and Samuel had chosen to take the two sisters. She hadn't had this much fun since she didn't know when. It was cold outdoors, but she was able to endure it. The extra layer of clothing was helping tremendously. She didn't feel chilled to the bone as she had without the double layer of warmth. The leather gloves had lamb's wool on the inside and really kept her hands warm. The hood on her jacket was pulled up with the strings tied under her chin.

Weston didn't necessarily drive the snowmobile recklessly, but he made enough dramatic twists and turns over the snowswept terrain to make it fun and exhilarating. Jessica screamed out of fear a few times. Samuel also had Jennifer howling. She had done this with her husband before so she was no stranger to the fun sport.

Samuel and Jennifer always had loads of fun together.

They had learned about a salsa class to be held at the resort and had just about convinced Jessica and Weston to join them.

The snowmobile-rental time had flown by. Weston and Samuel had gone to turn in the vehicles and settle the accounts. This was Jessica and Jennifer's first time alone since the families had arrived in Aspen and they were seated in the lodge's lounge sipping on hot drinks.

"You really like him, don't you, Jess?"

Knowing her secret was no longer just hers, Jessica lowered her lashes. "I've always liked Weston. The truth of the matter hit me square in the heart yesterday. Guess I've known it all along but have refused to admit it. Even to myself. I felt so hurt only because he rejected me. Been kidding myself for years by saying I couldn't stand him. I just wanted him to notice me, acknowledge me in some way—and he didn't."

"He notices you now, big-time. The look on his face when he saw you yesterday was so revealing. Had his parents not hugged you and called you by name, I'm not sure he would've guessed that you and the girl he used to torment were one and the same."

"Maybe so. I'd think he would have seen all the updated pictures of us that Mom and Dad always send to his parents." Jessica looked at her sister with open curiosity. "Did you ever have a crush on Wes, Jen?"

"Heck no!"

"Not even a teeny-weeny one?"

"Hardly. I loved Sam even before we started dating in junior high. That is, for as much as I did or didn't know about love back then. But you already know our history.

Took Sam a long time to notice me, too. At any rate, Wes is just not my type."

"I don't know if it's even about them noticing us. Most boys just don't start liking girls until they reach a certain age. Up until then, they believe their one purpose on this planet is to torture girls. Adolescent boys *are* cruel."

"Don't leave out the girls. There were some mean, overbearing chicks out there when I was in junior high. Talk about cruelty. They seemed to have had a monopoly on it. Don't you recall all the trouble I had with the so-called upper-class brat pack? I also agree with everything you've said. But look at what happened when Sam *did* notice me. We've been inseparable ever since." Jennifer was a nurse and Samuel a paramedic.

Jessica smiled broadly. "You guys got it going on. I want so badly what you two have. Not ready for marriage, though. Yet I desperately desire the romance. Eating dinner every single night by candlelight has to be the bomb."

"That and more." Jennifer blushed at a couple of other things Samuel and she indulged in by candlelight. "We do more than eat by the light of burning candles. The more sensual stuff keeps us hot for each other."

Jessica put up her right hand in a halting gesture. "No details, please! It'll only let me know how lonely and pitiful I am. Passion is lacking in my life."

"Don't say that."

Jennifer went on to remind Jessica that she had a great job and a wonderful group of girlfriends who loved doing adventurous things and taking exotic vacations. "You guys always do something fun and unique. And you also have a great male friend in Jarred. I'd say you have it all. All but the husband you admitted to not wanting now."

"Put like that, I don't have a choice but to agree. Thanks for always showing me the glass is half-full as opposed to half-empty." Jessica gently nudged Jennifer's arm. "Here come the guys. We should cool it."

"Yeah, wouldn't want Wes to know you're out of your mind over him."

Jessica frowned. "It's not that bad. But the potential for such is great."

Both women laughed at that.

All Jessica could do was sit and stare in utter amazement when Samuel sat down next to Jennifer. Taking her in his arms, he kissed her as if he'd been apart from her for weeks instead of twenty minutes or so. Their passion couldn't be charted since it was off the scale. Those two couldn't keep their hands and mouths off each other.

Weston sat down next to Jessica. "Wow! Your sister and her husband are sure deep into each other. Their love is so strong," he whispered.

"Been that way forever," Jessica whispered back to him. "Some people call it sickening. I call it incredible. If Jen weren't my sister, I might envy her."

Weston raised an eyebrow at that statement. Jessica's remarks made him think she wanted exactly what her sister had. Well, he thought, didn't everyone want to be involved in a true-blue, passionate love affair? His eyes softened even more as he looked closer at Jessica. He had to wonder if they could ever have what their parents and Jennifer and Samuel had an overabundance of, together or separate. He had to admit he preferred together to separate.

Chapter 3

Entering the town house, Jessica was immediately drawn to the kitchen, overwhelmed by the delicious aromas. *So much for ordering food in for the evening meal.*

Sahara had cooked and Jessica was sure her father had helped out her mother. Both were excellent chefs and they often worked side by side in preparing meals. Her parents loved to whip up delicious foods and Jessica hated everything to do with cooking, period. She liked cleaning up the kitchen even less than the meal preparations. No man in his right mind wanted a woman who couldn't or wouldn't cater to the needs of his stomach.

Sahara walked up and lightly popped Jessica on the hand. "Stay out of my pots and pans, girl. All the food is for our little get-together this evening. Want me to fix you a sandwich?"

Jessica looked at Sahara as if she had to be kidding. "You fixed all this delicious food—and you want to feed me a measly sandwich? That's scandalous, Mom."

"Okay, you win, number-two daughter." Sahara referred to her daughters' order of birth, not to how they ranked in her sight. She loved her girls equally. "Get a plate from the cabinet and take some of whatever you want. You know I can't stand here and deny my youngest child a meal."

"Thanks, Mom." Jessica kissed Sahara on the cheek. "Where's Dad?"

"Off somewhere with Jacque. He left here right after he finished helping me out. They're probably sitting somewhere talking shop. Those two eat and sleep real estate."

"And they both have their kids doing the same thing." Jessica put small samples from each pot on her plate and then took a seat at the table.

Sahara retrieved a cold drink from the refrigerator before joining Jessica at the table. "Speaking of our kids, how was the snowmobiling outing for you and Jen?"

"Lots of fun. The guys were acting a little crazy while driving the snowmobiles, making sharp twists and turns all over the place, but they pretty much stuck to most of the safety rules. I liked it enough to want to do it again. I think I'd like to drive one the next time. It might take a minute or two to get the hang of it. Jen and I were whooping and hollering it up out there. The guys had a tremendous time, too."

Sahara pressed her lips together, choosing her next words carefully. "Having a good time with Wes?"

Jessica looked down the length of her nose at her

mother. "Why don't you go right ahead and ask me what you really want to know? Your curiosity about us is written all over your face and you're dying to get up in our business."

"Just asked a simple question. Why are you trying to make a federal case out of it? My goodness, you're really sensitive on the subject."

"The only thing I'm sensitive about is you and Daddy trying to choose a husband for me. It's not like that with Wes and me. But to answer your question, I'm having a grand time. On January third the vacation will be over with and so will Wes and I. All we're doing is having some fun and trying to make the best of this situation our parents have thrown us into. Mom, it's *not* going to happen for us. Please share that with Dad and the Chamberlains so you all don't continue speculating."

"I think you are making way too much out of us wanting to share our holiday time with the Chamberlains. However, I'm glad you're having a good time."

"Whatever, Mom. Okay for me to eat before the food gets cold?"

Sahara knew that Jessica meant she wanted to be left in peace. "If you need anything, I'll be in the bedroom." Sahara got up from the chair, her head hung low.

Jessica could tell by the look on her mother's face that she had hurt her feelings. That hadn't been her intent, but she needed everyone just to get off her and Weston's backs. No one could choose a mate for another person, even though she knew there were many cultures in the world that still arranged marriages.

"Sorry, Mom," Jessica yelled out before Sahara could

disappear. "I'll try to be a little less sensitive, but please just let Wes and me be ourselves."

Jessica knew Sahara was a bit upset with her when she didn't accept her apology or even bother to respond to her plea. Sahara wasn't the type who stayed upset long, nor did she hold grudges, so Jessica wasn't worried that their little tiff would ruin the rest of their stay in Aspen. Both she and her mother would soon forget this had ever happened.

Keeping a covert eye on Weston was difficult to do, especially when Jessica kept catching herself staring at him outright. He looked so darn sexy, though he was only dressed in a neatly pressed burgundy shirt and heather-gray wool slacks, all of which appeared to be of excellent quality. It was how his athletic physique filled out the attire that turned Jessica on; it looked as if it all fit him to a T. His broad shoulders were more accentuated when they weren't buried beneath a bulky sweater.

Like the rest of the men, Weston was intent on seeing that the full Douglas fir Christmas tree was put up correctly. No one wanted to see it topple over at some point during the planned festivities. Jacque had suggested that the group purchase an artificial tree just before they had gone out to shop for a fresh one. His not-so-brilliant idea had met with clucking disapproval from the four women.

Looking down at her own attire, comparing it to what the other females wore, Jessica was still pleased with the outfit she had chosen for herself. Tucked neatly into the waistband of slim, black wool crepe pants was a long-sleeved black-and-white striped Ralph Lauren shirt. Over the designer shirt she wore a stylish black quilted vest.

Jessica's long, light-brown layered hair had been blow-dried straight but curled slightly at the ends of each layer to allow her shiny tresses to flow softly about her shoulders. Just the right amount of makeup to her pretty face and hazel eyes gave a gently dramatic flair to her normally wholesome appearance.

Weston thought Jessica looked cover-model perfect, though she hardly measured up in height. Her five-foot-even frame fell way short when compared to many statuesque, leggy models. But he liked how she carried herself. She was every bit as graceful and stylish as any top model in the country today. Jessica was a far cry from the preteen he'd once known, and he was still amazed by her unbelievable transformation. He loved how she was gently curvaceous in all the right spots, the ones his hands craved to tenderly caress. Though she had a small bustline, the twin mounds appeared to stand proud. The vest she wore over her shirt didn't allow him nearly the exciting view of cleavage he had seen the first day.

Christmas music, the popping and crackling of the fire burning brightly in the fireplace and the sounds of joyous laughter created a wonderful holiday setting. A wondrous winter scene of mountains, snow and large evergreen trees through the large picture window delighted the senses. The draperies had been pulled completely back, making it look as if the scene had been painted onto the glass pane.

Gaily colored rolls of foil wrapping paper, with every kind of decoration on them, from reindeer to Santa Clauses, were laid out on the table, along with bunches of ribbons in bright colors of green, red, gold, silver and white. There were also bows made up of more than one hue. White gift boxes waiting to be filled with presents and then wrapped in the paper were stacked high in one corner of the dining room.

Weston quickly snapped out of his reverie when he heard the others howling. He couldn't help but join in the laughter even though a sudden rush of empathy for Jessica had just hit him. It looked to him as if she had gotten herself all tangled up in the tinsel she was working with. The bewildered look on her face was comical but so endearing.

Jessica didn't like the glittery stuff, anyway, so it didn't bother her that it might be ruined. The tinsel had been Sandra's bright idea. The Harringtons had never used it on one of their family Christmas trees, although its use was traditional in many a household. Now that the tinsel could no longer be used, Jessica grabbed up the tray of delicate gold- and silver-edged angel and snowflake ornaments to hang on the tree's sweeping branches.

The delicious aromas of food, hot apple cider and freshly popped popcorn filled the air, mixing with the heady pine scent of the Douglas fir. Jennifer and Samuel had just finished popping the corn and warming the cider and putting out all the reheated foods Sahara and Roman had prepared earlier. The smell of the baked hot wings and grilled chicken tenders eventually ruled over the other scents. Swedish meatballs and beef cocktail wieners simmered in a light but very flavorful teriyaki sauce. Three kinds of pasta had also been made: spaghetti, penne and an angel-hair/vegetable salad.

The group hadn't finished trimming the tree, but they decided to stop long enough to enjoy the evening meal

together. The ladies quickly began to hustle around the
room to tackle several chores. Jessica laid out the plates
while Sandra took care of the silverware. Sahara busied
herself filling the drinking glasses with snowball-shaped
ice cubes. She had seen the cute trays on one of the aisles
inside a convenience store in town and she hadn't been
able to resist purchasing a few of the cleverly designed
items.

Roman requested that Weston ask for the blessing on
the food and all the hands that had prepared it. Jacque and
Sandra had prepared the sinful desserts. Apple cobbler
was their son's favorite and the triple-layer devil's food
cake was the one dessert Jacque loved most. Sandra and
Jacque had also baked sweet-potato pies, an absolute
favorite of all the Harringtons, including Jennifer and
Samuel. Once the simultaneous "amens" rang out, the
group wasted no time at all digging right in.

The tree duties had resumed right after the two families
had polished off their dessert. The group worked well
together and had worked rather quickly to complete the
fun tasks. Everyone had been designated a job and each
person had taken it seriously. The families finally stood
back to view the end results of their handiwork.

It was now time for the colorful and brilliant show of
light. Roman was to do the honors. Jacque scurried around
the place, turning off all other lights.

"Lights, action," Roman breathed excitedly. One flick
of his finger on the switch caused the tree to come to life
with hundreds of dazzling miniature white lights.

The magical moment had taken everyone's breath

away. All hands were linked together as the oohs and aahs continued to ebb and flow. There was not one pair of eyes without tears of holiday sentiment. Then the laughter broke out, loudly and freely.

"Oh, we forgot one thing," Weston said. He ran over to the kitchen counter and picked up the mistletoe, holding it up for everyone to see. "Who wants the honors?" Weston looked directly at Jessica, hoping she might step forward. He would like nothing better than to kiss her breathless beneath the fresh sprig of mistletoe.

"I'll hang it," Jennifer sang out, moving toward Weston. As soon as she reached for the mistletoe, she saw the disappointment in Weston's eyes. She didn't have to be a genius to figure out what was wrong with him.

After Jennifer took possession of the mistletoe, she walked over to Jessica and handed it to her. "You should be the one to do the honors. Does everyone agree?"

Enthusiastic hand-clapping thundered in the room.

Jessica knew what everyone hoped for; she would hang the mistletoe and Weston would kiss her while she stood under it. She had no desire to disappoint anyone, especially herself. Jessica took the offered mistletoe from Jennifer and quickly stepped up to the plate, her heart beating rapidly. The thought of Weston kissing her had her heart rate going berserk. She couldn't wait to feel his mouth on hers.

"Get the camera," Sahara told Roman. "This is a special holiday moment." Although the video camera had been running throughout their time in Aspen, its adapter plugged into the electrical wall outlet, Sahara also wanted still photographs.

Jessica ended up having to get a stool to stand on because the space at the top of the kitchen entry was too high for her to reach without one. Weston rushed over to help her up on the stool, holding it firmly in place as she tacked up the small green and white sprig. Once the mistletoe was set in place, Weston reached up and brought Jessica down and into his arms. Without allowing her feet ever to touch the ground, he tenderly kissed her mouth, doing his best to stave off his desire to use his tongue to deepen the kiss.

In the next second Weston lost himself in the sweetness of Jessica's lips. She had also slipped away into paradise. The arms that held her so securely made her feel safe and protected. So this was what it felt like to be in Weston's arms. She had waited a long time to find out, believing she would never experience such an enchanting moment.

Jessica could only imagine the expression on her face once Weston set her down on her feet and released his hold on her. If hers was anything like the bewildered look on his face, he more than likely had also experienced what she had. A brief kiss could be every bit as sensual as a long, passionate one. His kiss had just proven that. It had also left her trembling inside and desperately wanting more of the same from him.

Jessica was relieved that no one had resorted to cat-calling, whistling or clapping. Hiding her embarrassment was hard enough without all that. However, Weston didn't look the least bit embarrassed. After all, he *had* initiated the kiss between them.

The other three couples went back to chatting with each other, taking their focus off Jessica and Weston purposefullly. Jessica was happy about that. She had never liked to be the center of attention.

Jessica wanted to gently touch her lips with her fingers, hoping she might still feel Weston's kiss there. Her mind was somewhat befuddled, making her feel as if she were in a daze. She wanted him to kiss her again and again, but she wasn't so sure it would ever recur. At any rate, Jessica knew she shouldn't be having these types of thoughts.

Although Weston's kiss had been soft as a whisper, the impact on Jessica's senses was profound. Weston had her rocking and reeling and wishing they were off somewhere alone. As far as she was concerned, his kiss had impacted her way more than her first kiss had. Logan Langston had been the first male to deliver the first kiss to her "sweet sixteen" lips. She had been kissed many times since, but she hadn't ever felt anything akin to what she now felt. The floating sensation she experienced was rather surreal.

Weston was very pleased with the ardent response his mouth had received from Jessica's. His body was still tingling all over from their brief but very impressionable encounter. He had already begun to crave the sweet taste of her full lips. Weston knew he was addicted and he couldn't help wondering when his next fix might come, hoping he never had to go into withdrawal. No doubt that would be painful. He thought perhaps he should say something to Jessica, but he just didn't know what to talk about when his mind was only on one thing. Making love to her until she begged him never to stop.

Weston was positive that he and Jessica had more than just a little bit of chemistry going on between them. He hoped she had experienced the same wonderful sensations as he had. Was this the beginning of something beautiful for them or had their intimate kiss marked the end? Intimacy between a man and woman more often than not resulted in the couple taking things to the next level or it could have just the opposite effect.

Did either of them even want things to go to a higher level?

Although Weston couldn't speak for Jessica, he was sure he wanted to take their relationship as far as it could go, wanting that more than he'd ever wanted anything. He had never desired any woman this way. Jessica had him seriously interested in making her an integral part of his life.

After deciding to put a hold on his thoughts, Weston went into the kitchen and poured two cups of hot cider. One cup was for Jessica even though she hadn't asked for anything to drink. His desire was to reconnect with her as soon as possible so she wouldn't find a reason to disconnect from him, period.

Weston made it back to where Jessica was and then handed over the hot drink to her. "Here you go. Be careful. It's still hot."

Jessica smiled at Weston as she accepted the cup from him. Although she wanted to speak to him, she was afraid of how her voice might sound. If it came out as high-strung as she felt, that would prove embarrassing. Jessica swallowed hard.

"The tree is beautiful, isn't it? We all did a great job," Weston said.

Jessica looked over at the Christmas tree. It *was* magnificent. Positioned in front of the picture window, it appeared as part of the outdoor scenery. "It's stunning! This group has skills."

Weston had to agree with Jessica. They had really delivered on a beautiful tree. "Think you might want to take another walk later on? It's another great evening."

"I'd love that."

Jessica hadn't hesitated in the least to reply to Weston's query because she was very eager to spend as much time with him as he desired to spend with her. She no longer had to wonder where he was coming from. His intent toward her had been right there in his kiss. She had no desire to thwart a single intimate advance from him. Jessica recalled earlier wishing for them to be off somewhere alone—and that lofty wish was about to come true.

Weston had Jessica in his arms no sooner than they had stepped outside. His hands brought her in to him until there was nothing between them but their bulky clothing. His mouth hungrily sought hers and she responded with no less fervor. More kisses from Weston, all in the same day, had her beyond excited. Despite the heavy clothing he wore, Jessica could still feel his heat, not to mention her own. Her body felt on fire, in spite of how cold it was.

Although Jessica wished she could stay in Weston's arms forever and a day, she slowly pulled away, hoping his feelings wouldn't get hurt. She certainly wasn't trying to reject him, but making a spectacle of herself in public wasn't her cup of tea. Since they were both staying in the town houses with their parents, there was nowhere else for them to go to ensure privacy.

Weston pulled Jessica back to him. "I just leased a

cabin this morning. Come back there with me? It's close by, near the middle of the forest."

Jessica looked surprised by Weston's revelation. Why had he suddenly decided to get his own place? If he had leased the cabin with the intent of seducing her, shouldn't that make her feel a bit weird? It didn't. Did he think she was easy? Perhaps she should be concerned with what he thought about her, but she really wasn't offended by him wanting to be alone with her. She wanted the same thing. They were adults, not teenagers.

Weston lifted Jessica's chin with his two fingers. "What's wrong? Did I do or say something you didn't like?"

"What would make you think that?"

Weston stroked with his gloved hand the length of Jessica's hair, the section that wasn't covered by the brand-new cute winter hat she wore. "You look surprised. That's why I asked."

"The cabin. Why are you no longer staying with your parents in the town house they leased?" She began walking. It was really cold enough to freeze her solid.

"Oh, that." Weston stifled his urge to laugh. He bent down and grazed her lips with his own. "Do you know how long I've been living on my own? I'll tell you. Nearly ten years if you count college-dorm time. A time came when I realized my mother and father made love—terribly shocking. It's one thing to know what your parents do in their bedroom…and another one to hear evidence of it. Let's just say my mother was a little overzealous last night in vocalizing her physical state of euphoria."

Jessica knew exactly where Weston was coming from,

which caused her to blush heavily. Her parents had also gotten a bit rowdy a time or two in their bedroom, but those incidents had occurred way back when she and Jennifer were teenagers.

"Think they forgot I was in the house?"

"That's pretty obvious. No parent, especially a mother, wants their child or adult son to hear them making love. I'd be mortified if it happened to me. What went down when you two saw each other this morning?"

Weston shrugged. "Mom tried not to let on. I know she knew I knew. The expression on her face changed the minute I walked into the kitchen—like she had suddenly remembered the wild escapades from the previous night. Like you did a few minutes ago, Mom blushed hard. On top of that, she looked thoroughly embarrassed. For the next half hour or so she and Dad kept exchanging questioning glances."

"*Does he know or doesn't he?* That's what they were probably thinking."

"Oh, no doubt. They'd like to know the truth but won't ever ask. This is one of those uncomfortable situations they'll always wonder about. I know that because they didn't even ask me why I'd leased the cabin."

"I wouldn't have asked, either. Speaking of the cabin, we can go there now. I was just curious about you getting your own space."

"Like my parents, I won't ask what you thought before I told you the story. I don't want to know, especially if it's not favorable to me."

"Nothing unfavorable. Not at all."

Weston looked relieved.

* * *

The two-bedroom cabin was smaller than the town houses the Harringtons and Chamberlains had leased. Though very rustic, it was every bit as comfortable. On the way there Weston had told Jessica how lucky he had been to rent it. The guest who had held the reservation on the cabin had called to cancel only minutes before he had walked into the leasing office. The entire lodge had been booked solid up to that point; not unusual for such a major holiday.

Weston had gone to the local store to purchase some of the items he needed. He had had Jessica in mind when purchasing the Earl Grey tea, her favorite. Figuring how cold she had to be after their walk, though much shorter than their previous stroll, he went into the kitchen and turned on the teakettle.

Jessica was busy looking the rest of the place over, so Weston began lighting the candles. He burned candles at his home all the time, even in broad daylight, something his parents had done all his life. He always enjoyed the relaxing ambience they created. Lighting the fireplace came next.

Jessica stepped into the room at the same time Weston finished with the fireplace. He preferred to burn real wood, but a lot of the resorts had begun using gas-burning equipment. The firelight was just as beautiful, but he regretted the absence of the woody scents he loved. The town houses had wood-burning fireplaces.

The warm sensations Jessica experienced over the tea Weston had prepared made her smile. He had been a busy man in her absence, since he had also taken care of the fireplace. He seemed to like to take care of her and his attentiveness made her feel special.

Chapter 4

Curled up on the large rug in front of the fireplace was right where Jessica longed to stay. Positioned right behind her, his hand lying flat on her abdomen, Weston pressed his body against hers. She hoped she wouldn't need to disrupt their serenity for a bathroom break, feeling as though she had drunk enough tea to float a small ship. She also felt very drowsy. A short nap could only do her body good. Sleep should be the last thing on her mind when she had such a sexy live wire lying next to her.

Weston nibbled at Jessica's ear, slowly outlining it with his tongue. He felt her tense up and then relax in the next instant. "Warm enough?"

If Jessica's anatomy got any hotter, she'd find herself begging Weston to help cool her down by any means necessary. Being in such close proximity to him made her feel as if she was amidst a firestorm. The inability to get his earlier kisses out of her mind had only added more heat to the mix. The man definitely knew how to dole out the passionate kisses. His full, pouting lips moving over hers was one of the most sensual experiences she had ever encountered.

It was very easy for Jessica to imagine Weston making wild, hot and heavy love to her. All she had to do was close her eyes to envision them entwined in a compromising position. She had only conjured up that very erotic image of them hundreds of times over the past years. He was an expert in keeping her mind and body turned on, even when he wasn't in her presence. A cold shower would work wonders for her right about now.

Jessica had decided not to answer Weston's question about being warm enough, since she couldn't answer it candidly. The truth could set them both on fire. If he knew how often she thought of them making love, he would want to make certain all of her dreams and fantasies about it came true.

Weston buried his nose in Jessica's hair, inhaling deeply of its fresh scent. As he tenderly kissed her neck and ears, periodically allowing his tongue in on the action, he had a hard time suppressing his arousal. Over the past twenty-four hours he had had his own erotic thoughts about the two of them. He couldn't help wondering what kind of intimate apparel she wore. *Silk, lace or cotton? A thong, bikinis or briefs?*

It wasn't hard for Weston to conjure up an image of Jessica wearing a hot lace or silk teddy. Her long hair swinging loose and free over her perfectly rounded breasts caused him to have a painful stiffening. The image of her in nothing at all was the one he loved most. He wanted her in the worst way, desired to lose himself deep inside her. He couldn't wait until Jessica was ready for that.

Weston wasn't the kind of guy who indulged in any sort of casual sex and he was pretty sure Jessica wasn't into that lifestyle, either. There just wasn't enough time for them to develop a deep, meaningful relationship before they had to go their separate ways.

Weston knew he had to remedy that. Seeing her beyond Aspen was the key. Jessica agreeing to his proposition was anyone's guess, but he would suggest visiting her in California soon. It wasn't about sex, either. He wanted her, period.

The intense heat burning between Jessica's thighs had her turning over and pressing her body fully against Weston's. Foreplay had its benefits even though it could get a body into lots of trouble, literally. Turning off the turn-on wasn't always easy to accomplish. Despite her warning thoughts Jessica engaged Weston in a hot, wet kiss.

Weston responded to Jessica's kiss with the same degree of passion, loving the way her mouth fitted perfectly against his. He couldn't get enough of the sweet taste of her soft, crushable lips. He hated that he had missed out on all this sweetness and heady passion over the past years. Wishing he had gone along to California with his parents on their visits was no good. Those particular opportunities were lost, never to be recovered. *Get over it.*

Jessica pulled her head slightly back, eyeing Weston intently. "You seem to be quite a guy, directly the opposite of what I'd thought. I'm astonished by how well you turned out. I love who you've become. I love how you make me feel."

"How *do* I make you feel?"

"Special. Whether we're alone or with the group, I know you're with me in mind, body and spirit. You are attentive to me. Your entire being is expressive. You don't make a woman guess what's going on with you. That's a unique quality to possess. Not a lot of people can lay claim to that."

Weston's eyes had an undeniable way of telling Jessica he thought she *was* special. His hands and body language easily conveyed the messages he intended to get across. He wanted her—and his body language was easy to read. "I don't know how I should feel about all that. You make me sound like an open book, one that's pretty easy to read. Do I really put it out there like that?"

"Right out there in plain sight. I'm not usually bold in speech or in deed, but you are one hot man. If I were the kind of person who indulged in meaningless sex, we'd be getting it on right now. The chemistry between us is scorching hot yet so magical."

If Jessica didn't look so serious, Weston would have laughed. As he went over in his mind her galvanizing remarks, he sobered. She wasn't opposed to making love under a different set of circumstances. She had voiced aloud her desire.

How was that for bringing it on home?

Weston couldn't help wondering if Jessica already regretted her boldness. He hoped not. He also hoped she wouldn't withdraw from the sexually charged arena. Things were just beginning to heat up...and the temp was at the top of the thermometer. Weston was a man who liked the chemistry to be hot, hot, hot.

As if Jessica had read Weston's mind, she indulged him in another lingering kiss. Just as before, the kisses grew in intensity, making both parties wish they had been together over the past years.

Weston deeply regretted he hadn't been able to see Jessica for who she was inside. He had focused too much on her outer appearance, but he hadn't been anything to write home about, either. Maybe that was the reason he had mistreated her. Had she rejected him during his awkward teen years he couldn't have handled it. Life for him as a teenager had been very difficult. Surprisingly, he could now admit to himself that he had had a serious crush on Jessica. Perhaps he hadn't known how to show it.

Jessica pulled away from Weston and smoothed her clothing. She quickly got to her feet, leaving her companion looking bewildered. After crossing the room with deliberate strides, she stood in front of the large picture window. Why had she come to the cabin with Weston? Deeply conflicting thoughts and emotions had her at war with herself. One part of her wanted to throw caution to the wind and make steamy love to the man of her dreams. The sensible part of her makeup was telling her to run for her life, get out while she still had the strength to do so.

Weston came up behind Jessica and circled her waist. "You're trembling. I've frightened you, haven't I?"

Jessica leaned her head back against his chest. "I've

scared myself. What we're doing scares me even more. We're strangers, Wes. We haven't seen each other in ages yet we're all over each other like two silly teenagers. Is that stranger than fiction, or what?"

Weston kissed the top of her head. "It's called attraction, sweetie. I don't know about you, but it's more than just a physical magnetism on my part. If you think all I want to do is get you into bed, you're wrong. I really want to get to know you."

Jessica turned completely around and looked up into his eyes. "Are you serious?"

As Weston's lips connected with Jessica's, he closed his eyes for a moment. "I've never been more serious. This is not a holiday fling for me. What's happening to me has nothing to do with a festive atmosphere. My heart is compromised. I hope that's not too much information."

Jessica stood on tiptoes and kissed him deeply. "Just enough information to keep me from questioning my sanity. So, do we just wait and see what develops between us?"

"I think to do otherwise would be insane. I'm in. Are you?"

Jessica smiled sweetly. "In."

The couple fell into an easy, warm embrace, hugging each other to show they were on the same wavelength.

"I have an idea, Jessica. What about ice-skating away the rest of the evening?"

"I'm all for your idea, though I'm afraid I might kill myself on the skates. I'm terrible at skating. Will you help me up when I fall?"

"You bet I will."

"Should we see if the others want to go?"

"This is a family holiday. Let's stop by and see what they're up to." Weston looked down at his wristwatch. "We'd better get a move on since the ice rink closes at eleven and it's almost eight-thirty now."

As the two families filed out of the vehicles, Jessica could see that the arena was filled with patrons. All the colorful winter clothing worn by the skaters, not to mention the dazzling lights strategically posted around the place, brought the outdoor arena to life. Once both vehicles were unloaded, everyone made their way inside the ice rink, where the skate-rental booth and refreshment bar were located. The place was also equipped with a wood-burning fireplace.

"What size skate do you need?" Weston asked Jessica.

It was time for Jessica to get her payback against Weston. She laughed with enthusiasm. After reaching down into the small duffel-style bag, she pulled out a shiny pair of white ice skates. "Ta-da," she exclaimed, holding up the skates for him to see.

"Oh, no! You set me up, girl. I've been had. You lied about not knowing how to skate, didn't you? How you going to play me like that?" Because she came from Southern California, he'd been sure she wouldn't know a thing about ice-skating.

Jessica howled. "Just as you lied about your spelling skills. Now we're even." She had the most devilish expression on her face. "Two liars, and we're not ashamed," she sang out, using the tune to Mary Wells's song "Two Lovers," a great Motown sound.

Weston laughed heartily. "You have the gear. Now let's see what the little girl from Southern Cal can do. I'm putting twenty bucks on myself. Before you take the bet, keep in mind that you're competing with a guy who skates in New York's famous Central Park. Among some of the best ice-skaters around, I might add."

Jessica smirked. "Cut the boasting. Let your feet do the bragging. Twenty bucks is all you're in jeopardy of losing. You probably drink up at least that much at Starbucks in a week's time. You won't miss the money."

"That's not too far-fetched. I *do* need my caffeine fix, but you'll be the one paying my coffee bill the first week I'm home."

"We'll see. If I were you, I wouldn't count my chickens before they hatch."

After Weston was in possession of his size-eleven rentals, he and Jessica found an empty bench, where they sat down and laced up their skates. She couldn't wait to hit the ice to show off her talent. Weston wasn't as eager about revealing his skills after seeing Jessica's skates. They looked somewhat used so he knew they hadn't been purchased for show. He hadn't given any thought to indoor ice rinks, but he had known they existed. Los Angeles wouldn't have come to mind.

Whether Jessica was talented enough to compete against him remained to be seen. However, the only competition he was interested in was the one that'd win him her heart. She had already won his.

The songs being played were up-to-date rhythm and blues hits. A song by Usher and one by Lionel Ritchie had played while everyone had laced up their skates. The tune currently playing was Beyoncé Knowles's "Crazy In Love." Jessica couldn't remember if it was off the first or second album, but it was one of her favorites, a really upbeat song to skate to.

As if Jessica was playing a game of tag, she hit Weston playfully and then took off for the ice, hoping he'd chase after her. He did. Seeing that he was up to the challenge, giving her the opportunity to skate circles around him, Jessica started whirling around the ice as though she owned it. She was good on the ice.

Weston nearly fell when he had a hard time taking his eyes off Jessica's fascinating technique. That made him more determined to win. He was darn good at ice-skating, too, much better than she gave him credit for. He had learned to ice-skate as a young boy, taught by his parents. It was often considered a sissy sport in many circles, but not among his New York City friends. Men were always seen skating in Central Park's ice arena during the winter; it was a favorite pastime for a lot of couples Weston knew personally.

When Jessica saw Jennifer hit her behind on the ice pretty hard, she started toward her, hoping she wasn't hurt. Before she could reach her sister, Samuel was already assisting his wife. Once Jessica saw that Jennifer was okay, both husband and wife laughing about the mishap, she took off again.

After Jessica had covered the entire arena, skating a fun routine with lots of enthusiasm, the music slowed down. Weston quickly skated over to her and engaged in a couple's skate. The competition was over. His skills were no match for Jessica's. He planned to dig into his pocket and hand over the twenty-dollar bill. She had won it fair and square. The lady from sunny California was a dynamo on the ice.

Jessica liked the protective feel of Weston's arm wrapped snugly around her waist. As they glided atop the ice, she laughed inwardly, thinking of the romantic ice shows on television. Pairs skating was her favorite. She imagined the two of them executing a great lift. Slithering seductively down his body would make a great ending. He would then look at her as though she was the only woman in the world for him.

Weston was McDreamy, McSteamy, McSweetie and McSensitive all rolled into one sensuous human being. *Life is good. Sooo good.*

"Hey, Miss Olympic champion," Jennifer yelled from the side rail, "you're looking pretty hot out there. Work those ice skates, girlfriend."

Jessica flashed her sister a bright smile and the thumbs-up sign. The others waved as she and Weston appeared to fly by on wings.

Weston gently tightened his grip on Jessica's waist. "You *are* good, you know."

"Yeah, I do. Wish I could reach my back with ease. I'd give it a good pat."

Weston couldn't help laughing. What kind of man laughed along with a woman who had just kicked his butt on a twenty-dollar bet? A man who had begun to fall in love with the same woman who'd dished out one can of whoop-butt.

"Instead of paying up twenty dollars, you can buy me dinner tomorrow night. How's that for a compromise?"

"You deserve both. I'd do anything to hang out with you. Dinner alone, just the two of us?"

"Just the two of us. Sounds nice and cozy. I don't think

our families will protest, seeing how badly they want us to become an item. Ugh, we're starting to fall right into their perfectly set trap."

"Hmm. Maybe, maybe not."

As Jessica and Weston joined their families, he looked at her and sighed heavily. "I don't know why I ever thought we'd get along with each other. You're still insufferable. The older you get the more unbearable you are. You need to grow up, Jessica. Life is passing you by while you're still stuck in your adolescence." He looked at his mother. "And to think I let you guilt-talk me into this trip. I must've been insane."

Jessica's brow furrowed. "What?" She looked totally puzzled. Where had Weston's sudden flash of anger come from? His odd behavior was so off the wall.

His unexpected outburst made no sense at all to Jessica; they'd just been laughing and joking up a storm. The concerned looks made her wish she could sprout wings and fly away. How dare Weston embarrass her like that...and in front of both their families? It looked as if perhaps he hadn't changed at all.

Had McBratty risen from the ashes?

The others looked like they felt sorry for Jessica. She felt kind of sorry for herself. Weston's tongue had been rather sharp. Then she saw his barely noticeable wink. She had to work hard to hide her astonishment. The "maybe, maybe not" response made sense now. He'd been trying to make the others think they weren't getting along. The funny thing was it looked as if everyone had bought into his melodrama. Weston had even sold her on it.

Jessica smiled inwardly as she returned to the ice.

As Weston joined Jessica, he got out in front of her and began skating backward.

Smiling with admiration, Jessica gave him an approving nod. "You were very convincing. But there's one problem."

"What's that?"

"How do we continue hanging out and enjoy each other's company when we're supposed to be at odds?"

Weston scratched his head. "Hadn't thought about it like that. Anyway, let's let them think we're making up. You know what they say about making up."

Weston winked at Jessica again. She stopped and he skated up to her. Taking her into his arms, he gave her a warm hug. "We don't want to pour it on too thick. Everyone will be watching our every move from here on in. When we're in private, we'll do the make-up bit right."

"As if they haven't already been watching us," Jessica said. "I bet our relationship is their first topic of discussion and the last one."

"You're probably right. Can I interest you in a cup of hot chocolate?"

"Sounds divine. I'm also intrigued by the promised make-up session."

The Commodores' "Brick House" came pounding out from the speakers before Jessica and Weston could clear the ice. Loving the oldie song, one of her parents' favorites, Jessica whirled away from him and began ice-dancing. As if she were the only person out there, she lost herself in the hip-stirring rhythm. Jessica ice-danced every bit as well as she danced.

Watching Jessica's seductive moves had Weston

hurrying across the ice to join her. As his hips gyrated wildly to the funky beat, she moved to the center of the rink, summoning him to follow her. It didn't take long before many of the other skaters decided to join their routine. A line dance ensued as the next song came on.

Back inside Weston's rented condo, seated at the breakfast bar, he dropped several tiny marshmallows into Jessica's cup of hot chocolate. "Want more?"

"That's plenty. Thank you." Jessica scooped up a handful of marshmallows and dropped them one by one into his mug. "I'm worn out. What about you?"

"Same here. We've had a very long day, an even longer evening. I've enjoyed every second of it. Not only that, the time is moving too quickly for me. Our winter wonderland vacation will be over before we know it."

Jessica was saddened by his remark. It would be over soon, much too soon, as far as she was concerned. She'd had no idea that Weston could be this much fun, not to mention how romantic and sensual he was. She'd miss him. "It *is* going by pretty quickly. Getting back to work will be tough after I'm finished playing so hard."

Wearing a serious expression on his face, Weston made direct eye contact with Jessica. "Now that we're on this subject, I want to ask you something. What's the chance of us getting together after we leave Aspen?"

Jessica shrugged. "We live on separate coasts. I don't know how we'd manage it. California to New York is at least a five-hour flight, one way."

"What if I agree to do the traveling? Can I visit you in L.A.?"

Jessica looked surprised by the questions. "You'd be willing to do that?"

"In a New York minute." He grinned. "No pun intended. What about it?"

"I'm okay with it if you are. I have a guest bedroom. Just let me know when."

"We're on!" Weston was obviously pleased by the outcome of his probe.

Jessica fished out a melted marshmallow from her cup. She then held the tiny morsel up to Weston's lips. After taking the tidbit from her hand, he licked her finger in a provocative way. "Sweet, so sweet. Think I can get another one?"

Jessica repeated the act. This time he drew her finger into his mouth and sucked on it gently. His eyes connected soulfully with hers, causing her to blush. "I think it's time for us to make up. What do you think?"

Jessica responded to Weston's question by offering up her lips to taste. He quickly accepted the sweet offer in the spirit it had been presented. Kissing her had already become his most favorite thing to do.

Jessica's cell phone abruptly interrupted the intimate moment. After identifying the caller, she thought about not answering. She then thought better of it. It could be something important. She really cared about her friends. And Jarred might be having a hard time over the bad breakup with Melanie. She wanted to be there for him.

"Where are you?" Jarred asked Jessica, sounding rather anxious.

"You already know where I am. What's up?"

"You're not with your family, because I just called there."

"And? What's that supposed to mean?"

"Nothing, really. I just wanted to make sure you're okay. It bothers me that you're in Aspen with some guy who doesn't value you as a person. Please tell me you are not off somewhere alone with him."

"Why does that matter to you one way or the other?"

"I just told you. I'm really worried about you being around someone who has a history of being mean to you. Is that a sin? It's also very late."

Jessica's heart instantly softened toward Jarred despite the fact he had just interrupted a very intimate moment. "No, it's not a sin. Please don't be concerned. Everything is under control. I'm a big girl. Okay?"

"I guess. When are you coming home?"

"You already know that, too. The dates still haven't changed…and they won't. Is something going on that I don't know about? Are you missing Mel?"

"Not in the least. It's *you* that I'm missing. It's *you.*"

Jessica was a bit stunned by Jarred's candid remarks. She didn't want to read more into what he had meant by it, but it sounded like he missed her in a way different from the norm. She didn't want to entertain this. Besides, it was a ludicrous notion. "You're just lonely. It's the holidays. I understand what you're feeling. You need to get with the crew and stop isolating yourself."

"Maybe you're right. Call me before you shut down?"

"In the morning. Like you said, it's late."

"Good enough." Jarred disconnected without further comment.

Wondering what was really up with Jarred, Jessica scowled, flipping her phone shut. Her best friend was acting terribly strange. Breakups caused a person to feel lonely, but Jarred had said it was the best thing. If that was the case, why was he acting so weird? Jessica wished she had the answers.

Feeling the intensity of Weston's eyes on her, she looked over at him and pointed at her cup. "It's cold now. Refill, please?"

Weston nodded. The last thing he wanted to do was move away from her side. The phone call had him more than curious. Although Jessica hadn't referred to the person by name, he was sure it had been the same guy who'd called before. Who was he, anyway? He wanted to ask her about it, but since he didn't know how to go about it, he'd let it ride. The last thing he wanted was to come off as jealous and insecure.

Once Weston had poured a refill, he carried it over to the coffee table in the living room. He then went back for Jessica, reaching for her hand. Moving from the kitchen to the living room would allow them to sit closer together. The setting was also more comfortable. He needed to have Jessica right up under him. The odd phone call had Weston feeling a tad insecure, something he wasn't used to.

Weston brought Jessica in close to him. As he put his arm around her shoulder, his lips met tenderly with her cheek. "The firelight is pretty, isn't it?"

"Beautiful. I love the roaring colors. I can sit and stare into a blazing fire for hours on end. It has a way of mesmerizing me. Many people have misconceptions about California living, mainly because of the weather. I have two stone fireplaces in my town house. And I use them both, especially the one in the bedroom."

"Real wood or gas logs?"

"Both. I prefer to use the gas log. Cleanup is difficult with wood. I don't want my place to smell like unpleasant ashes, either."

"There are ways around it, but you have to clean it after every use. My housekeeper's husband sweeps out my fireplace after each use."

Jessica raised an eyebrow. "Housekeeper? What size place *do* you have?"

"A pretty good-sized one. Four bedrooms and a nice-size loft."

"Hmm, sounds really nice. Maybe I'll get to see it one day."

"I'd like that. If you could go anywhere in the world, where would you go? Right now?"

Jessica closed her eyes for a second. "Paris. Definitely Paris."

"Have you been there?"

"I wish. One day, though."

"We can go there right now."

Jessica looked perplexed. "Come again?"

"Close your eyes, sweetheart. Let me take you right into the heart of Paris."

Obedient to Weston's gentle command, Jessica closed her eyes. As his hand tenderly squeezed her shoulder, she laid her head against his chest.

"We'll visit the Eiffel Tower first," Weston soothed, "then the Arc de Triomphe. Later on we'll tour the Louvre, where Mona Lisa hangs out."

"Sounds fantastic!"

Weston reached down and took off Jessica's shoes and

then had her stretch out on the sofa. Grabbing hold of a throw pillow, he placed it on his lap, summoning her to lay her head there.

Jessica obeyed Weston's commands again.

Weston looked down into Jessica's eyes and smiled broadly. "Once upon a time there was a beautiful young princess named Jessica, the fairest woman in all the land. But she was awfully lonely because there weren't any guys good enough for her. She was the kind of woman who set her standards high, worthy of such…and so much more. You see, Jessica deserved the very best in a man because she was a wonderful woman.

"Then one day Prince Weston, who lived far, far away, stopped by a remote palace for a brief respite for himself and his steed. When he asked the groundskeeper for water for himself and his powerful animal, he was told to see Princess Jessica, the mistress of the castle. He found her out in the Garden of Love, looking sad and feeling down-right lonely.

"Princess Jessica told him she'd been praying for her Prince Charming to come along before his arrival. She asked if he was *the one*. His passionate kiss gave the answer.

"Prince Weston was the one, the one and only.

"Prince Weston then offered to take Princess Jessica for a ride on his magnificent white steed. When she asked him where to, he told her Paris, the magnificent City of Light."

Chapter 5

With both families seated near the Christmas tree in the Harrington town house, holiday sounds by Nat King Cole played softly in the background. The tree lights and fireplace were in service. Dozens of red and green candles burned brightly, adding a dash of cinnamon and spice scents to the fresh pine.

The two families were having a grand time viewing photos from past vacations. Many pictures had been taken when the kids were younger. Jessica moaned at how pudgy she had been in her preteen years. Weston wasn't happy about the numerous photos clearly capturing his acne.

Jennifer gushed over all of the pictures of her, especially those including Samuel. Her parents had started taking him on family trips after they'd been dating a couple of years. Jennifer would've been miserable without him.

Sahara and Roman had closely chaperoned the young couple, carefully monitoring all their activities away and at home.

To share something special with Jessica, Weston excused himself and asked her to come along. The couple entered the unoccupied bedroom and it surprised her to see the spacious room filled with toys and other presents. She turned questioning eyes on him. "What's all this? How did it get here?"

Weston picked up a sweet-looking baby doll and hugged it to himself. "Our dads helped me out when you ladies were shopping. I need some help wrapping these presents. Can I count on you?"

With no children in their group, Jessica gave him another puzzled look. "Of course, but who are these gifts for?"

Weston's eyes suddenly glistened with moisture. "We're taking them to an orphanage. Something I do every year. I delivered gifts to orphanages in Harlem and the Bronx before leaving New York."

Jessica was totally bowled over by Weston's altruistic spirit, her mouth agape. "What a glorious and loving gesture. Why do you do this?"

"Just something I truly enjoy. When I'm home, a couple of my buddies and I dress up like Santa on Christmas Eve and then make a visit to the orphanages to pass out presents to children and employees. We leave the majority of the gifts for discovery on Christmas morning."

Jessica rushed across the room and threw her arms around Weston's neck. She then pinched him. As he reacted to the pain, she laughed heartily. "Sorry, but I had to make sure you were real. You amaze me. I can't express how I feel about this. God is no doubt smiling on you."

"God inspires me. All the glory goes to Him."

"I'm so impressed. Well, enough of this. Let's get these presents done so you can deliver them. Where are the wrapping paper and ribbons?"

Weston opened the clothes closet and pulled out large bags of decorative Christmas paper and a bunch of assorted bows. "Think we should ask the others to help?"

"Duh! If we don't, it'll take us a few days to do it all. I think everyone would love to help. It's a worthwhile cause. Let's go ask."

Weston pulled Jessica to him and gave her a warm hug and kiss. "I knew I could count on you. Thanks, sweetheart, just for being you."

"You're the one who deserves the thanks. You keep earning favorable points with me. I never dreamed you'd turn out to be this special."

"I know why that is. Sorry I was so mean to you. Do you think maybe I had a serious crush on you and didn't know how to show it?"

"I guess that's possible, but we'll never know for sure. It's a really nice thought."

"It *is*. I can show how I feel about you without scalping you, leaving you without a shadow of doubt."

"Another nice thought. Let's get the others before we get into some serious showing and telling. I have the desire to kiss you breathless."

"Oh, please hold that thought until later, since I plan to take you up on it. We have a lot to show and tell each other."

* * *

Just as Jessica had thought, the others were eager to help wrap the packages. An assembly line was quickly established. Weston, Roman and Jacque opted to measure and then cut the wrapping paper. Jessica, Sahara, Sandra and Jennifer wrapped the gifts. Once gifts were handed to Samuel, he placed the bows on them. *Boy* or *girl* name tags were also added by Samuel to show the gender intent.

The variety of toys Weston had picked out was sure to delight all the boys and girls. Baby dolls, stuffed animals, footballs and basketballs, board games and a host of other entertaining items would make someone's day.

Jessica would love to see the smiles on those little faces.

The sudden chiming of the doorbell had Jessica scrambling to get up. Since no one was expected, Weston got up and went with her as a safety precaution. These days no one ever knew who might be on the other side of a door.

The moment the door was opened a group of men and women began to carol softly. Weston instantly called for the others to join them. Jessica, forgetting about the presence of everyone else, laid her head back against Weston's chest, overwhelmed by the Christmas carolers. Normally her family and their neighbors were a part of the caroling festivities back home. Like the special gift-giving, it was something the Harringtons loved to do.

One of Jessica's favorite holiday tunes, "The First Noel," was sung beautifully. She couldn't be happier about her decision to join her family. Though she had remained undecided up to the last minute, she was aware of how much she would've missed out on. Although she loved spending time with her friends, what she missed most was the group shopping sprees they took.

"Shop until you drop" was their motto during the holiday season.

Each female in Jessica's circle hosted a girls-only breakfast, brunch, luncheon or dinner during the holiday season, beginning on the fifteenth of December and ending Christmas Eve. The guys did something similar, but their events were held in the evenings. The two groups joined together for the last event, a potluck dinner held at the home of the host person for that year.

Once Jessica realized she and Weston were giving the others cause for further speculation, she moved slightly away from him. Before she got out of his reach, he grabbed hold of her hand. Squeezing her fingers was his way of letting her know he understood. Jessica fleetingly contemplated making their feelings known to the others, but then she thought better of it. There'd be no peace for either of them if their families got the idea they were falling in love.

Falling in love. What an interesting choice of words, Jessica mused.

Jessica had to wonder if she *was* falling in love with Weston. It didn't take her long to deliberate. Even though she suspected she was already in love, she wouldn't allow herself to admit it. The reality of such a magnanimous occurrence was scary.

Once the carolers moved on down the outside corridor, Roman closed the front door. His offer to fix drinks and snacks was met with loud shouts of approval. Jessica quickly offered to help her father. After Roman nodded his agreement, she followed him into the kitchen, where she retrieved a box of assorted crackers, a summer sausage, apples and two blocks of cheese.

While Jessica cut the snacks into bite-size cubes and slices, Roman began mixing up a variety of drinks. Preparing a pitcher of strawberry margaritas came first; Jessica's preference. Since Sahara loved apple martinis and Sandra loved cosmopolitans, he planned on mixing those, too. His choice in drinks was a white merlot or a zinfandel, which Jennifer and Samuel also liked. Scotch on the rocks was Jacque's.

Roman suddenly realized he didn't know Weston's drink. "What does Wes like to drink? I see how cozy and comfy you two have gotten with each other."

Jessica rolled her eyes. "Why ask me? How would I know?"

Roman chuckled. "If you both would stop trying to prove you don't like each other, you'd do a better job convincing us. You aren't fooling a single soul. You guys can barely keep your eyes and hands off each other."

Jessica's cheeks flushed with color. "That's simply not true."

Roman took Jessica into his arms. "It *is* true...and we all know it. Stop fighting the feelings, honey. It is okay to be attracted to each other."

"What's not okay is for you guys to put so much pressure on us, Dad. Wes and I could become great friends if everyone wasn't expecting anything more to develop. We *are* enjoying each other's company, but we're both fearful of the high expectations. We're not interested in our parents setting us up for marriage."

Roman looked concerned. "I can see you're really upset about this. What can we do to make the rest of your vacation more enjoyable?"

"*Back off,* Dad, please. You guys need to give us our space. I have enough pressure in my life without thinking about marriage. Actually, you and Wes's dad are more on this kick than Mom and Ms. Sandra. Someone is always hinting about Wes and me. I'm totally sick of it."

Jessica hadn't intended to go off like that. Her frustration had gotten out of control. Wasn't it bad enough that she was falling or had already fallen in love with Weston? Where they lived was a major obstacle, a painful one. A long-distance relationship was impossible to maintain. She wished everyone else knew that. Jessica just wanted to enjoy the holidays and move on.

Jessica looked up and managed a believable smile. "We only live on opposite coasts. I'm not moving to New York. He's not moving to L.A. We have established that much. We both love where we reside. Compromise just isn't in the cards for us."

Jessica didn't feel it necessary to explain they planned on seeing each other beyond Aspen. It would only add more fuel to the bonfire. She couldn't stand the stressful situation as it was.

Regretful, Roman nodded. "I'll tell everyone to back off. Good enough?"

"It has to be. But if it doesn't happen, I'm leaving. I didn't come here to make a love connection." *Yet it happened. Big-time.* "I came to relax and have a good time."

"That's *just* what you'll have. I'll see to it. Okay?"

"Okay." Jessica smiled nervously as she gave Roman a warm hug.

Weston walked into the kitchen as Jessica resumed her duties. He immediately noticed her discomfort. With Roman there, he decided not to ask what was wrong. Showing concern wasn't an option, either, since their every move was closely scrutinized.

Roman made small talk with Weston while mixing up the remaining drinks. After pouring the green liquid into two martini glasses, he plopped in green olives. Once the frozen-strawberry margarita mix had blended well with the tequila and triple sec, Roman poured it into a margarita glass, with a powder-sugared rim. Pouring the white wine came next. Before leaving the kitchen, Roman gave Jessica a margarita with a lime wedge.

"Thanks, Dad."

"You're welcome." Roman leaned over and kissed her cheek.

Finished up with the snack platters, Jessica placed them on a serving tray. She asked Weston to carry them into the living room, but Roman offered to come back for them once he served the drinks.

Weston watched after Roman until he disappeared. "What was going on in here?"

Feeling sorry over her earlier behavior, Jessica sighed. "I sort of lost my cool with Dad. I'm sorry about it, but maybe it'll stop the nonsense once and for all. Dad promised to have everyone back off."

"Do the hints and suggestive remarks upset you that much?"

"It's more frustrating than anything."

Roman reentering the kitchen caused Jessica to go mum. Feeling that he had interrupted something important, he grabbed the snack tray and left.

"As you were saying?"

Jessica waved her hand in a dismissing way. "Don't want to go there. We're supposed to be having a good time. Everything will be okay now. I'm sure of it."

"Are you positive you don't want to talk about your feelings? I'm here for you."

Jessica smiled sweetly. "I know that…and I am sure." She crossed the room and stood up under the mistletoe. She then pointed up at it.

Weston rapidly closed the distance between them. Tenderly, he pulled Jessica into his arms, looking down into eyes filled with a gentle spirit. His mouth instantly covered hers, causing her to shiver with pleasure. Her hand sought out his hair, entwining her fingers in its softness. Jessica first flattened her palm against his chest, then stuck her hand inside his shirt, meeting up with a thatch of thick hair.

Jessica moaned softly, conjuring up a nude image of Weston. What she imagined was nothing similar to his teenage body. There hadn't been chest hair, or rock-hard abs and rippling muscles back then. Jessica loved the great changes.

Knowing she was quickly losing the battle over her desire to touch Weston all over, Jessica groaned inwardly. She enjoyed touching him, loved the way his skin felt beneath her fingertips, craved the jolt of electricity she felt every single time they joined hands. "Please kiss me again. All day long I've been thinking about our lips engaged in passion. Kiss me, sweetheart. Kiss me again and again."

"My lips are all yours, to do with as you please."

"I hope you mean that." Jessica wrapped herself up in the strength of his arms. Knowing she was right where she belonged caused her heart to rejoice.

Weston kissed the tip of Jessica's nose. "I try not to say anything I don't mean."

"I like that. We should never say anything we don't mean." She lazed her knuckles down the side of his face as she claimed his mouth again. "Once the evening quiets down, we should slip away to the cabin. You think?"

"Most definitely. I love being alone with you."

"Go ahead and join the others. I'll follow in a minute." Jessica needed a minute to regroup. Besides that, she didn't want them returning together.

Weston started for the door, only to turn around. "This doesn't feel right to me. I have a suggestion. Willing to hear me out?"

"No doubt."

"Why don't we just tell our families we're trying to establish a bond to see where it takes us? We can ask them to let us go at our own pace, without any interference from them. Can we at least consider it?"

Jessica grinned. "I like your suggestion, but I want to do it separately. You tell your family and I'll tell mine, at an opportune time. Good enough?"

"Perfect." He took her hands in his and kissed her forehead. "See you in a few minutes. Don't give my heart time to get lonely."

Jessica winked. "You got it. Now move it, buddy."

Closing her eyes tightly, Jessica leaned back against the sink, wishing her heart would stop this wild ride. Weston caused such crazy feelings to stir inside her. He was the only man ever to make her heart rate soar. She didn't want to think about the arrival of January third, but it was hard not to ponder.

Jessica didn't look forward to leaving Weston behind. She loathed the very thought. The man was in her blood hotly. Admitting her deep feelings for him was sweetly unbearable. The song "Ain't No Sunshine" suddenly came to mind, causing her to shrink within. She had to get back to the others, but first she had to pull herself together.

Jessica immediately got caught up in all the hoopla as she walked back into the room. Everyone was caught up in wrapping the gifts and having fun accomplishing it. Laughter and animated chatter abounded.

The large red bow Sahara had placed in her hair caused Jessica to laugh. It reminded her of how their parents used to wrap her and Jennifer in bright ribbons and place bows in the center of their foreheads. The girls were often told they were the best presents their parents had ever received. All the family holidays were special ones. Jessica missed both sets of grandparents, who had died. Their presence during the holidays had made the festivities even more special.

Jessica discreetly wiped the sentimental moisture from her eyes. She hadn't acted quickly enough. Weston had already spotted the sparkle of tears. He instantly came to her side. Taking her in his arms to comfort her was thwarted. He didn't want to embarrass her. Until they told their families about their plans, they'd just have to cool it.

A loud honking sound caught Jessica's and Weston's attention. Roman held a toy car in his hand. Sounds of a baby crying came next. Sahara was playing with a baby doll. Samuel turned on a switch to a monkey manically playing a set of drums. Everyone fell into peals of laughter. Jennifer had fun putting the jump rope into commission.

Since everyone seemed to be enjoying themselves, Weston and Jessica decided also to pick out favorite toys. The bright red fire engine, equipped with all sorts of bells and whistles, caught Weston's eye. Jessica quickly became enamored with a stuffed white polar bear. It reminded her of the fluffy white one she had been given as a child.

Polo Bear had been Jessica's favorite toy, a security blanket of sorts—and she still had it. Polo Bear's permanent sleeping place was the comfortable chair in her bedroom, but there were times when it found its way into her bed.

Once the group had their fill of the toys, the wrapping duties were resumed.

Sweaters had also been purchased, along with jackets, pajamas, robes and slippers. Weston collected the money throughout the year for his charity cause in various ways, but he also gave a big chunk of his own money. Everyone was pleased he had invited them along to help deliver the gifts on Christmas Eve.

Seated on the sofa in the cabin, Weston held Jessica in his arms. Although it was long after midnight, they'd only been alone less than an hour. It had been harder to slip away than anticipated. All the fun at the town house had made it difficult to leave. The two families had gotten into a real party mode. Sahara and Roman had put on their seventies CDs and the dance grooves were on. Their folks were still dancing when both the younger couples had left.

Weston made sure Jessica was comfortable before he opened the long, slender book, written in large, bold print. He couldn't believe what he was about to do. Read to a woman, something he hadn't ever done before. He wasn't sure where the idea had come from, but the book of Christmas stories had somehow gotten left behind in the cabin. There was something sensual about reading to Jessica and he took in a deep breath before beginning "The Night Before Christmas."

Jessica loved the very idea, thrilled at Weston reading to her. It was a novelty for her, an extremely enjoyable one. His voice alone, deep and mesmerizing, made the reading interesting. Although it was a story she had heard hundreds of times, she had never heard it done in such an artistic manner. Every single word was pronounced clearly and distinctively. It was as if Weston were onstage delivering aloud a dramatic reading to an attentive audience. But she was his only listener—and she loved the way he held her completely spellbound.

Once Weston finished the moving story, he handed the book to Jessica. "Read something to me." With that said, he laid his head upon her shoulder.

Jessica chose a more biblical-based story, the birth of baby Jesus. In a matter of seconds she had proved that she was also quite a storyteller. He was enchanted by how softly yet expressively she spoke. Even though he wasn't looking at her, her emotions were easy to discern. He could tell the story had tapped into her soul.

After Jessica finished her read, she closed the book and laid it on the coffee table.

Weston drew Jessica in closer to him, smoothing her hair back from her forehead. Her slight tremors let him know she was affected emotionally. There was something special about that. He loved compassion in a woman. Jessica seemed to have lots of empathy to go along with her other appealing characteristics. "If you could have anything you wanted for Christmas, what would you ask for?"

"For hunger and poverty to be abolished," she said without the slightest hesitation. "Then joy for the world and peace and contentment for everyone." Jessica giggled softly. "Then I'd plead for lots of diamonds, a navy convertible Mercedes Benz and a different wardrobe to cover every day of the year. Is that selfish or what?" Tilting her head, Jessica looked up at him and smiled. "What about you? What do you want?"

"I'd ask for the same things you did, peace and joy and for hunger and poverty to cease to exist." His eyes softened, darkening at the same time. "I'd ask for you to love me, only me, for always and forever." Weston licked his lips. "You are my diamonds and Mercedes Benz. I'd be wealthy because of your love. If a man can get the woman he loves to love him back, he shouldn't ask for more."

Jessica felt breathless, her heart thumping wildly inside her chest. Her palms felt sweaty, her limbs trembling. Had this beautiful man just confessed his love to her? Had she heard him right? Was it just wishful thinking because it was something she desperately wanted? Jessica knew that she wanted Weston to love her the same way she loved him. *Yes, I do love him, with all my heart and soul.*

Totally knocked off-kilter by how easily she had admitted her love for Weston, Jessica found herself astounded yet again. It was hard to keep from hyperventilating. Admitting her love to him was a horse of a totally different color. Jessica wasn't sure she could put her heart out there like that again. The fear of him trampling on it was a real possibility, a serious threat to her serenity.

Weston lifted Jessica's chin with two fingers, kissing her softly on the mouth, repeatedly. His lips tenderly caressed her cheeks, nose and eyelids. Her ears then became the target of his moist tongue. Weston pulled his head back and gazed into Jessica's eyes. "In case you're wondering, I *do* love you. I *was* confessing my love to you."

Jessica closed her eyes and desperately tried to catch her breath. The moment was so surreal that she wanted to pinch herself. But she was awake and aware. She had never been more aware of the here and now. The moment was breathtaking. No man, other than Roman, had ever told her he loved her. Weston's confession meant everything to her.

It wasn't every day a woman had the man she loved love her back. Even though Jessica didn't think she should confess her love to Weston so soon this was the ultimate season for lovers. And she was madly in love with him. "I love you, too."

Jessica and Weston sealed their confessions with a flurry of staggering kisses.

At 3:00 a.m. Jessica awakened with a start. Looking at the clock caused her to shriek inwardly. Weston was completely knocked out; his head nestled in her lap. What was she to do? More importantly, how was she to explain this to her parents? There were only a few hours until daybreak; she had nearly spent the night in Weston's cabin. Although their parents desperately wanted them to come together, they might be embarrassed by the inconsiderate behavior.

Wakening Weston just to get up from the sofa had Jessica wishing they hadn't fallen off to sleep. He looked so peaceful. But she had to get back to the town house, so Jessica shook him gently.

Weston's eyes opened slowly. Seeing Jessica made him smile. "Hi, there." He then shot straight up. "Oh my God, what time is it?"

"My sentiments exactly." Frowning, Jessica pointed at the clock. "If you think I'm not in hot water with my folks, you'd better think again. I have to go."

Weston got to his feet. "Wait until I splash some water on my face."

"Don't bother. I'll see you later. I've really got to run."

"Not without me. If there is any explaining, we do it together. We're totally innocent. We simply fell asleep, so calm down. No one can fault us for that. Every day in Aspen has been action packed."

Jessica took a deep breath. "You're right. I think our parents understand. Besides, we're adults, living on our own. Still, we should go just out of respect."

Roman and Sahara and Sandra and Jacque were still up when Jessica and Weston crept in. Roman jumped to his feet when his daughter appeared. None of the parents appeared overly concerned or at all anxious.

Weston immediately began to explain what had happened, taking total responsibility.

Jessica didn't think he should shoulder all the blame. She would back him up. "This is no one's fault. We were just tired enough to fall asleep," she explained. "Sorry if we embarrassed you guys. It wasn't our intent."

"That you're both safe is all we care about," Roman said. "We haven't been sitting up waiting for you two, just catching up. Our evening hadn't come to an end." Jacque nodded. "You two are responsible adults. Your moms weren't even worried. In case you've forgotten, we were young once, too. Did you have a good time?"

Weston looked over at Jessica in a questioning manner. She immediately understood the query. It was time for them to explain. Although they had decided to speak on it individually, the timing couldn't be more perfect. Once he received her nodding approval, he summoned her to take a seat—and he did the same.

"Jessica and I know you guys want us to get together. We have resisted it, up until now. We are extremely interested in each other and we do plan to see where it goes." That was an understatement, but he wasn't ready to reveal more. "All we ask is that you give us space to do our own thing, at our own pace. Please, no pressure or any expectations for us. Can you guys do that?"

"Absolutely," Roman said. "I believe I'm speaking for us all." The others nodded in agreement. However, the four parents failed terribly at hiding their excitement despite the valiant attempt. Euphoria was all over their smiling faces.

Feeling good about how things had gone down, Weston

stood and reached for Jessica's hand. "That's settled, so you can walk me out. We need to get some sleep even if our parents are outdistancing us."

Everyone laughed.

Jessica was thrilled to step outside with Weston for a proper and passionate good-night kiss. This was the beginning of something special for them. Both were eager to see how far their feelings would go. The issue of distance remained, but they weren't dwelling on that for now. They still had time to figure out everything.

Chapter 6

Inside the One of a Kind Boutique, located in the center of downtown Aspen, Jennifer sat quietly, sipping on a cup of hot tea. As she patiently waited for Jessica to come out of the dressing room, she wondered what designer creation she'd wear next. The two sisters had been shopping for nearly two hours. This was the last store on the list.

The formal-wear boutique owners, three biological sisters, generously offered refreshments daily to their customers. The upscale boutique proudly boasted a vast collection of original one-of-a-kind designer creations.

Shopping in special boutiques for formal wear was exciting and fun for Jessica and Jennifer. Jessica had brought along an evening gown, but it wasn't what a woman in love wore on a special-occasion date with the man of her dreams.

Although Jennifer was satisfied with her dress, she was having loads of fun helping her sister choose the perfect formal. Besides Weston, Jennifer was the only person who knew that Jessica had fallen in love.

Sahara and Sandra were also out on a shopping spree. Instead of looking for clothes, they were scouting specialty stores for unique gifts for hard-to-buy-for spouses. The four men had left early in the morning to tackle the slopes of freshly fallen snow.

Jennifer gasped as Jessica stepped out of the dressing room. Jessica had only achieved a half pirouette before Jennifer decided it was the perfect dress for the New Year's Eve gala. Her sister looked like a million bucks in the gown. Jessica could easily pass for royalty.

The red-hot, floor-length gown Jessica modeled had been fashioned in a winter-white silk crepe, beautifully highlighted with shimmering mother-of-pearl sequins. The dress hugged every one of Jessica's luscious curves, outlining her firm breasts in a flattering way. The fit was absolutely perfect. It looked as if her figure had been melted down and then poured into the gown.

Several customers had gathered around Jessica to get a closer look at the gown. Jessica was thrilled that she had first dibs on it. If she decided to make the purchase, no one else in Aspen would show up at the gala wearing a duplicate. A few more twists and turns in front of the mirror helped Jessica make the final decision. "Ring it up," she called out to the store clerk.

Jennifer looked pleased. "I'm glad about your choice. It's perfect for you. Wes won't be able to take his eyes off you. You look stunning, baby sister!"

"Thank you, Jen. That was sweet. It *is* stunning. I feel like a dream."

"You look like a dream, every man's dream come true," the store clerk voiced. "We received this marvelous creation this morning. You're the first person to try it on. Congratulations on a wonderful One of a Kind find!"

"That seals the deal. The dress was made for me," Jessica gushed. "I promise to wear it proudly and tell everyone where I purchased it."

"That's kind of you. Word of mouth is the best advertisement. The gown on you is a walking endorsement for us. By the way, my name is Mary Moore. My sisters, Maria and Marsha, are co-owners."

"Nice to meet you, Mary," Jessica and Jennifer said in unison, laughing afterward. The Harrington sisters also shared their first and last names with Mary.

"Do you have the right kind of shoes?" Mary asked Jessica.

"No to go with this. Any recommendations?"

"I'll be right back." Mary disappeared into a back room. Jessica shrugged. "They don't sell shoes, do they?"

"I didn't see any on display," Jennifer responded.

Mary returned with a catalog and handed it to Jessica. "You can find the perfect shoes for your dress in there. If we phone in an order today, I can have them in time for your holiday event."

Jessica handed the catalog to Jennifer. "Start looking while I change out of the dress. I'll only be a couple of minutes."

"Sure thing." With that said, Jennifer began flipping through the catalog.

* * *

The resort weight room was fully equipped with state-of-the-art equipment, the best money could buy. Jessica had finished with the weight machines and was now on the stationary bike. She planned to work out on the treadmill before using the wet sauna and hot tub. She felt hot and sweaty and had already reached her target heart rate. That made her feel really good.

Jessica thought she was alone in the workout room until she heard a noise. She turned with a start, surprised to see Weston there, dressed in dark sweats. Because her body glistened with sweat, she was pretty sure she didn't smell pleasant. That slightly embarrassed her. "Hi. I didn't expect to see you in here."

Weston took a cursory glance around the place. "We just got back from skiing so a soak in the hot tub might keep my leg muscles from tightening. Want the rest of why I'm here?"

Jessica laughed. "Sure."

"I called the town house. Jennifer said you were here. I then recalled your plan to work out after shopping." With his eyes fastened on her, he walked over to the bike. Removing the white towel from around his neck, he patted dry the moisture on her face and shoulders. "Are you about through?"

"Not quite. I plan to use the hot tub, but the wet sauna is next."

"I can benefit from the sauna, too. Mind if I join you?"

There was no way to discreetly raise her arms and smell her pits. She'd love to share the sauna and hot tub with Weston, but her sweaty scent was a strong deterrent.

She didn't want to turn him off. Her desire was to keep him turned-on.

"Don't worry about how you smell. It's a natural one. We all sweat, honey."

"Mind reader, huh?"

"Expression reader. Your face has a way of telling all." He leaned over and inhaled her scent. "I wonder what you smell like after a night of hot, tantalizing lovemaking. Delicious, I bet." Her blushing made him smile. "I'd let you take a whiff of me, but it won't be delightful. I only rinsed off after skiing. I plan to shower before we go to the orphanage later."

Weston's comments had Jessica burning with sexual desire. Blowing off her worries, she quickly dismounted. "Let's hit the sauna."

Weston grinned widely. "That's what I'm talking about!"

Hot, sweaty bodies were sexy to people madly in love. The thought of their sweat mingling during a heated love-making session had Jessica gasping inwardly. Her body temperature had already soared a few degrees.

The sauna swirled with hot steam as Jessica and Weston stepped inside. After stretching out on the wooden benches, Jessica closed her eyes. Seeing Weston with his shirt off was a thrill. He had also stripped off his sweat-pants to reveal boxer-style swim trunks. Concentrating on anything but his nude upper body, bare thighs and sturdy legs was next to impossible. His strong abs were well-defined beneath the muscle-enhancing attire he some-times wore.

Although conscious of the one-piece bathing suit she had stripped down to, Jessica was sure Weston had seen women in a lot less. Seeing the ladies in nothing at all was probably more like it.

The sudden feel of Weston's tender touch on her abdomen had Jessica afraid to open her eyes and look up at him. She had to wonder where his roving hands would go next. Where did she want them to go? She refused to answer her own question. The response might be incriminating. It only took a second for her to find out, as his fingertips outlined her thigh at the edge of her swimsuit. He was a little too close to her molten treasures for her to relax under his expert touch. Relaxing totally could be her undoing.

Jessica bit down on her lip to keep from crying out from the bliss. As she squeezed her eyelids tighter, Weston's moist tongue feathered across her lips, his sweet breath mingling with hers. Butterfly kisses followed his delightfully tormenting tongue.

Please don't let your hands and mouth go any lower.

Jessica basked in the heated intimacy, wanting to welcome him inside her. Her bared thighs were now the lucky recipients of his gently stroking hands. The tender kneading and massaging of her legs felt outrageously wonderful. As the tip of his tongue outlined her cleavage, her body turned to liquid fire. Begging him to stop the seduction of Jessica Nicole Harrington was totally out of the question.

Weston took hold of Jessica's hand and directed it to his chest. "Touch me. Make me feel as good as I'm making you feel. How good *do* you feel?"

Jessica allowed her forefinger to circle his right nipple.

"Wonderful! I feel wonderful." Her hand moved over to his left pectoral and massaged it with her palm. "How does that feel?"

Weston only moaned in pleasurable agony. He again covered her hand with his. Directing it to his abdomen, he pressed it into his midsection, as if wishing she'd take it lower without any prompting from him. His rigid manhood throbbed and relief would be only a few fiery strokes away.

"I don't want to push the envelope, but I hope you feel confident enough in our love to let me make love to you. I want you desperately."

Keeping her eyes shut tightly, Jessica blew out a stream of breath. "The feeling *is* mutual, Wes, but the timing isn't. Can you be patient?"

"I'm a patient man. There's no rush." He kissed her thoroughly. "No rush at all."

Jessica rewarded Weston's patience with another staggering kiss.

The two families filed out of the van. With their arms and hands piled high with wrapped presents, they rushed toward the entry to St. Anthony's Orphanage. The extreme cold would keep the women inside the toasty warm building while the guys made return trips. Fresh snow fell and the temperature had dropped drastically again.

Sisters Carmen, Bernadette and Natalie welcomed the visitors with smiles and holiday greetings. The children were inside one of the rooms, waiting impatiently. The grateful sisters had invited Weston and his group of friends to join them for a bit of Christmas caroling and early-evening snacks. Hot drinks were quickly served.

Since this charity event was Weston's baby, he was the spokesperson for the group, taking pleasure in the introductions. More warm smiles and handshakes followed. Sister Carmen then led the way to the recreation room, where the Christmas tree was. As she opened the double doors, the children welcomed their visitors to St. Anthony's.

Jessica instantly took to the children. She hardly ever had the opportunity to be around young kids. None of her friends had children so this was a real treat for her. Jennifer and Samuel had talked about starting a family. She could barely wait to become Auntie Jessica. Holding a baby securely in her arms would be a thrill.

Not long after Jessica sat down in a folding chair, a little boy of five or six cautiously inched his way over to her. He beamed at her with a toothless grin and then practically jumped into her lap, catching her by surprise.

The child rested his head against Jessica's chest and stared at her as though he was looking into the face of an angel. "I'm Matt." He gave a cute little infectious giggle.

"Hi, Matt, I'm Miss Jessica." She kissed his forehead and smiled. His dark-brown eyes smiled back, leaving her hopelessly enchanted. "Looking forward to Santa Claus coming to town?"

Matt suddenly eyed Jessica with suspicion. "There's no Santa," he said, his childlike voice endearing and raspy.

Swallowing hard to clear her throat, Jessica was caught off guard again. That this little guy didn't believe in Santa was hurtful to her spirit. "Who told you that?"

Matt pointed at an adorable little boy seated on the floor. "Jimmy said so. He says Santa sucks and his reindeer can't fly."

Jessica's heart ached over Matt's sad expression. "That's not true. Santa *is* real."

"Is Jimmy a liar?"

This kid was so amazing, quick-minded, too. She'd have to tread lightly with him or end up falling prey to disaster. "No. He just might think there's no Santa and that reindeer can't fly. When Santa stops here on Christmas Eve, maybe Jimmy will believe it then."

Matt shrugged his little shoulders. "I hope so. I like Santa and his reindeer. Rudolph is my best bud. He has a red nose. It lights up, too. Do you think his nose is red because he has a cold?"

Jessica cracked up. "The bright red nose helps Rudolph guide the way. I like Santa and Rudolph, too. I used to read about Rudolph when I was small."

Matt looked terribly disappointed. "I can't read yet."

Patting Matt's tiny arm, Jessica smiled with empathy. "You'll learn to read soon. Do you like looking at pictures in books?"

Matt nodded. "I do it a lot."

"That's good. You're a pretty special little guy, you know."

Matt's eyes took on a liquid sadness. "I wish a nice mommy and daddy knew that." Matt jumped out of Jessica's lap as quickly as he'd landed there. "Gotta go." He turned and gave Jessica another grin and waved. "Bye."

Jessica's heart ached for Matt as she watched him join a group of his peers. Had he left her because of sadness?

She wasn't sure why he'd run off. It was hard to keep her tears at bay. Then Matt's laughter rang out. That lifted her spirits tremendously. The kid was so real. She had never met anyone like him. Jessica would never forget Matt, the little boy who desperately wanted a nice mommy and daddy.

Weston sat down at the base of Jessica's chair. The large family-style recreation room had wall-to-wall carpeting, allowing him to sit comfortably. "You made a fast friend, huh? He's a cute little guy. You held him so tenderly. What's his name?"

"Matt. He came over quickly and left the same way. He seems to be a great kid, but also a deeply wounded one. I pray someone takes him out of here soon."

"He's probably hoping for the exact same thing."

"He is. He wants a nice mommy and daddy. I wish I could help him get one."

Weston clearly heard the raw emotion in Jessica's shaky voice. The hurtful look on her face revealed her pain. He wanted to hold and comfort her, but he let her have her space. She'd reach out if she needed him.

"This is a wonderful orphanage. How'd you find it?"

"The Internet." Weston was relieved to see Jessica recovering from her emotional agony. If one more thing out of the ordinary occurred, he feared she'd bolt out of the room in tears. Her heart was out there on her sleeve.

"O Holy Night" streamed into the room like a bolt of lightning, ushering in the true spirit of Christmas. Powerful vocals from the voices of Il Divo had Jessica listening up. She knew those fabulous voices, had already purchased their Christmas CD.

As Jessica looked around at Weston and the others, she could see they were also moved. The song was a perfect example of what Christmas was all about. Many folks had lost sight of the true meaning and some didn't know the truth.

Weston took hold of Jessica's hand and squeezed it tightly. "This is an emotional moment. I know what you're feeling. I feel it, too. Everyone does."

Jessica smiled weakly. "I don't think we always realize how blessed we are. These little children should be blessed, yet they're in an orphanage hoping and praying for a set of loving parents."

"I hear you. But they *are* blessed. It could be much worse. They could be homeless. What we can't ever do is become indifferent to the sufferings of others. That's why I do this. Wish I could do more. As I prosper, so will my charitable causes."

Jessica's respect for Weston shot through the roof behind his comments, truly a man after her heart. She was already a better person for knowing him, felt fortunate to spend so much time with him. She looked forward to the future. She and Weston seemed to be good for each other. Two giving spirits could only double the pleasure of helping others less fortunate.

All the children began to crowd together, lining up by height in front of the marble fireplace. The movement quickly captured Jessica's and Weston's attention. When Sister Natalie seated herself at the piano, Jessica knew the kids were going to sing. She was eager to hear the songs, feeling giddy with excitement.

"Santa Claus Is Coming to Town" was the first carol the children belted out in an impressive manner. Such little people with such big voices sounded amazing to Jessica. The residents of St. Anthony's Orphanage treated the guests to a miniconcert, a highly memorable performance.

Most presents would be saved until Christmas morning, but each child was allowed to open a large and a small package. Weston donned a Santa hat, surprising Jessica when he handed her one. Sure they were being perceived as Mr. and Mrs. Claus, the happy couple were about to go to work. Weston said all his helper elves had to wear hats, too. He then pulled from his pillowcase sack red hats for the group. After the hats were in place, eager hands began passing out the gifts according to the gender tags.

Loads of laughter and animated chatter were heard, along with sounds of ripping paper. Loud whoops and childish giggles followed. Eyes were all aglow as the promise of a merry Christmas was fulfilled. It was easy to see that the children were grateful for the nice gifts they had received. Everyone seemed pleased.

Matt quickly found his way over to where Jessica sat on the floor. Giggling, he plopped down on her lap to show off the metallic blue truck and a handheld electronic game. "See what I got."

"I see! Nice. Are you happy?"

Matt nodded, clapping with enthusiasm. "Show me how to work it?"

"Sure." Jessica took the game from Matt's hand and figured out how to turn it on. Once the game pad lit up, she saw several games for him to enjoy. After lining up the arrows for one game, she pressed it into service. It took a couple of minutes for her to get the hang of it, but once she had it down she taught Matt.

Matt had nearly mastered one of the sports games within a few minutes. He was all smiles and silly giggles over his accomplishments, yelping with childish glee every time he scored a point. As bells and whistles sounded, he laughed louder. When he messed up, a loud honking noise sounded. The honks frustrated him, but he kept at it.

The children brought the room to life with lots of noisy animation. They were having a grand time. The adults had a wonderful time helping out the kids while watching them enjoy the great gifts provided for their playtime pleasure.

Jessica couldn't imagine the evening getting any better, yet she felt it would. She felt blessed to be a part of the holiday festivities. God had to be smiling. She closed her eyes and sent up a silent prayer of thanks.

Jessica felt apprehensive that Christmas Eve would never arrive. The time was moving right along. She found that disturbing since it meant that she and Weston would soon separate. The group had many things left on the agenda—things that would probably make the time move even faster.

The entire group would meet for dinner at a family-style restaurant in town. Upon returning to the Harrington town house, each person would open a few presents. The rest would be opened Christmas morning during the holiday breakfast.

Jessica tried to get comfortable in bed but continued to

toss and turn before finding a desirable position. She should go on and get up, but she also wanted to lie still a bit longer. Since she didn't have to go out with her family for a couple of hours, she felt like being lazy.

Last-minute shopping would take the Harrington women back into downtown. Jessica had no desire to visit another retail store. She had done all her shopping, but Jennifer still hadn't found the perfect gift for Samuel. This happened every year so she wasn't surprised. Jennifer's problem was thinking there wasn't anything good enough for Samuel, who'd be happy with anything from his wife. He'd be happy with nothing at all, as long as he had his beautiful wife by his side. No man loved his woman more.

Jessica's cell phone jangled, making her moan. Probably Jennifer calling to make sure she got up on time. The caller ID revealed an unfamiliar number, but she was very familiar with the voice on the line. "Morning, Wes. What you up to so early?"

"Thinking about you. Can't get you off my mind. Are you still in bed?"

Jessica giggled. "Sorta, kind of."

"Either you are or you aren't. Which is it?"

"Still in," she sang out. "Don't know why I'm embarrassed by it."

"Me, neither. I love the thought of you in bed. What're you wearing?"

"Let's not go there, pal."

"Oh, please, let's. Why don't I guess what you're wearing?"

Jessica closed her eyes. Weston was bent on playing a game that'd make her want him more than she already did, driving her physically crazy in the process. "You'll never guess. Not in a million years."

"Let's start with nothing at all. Am I close?"

"You're colder than it is outside."

"Hmm. Bikinis and a T-shirt?"

"Brr. That's even colder."

"Sweats?"

"Let me look and see." As though Weston could actually see her, Jessica lifted the covers and looked at her attire. "Sorry. Wrong again."

"Flannel pajamas or nightgown?"

"Not even getting warm."

"I give! This is no fun. Tell me what you have on in your sexiest voice."

Jessica gave a low, guttural growl. "Silk pajamas, leopard-print with black silk piping," she purred softly. "I'm on the prowl, baby. Looking for a sleek, hot-blooded panther to get into hot water with. Are you up for the hunt?"

"I'm there, girl. Just name the time and place."

"Time and place? If I tell you that, you won't have to hunt. Panthers are experts at tracking and trapping their prey. You want to come again?"

"*Again and again!* Imagining you wearing nothing already has me in hot water."

Jessica felt her face flush with color. She had stepped right into that one, had set herself up good. "You are sooo bad! What am I to do with you?"

"How much time you got? It might take a while to tell you all the things I'd love you to do."

"Your time is already up. This girl has to go shopping with her family."

"Ugh. How you gonna leave me hanging? And I do mean hanging."

Jessica cracked up. "I get the picture. Can't do a thing about it right now. See you at dinner tonight. I can hardly wait." She disconnected, howling as she imagined the look on Weston's face.

Jessica really couldn't wait to see Weston later on. She had no problem imagining the hot water they could get into together. A physical connection was inevitable? They loved each other? If all else failed, a girl could certainly dream about her sexual fantasies—she quickly closed her eyes to do just that.

Weston had a hard time believing Jessica had hung up. His manhood was stiff as a board, feeling as if it might break off. Just thinking about her lying in bed, looking sexy and ravishing, had him insane with desire. He knew exactly what she could do with him. And he couldn't wait for the day to come when he could show her. His feelings for her had been assessed and reassessed, over and over again. The outcome was always the same. Jessica was the right girl for him, the only girl.

If they managed to get a long-distance relationship under way, he believed they'd have a wonderful future together. Was it possible for them to live on both coasts? He wondered if Jessica would consider living in New York during the mild-weather months and in California when it was harsher on the East Coast. The real-estate market was better than good in both regions. They'd have to hold licenses in both states, but that wasn't insurmountable.

Weston's hopes soared at what could be a feasible resolution. Now all he had to do was convince Jessica. They could have the best of both worlds. He couldn't act on his idea too soon. Jessica wasn't ready to go at a faster pace.

After visiting Jessica in California a few times, Weston hoped she'd become more open to his idea. He had a lot to prove to her. Hurtful things in childhood had a way of carrying over into adulthood. He had hurt her back then, badly—no doubt about that. He couldn't change the past, but he could navigate a bright future.

Weston's ideas couldn't happen without Jessica on board a hundred percent. Though disheartened over all the obstacles to overcome, he couldn't let it throw him. Knowing he'd see her this evening helped lift his mood. Leaping off the bed, Weston made a beeline for the shower. The sooner he got his day started, the sooner he could be in the company of the woman he loved.

Chapter 7

One glance at Weston caused Jessica's heart to palpitate and flutter wildly. His camel cashmere sports coat was the bomb. The light-yellow, open-collar shirt gave her a sneak preview of thick chest hair. She itched to get next to him, yet he wasn't even looking at her. She decided to play it cool by not meeting him halfway. The closer he moved toward her, the sweatier her palms got. The skyrocketing effect this man had on her was downright crazy.

Weston finally made direct eye contact with Jessica, gazing at her intently. Putting his hand over his heart, he shook his head from side to side, blowing her a flurry of kisses.

Falling into Weston's arms was what Jessica could hardly wait to do. Too many prying eyes kept her from fulfilling her heart's desire. Even though they had explained their romantic interest, no one knew how deeply they'd actually fallen in love. Weston didn't even know that Jennifer knew since Jessica hadn't made him privy to it.

Jessica thought she smelled the scent of Weston's manly cologne from where she stood, an alluring blend of citrus and sandalwood. She closed her eyes to capture his essence and inhaled deeply. Hoping to see him standing before her, she reopened her eyes. A sharp twinge of disappointment hit her when he was nowhere in sight.

A handsome young man stepped up to Jessica, asking her name in a deep, sultry voice. She was both flattered and annoyed by his presence, yet she supplied the requested information. Since he blocked her view of the man she anxiously awaited, the man she loved to the depths of her soul, she tried to see around him.

"Joshua Gibson." He extended his hand to her. "Nice meeting you, Jessica. I've watched you since you first came in. Are you dining alone?"

Joshua couldn't have watched her that closely, Jessica knew. She had only arrived with her family. "My family and my boyfriend and his family are dining together."

"Boyfriend and families! I get the picture. Should've guessed someone as beautiful as you wasn't solo. Forgive the intrusion. It *was* a pleasure. Good evening, Jessica Harrington."

Joshua disappeared as quickly as he had come upon Jessica.

There was still no visible sign of Weston as Jessica looked all around. Where had he gotten to? He had been there only seconds ago. Her eyes had only been shut for a second. That was when Mr. Gibson had suddenly appeared, interrupting the flirtatious flow between her and Weston.

It was a large restaurant so Weston could be anywhere. But why had he disappeared like that? Was he upset by her talking with Joshua? Nothing about Weston indicated insecurity. She hoped he wasn't playing games. Jessica wanted to be with him badly, especially on Christmas Eve. Maybe he had suddenly taken ill. With that in mind, the worrying began. Jessica's mind was in a tizzy.

Ten minutes later and still no Weston. Since Jessica's family was already seated near the bandstand, she had no choice but to join them. Standing in the middle of the room alone made her stick out like a sore thumb. Jessica was really worried now. She tried not to show concern in front of the others, but Weston's sudden disappearance had gotten to her.

Unable to stand the mystery of Weston's disappearing act, Jessica got up and looked around for him again. The ladies' room had been her excuse. She thought of asking Samuel to check out the men's room for Weston, but she changed her mind. Why get the others worried, too? Her heart thundered with anxiety as she made her way up front. This was an unpleasant situation to find herself in.

Just as Jessica stepped out into the corridor, someone walked up behind her and covered her eyes with some sort of soft material. Panic quickly arose within her, yet she didn't feel in any imminent danger. That in itself was odd. The person who had blindfolded her propelled her forward. Joshua Gibson popped into her mind, making her wonder if it was him. Panic flared slightly again.

Was she really being kidnapped? Or was this a Westongenerated hoax? She prayed for the latter. Screaming her head off would bring attention to her, but if Weston was behind all this, how foolish would that make her feel?

As a pair of hands spanned Jessica's waist, she felt they were Weston's, but she wasn't positive. The touch was so familiar. She was then pulled along rather quickly. If she was anywhere other than a busy restaurant, the panic would be intense.

The blindfold was quickly stripped from Jessica's eyes, but it took a minute for them to adjust to the soft lighting. She then saw Weston standing in a candlelit dining room, where there was only one elegantly dressed table, romantically set for two.

Jessica gasped, feeling as though she had stepped into a fairy tale. Her Prince Charming was right there, looking as if he was on cloud nine. She felt the way he looked. This gorgeous hunk of a man had pulled out all the stops. When January third popped into her head, she felt a painful twinge of sadness.

Jessica reminded herself that the relationship wasn't going to end then. That was when it would really begin, when the moment of truth was upon them. Not seeing him every single day would be a real bummer, but seeing him again in L.A. was the silver lining.

Smiling smugly, looking fine as wine and sweetly arrogant, Weston held up a black silk scarf and then a leopard-printed one. "These silk beauties represent the panther and the leopard. You, my beautiful leopard, have been captured by the sleek panther. Without any effort, I might add."

All Jessica could do was smile at Weston. He *had*

captured her—heart and soul, mind and body. The sexy hunter had easily captured the game.

Weston took the leopard scarf and placed it around Jessica's neck, sliding it back and forth. His dark eyes thirstily drank in her heart-stopping sensuality. As he kissed her gently on the mouth, he inhaled her captivating scent. "You turn me on, woman. You have no idea what you do to me." Taking her by the hand, he led her over to the table and pulled out the two chairs.

In the background Freddie Jackson was softly crooning "You Are My Lady."

Weston waited until Jessica was seated before he knelt down on bended knee. "I wanted to be alone with you. I hope you don't mind."

Jessica was touched by his desire to be alone with her, yet she felt apprehensive. "What about our families? It's Christmas Eve."

"I know, baby. I know. They understand. We're joining them for dessert, but we're dining alone. Are you okay with that? If not—"

Jessica silenced him with a sensual kiss. "Thank you. This is special. You are special to me."

"As you are to me. Words can't begin to express how happy I am to be here. This is our private dining room for a couple of hours. Let's enjoy it."

Jessica blushed, smiling. "I feel the same way. Ready to order?"

"Absolutely." Weston brought Jessica to him and kissed her like there was no tomorrow in sight. "I love you."

"Love you, too, my darling."

Weston got up and took the chair opposite hers.

Prepared to take care of Jessica's and Weston's dining needs, a tall, slender waiter handed them both menus. Smiling brightly, he politely introduced himself to Jessica as Wayne. He had already met with Weston when he had arrived earlier to oversee his plans. After white merlot was poured into crystal glasses, Wayne walked away to give the couple ample time to be alone before examining the menus.

It was only when Weston asked Jessica to dance that she once again became aware of the soft music. She had been too busy looking at Weston and losing herself inside her thoughts. He gently pulled her up from the chair.

After moving a few steps away from the table, Weston took Jessica into his arms, holding her as close as possible. His arms went up under hers and his hand rested firmly on her shoulders. Still, she wasn't close enough to him. Closing his eyes he rested his chin atop her head, swaying gently to the music.

Jessica thought that Jill Scott's "Cross My Mind" seemed so fitting for the moment. It reminded her of all the times Weston had crossed her mind over the years.

Once Jill Scott's song ended, Brian McKnight picked right up with "Find Myself in You" from the *Madea's Family Reunion* soundtrack. The song wasn't really slow, but they continued to dance at a relatively snail-like pace, wrapped up tightly in each other's arms.

Jessica felt as though she were floating in space. The way Weston held her made her feel very secure. She reached up and entwined her hands in his hair and buried her face against his neck. She couldn't remember ever feeling this wonderful, this content. Lifting her head slightly, she planted sweet kisses on the side of his neck. "I love you," she whispered softly. "I don't know what I'll do without you."

"I do," he whispered back, kissing her forehead tenderly. "We'll talk every single day and night by phone, as often as you permit. We'll e-mail each other all the time. We can exchange pictures daily. We can even do the Web-cam bit if you're comfortable with that. Jess, we *will* stay connected. I promise."

Jessica believed in Weston's promise, believed in him, believed in their love.

Leaving her worries and concerns behind, hoping never to pick them up again, Jessica gave up herself fully to the intimate moments. By that time, "Me Time" by Heather Headley was playing. Jessica loved the song, but didn't think she'd ever need or want any "me time" from Weston.

Weston escorted Jessica back to the table, waiting until she was seated before seating himself. As if Weston had a magic button somewhere on his person, Wayne reappeared. He saw that they'd need a few more minutes to look at the menu, since the menus were still right where he had left them.

Food was the last thing Jessica had on her love-saturated mind. She was more interested in Weston continuing the heavy romancing. Because it appeared that he had gone through special pains for them to dine alone, she had to order something. He might be disappointed in her other-wise.

Jessica's entrée would be light fare. All she was hungry for was Weston's passionate kisses and those warm, heartthrobbing embraces he heated up her anatomy with.

Knowing she couldn't do justice to a big meal, she only ordered grilled tilapia, steamed vegetables and a garden salad with Italian dressing. Water with lemon was her beverage choice since she hadn't finished her wine.

Although Weston didn't call Jessica on ordering such a light meal he eyed her with slight concern. She was upset by their imminent separation and he hoped it hadn't ruined her appetite. On the other hand, his desire for food was big enough for both of them. He ordered his porterhouse steak medium-well, along with his favorite trimmings. He also ordered a glass of water with a twist of lime instead of the lemon. When he suddenly summoned the waiter back and addressed him in a secretive manner, Jessica strained to hear what was said, all to no avail.

The happy couple made small talk while awaiting the first course. It was hard for Jessica to fully concentrate. Her brain was busy figuring out what Weston had told the waiter. She wanted to ask him, but he would've said it aloud had he wanted her to know.

The mystery conversation was resolved when Wayne returned carrying a silver champagne bucket with a bottle of champagne nestled inside. He then produced two beautifully cut crystal flutes in the same pattern as the wineglasses. Once Wayne popped the cork without incident, he slowly poured the champagne. Then he was off again.

Jessica wanted to know how Weston had managed to reserve this lovely room for only two people. He had more than likely paid an arm and a leg for it. It really shouldn't matter to her one way or the other. His honorable intentions were probably obvious to most. His deep feelings for her were behind every move he'd made so far. If what he'd done for her was an indication of how he felt about her, she was one lucky sister.

Jessica was very grateful for Weston.

Weston picked up a flute and handed it to Jessica. He took hold of the other one and held it up in a toast. "To us, Jessica, to our love. May it keep us happy, content and optimistic about the future. For all seasons, for all reasons."

Fighting her emotions, Jessica touched the rim of her flute with Weston's. "Hear, hear! For all seasons, all reasons. To us and to our love," she said, just above a whisper.

The first course of the meal was then served, salads and hot sourdough bread. Soft, romantic music continued to play. It seemed like many songs from the same movie soundtrack were on the playlist, making her wonder if he'd made the selections.

Weston picked up a linen napkin and placed it on Jessica's lap. The kind gesture made her smile. She then returned the favor by thanking him with a passionate kiss. His eyes closed to savor the scrumptiously sweet taste of her mouth.

All through the meal Jessica and Weston fed each other food and sipped from each other's glasses. When they shared wine from each other's mouth, she got terribly hot and bothered by the sensuality of the intimate act. Each time their tongues mingled for a bit of wine-tasting, she nearly came unglued. At times she giggled like an infatuated schoolgirl.

Once the meal was over, Weston stood up and reached down for Jessica's hand. "One more dance before we join our folks for dessert?"

Taking a firm hold of his hand, Jessica got to her feet. "By all means."

Weston let go of Jessica's hand and then reached into his pants pocket. After pulling out a purple velvet jewelry box, he handed it to her. "Merry Christmas, Jess."

Jessica was scared to open the box. Her hands trembled badly when she finally did so. She gasped at the beautiful platinum band, simple yet delicately elegant. "Gorgeous! I love it. Thank you."

Weston took the ring from her hand. "Before I place this on your finger, please read the engraved inscription."

Jessica fulfilled his request. "Weston loves Jessica," she read aloud. Then she saw the date, the date of their very first kiss; the one under the mistletoe. Tears sprang to her eyes. "Jessica loves Weston, too. I'll cherish this ring always."

"I know that. You're a very appreciative person. The ring is my promise to love you the way you deserve."

Just as the couple fell into a warm embrace, their tears mingling, "Tonight" by Kem softly strummed the air, causing a ring of fire to encompass Jessica's very being. "Tonight" was a beautiful song, seductive and sweet, one that she loved. The lyrics spoke to all the goodness that was happening for them.

As Jessica and Weston joined the others for dessert, they boldly held hands. There were no benefits in hiding their feelings. Everyone had drawn their own conclusions anyway. All eyes were on the attractive couple as they strolled into the main dining room.

The two fathers beamed from head to toe, hopeful that

their lifelong dream would come true. Both mothers were extremely proud of their children and loved them no matter what, together or apart. All Sahara and Sandra wanted was happy kids.

Jennifer knew the real deal. Jessica and Weston knew it, too. Their love for each other was as explosive and recognizable as Fourth of July fireworks. Love wasn't supposed to be hidden. If the couple thought their love wasn't obvious, they couldn't see what both Jennifer and Samuel saw.

Samuel had already asked Jennifer if Jessica and Weston were in love. When she only shrugged, he didn't press the issue. He later told her he thought they were crazy in love with each other.

Jessica kissed both her parents and then hugged Jennifer and Samuel. She wired broad smiles to Sandra and Jacque. Weston repeated everything his lady did, giving his mother an extra-special greeting. He was a mama's boy and he didn't care who knew it. Being the apple of Sandra's eye wasn't anything to be ashamed of. It had never interfered with his fiercely tough-boy persona or his independence.

Sandra and Jacque had taught Weston about love, respect for women and also the importance of showing compassion. His mother had also taught him how to get and stay in touch with his spirit.

Once the waitress reappeared, the gentlemen let the women order first. There wasn't a shortage on dessert choices. Cheese, carrot and red velvet cakes were offered on the menu, along with apple, sweet-potato and pecan pies. Jennifer loved red velvet cake. Jessica opted for a generous slice of sweet-potato pie, one of her favorites. Roman, Samuel and Jacque ordered double slices of pecan pie. Weston had a taste for apple pie à la mode, also one of his favorites.

The band began playing just as the waitress left the table. According to the advertisement about the entertainment, the band played the top forty and seventies music. Most of the band members appeared to be in their early fifties. The choice in music was understandable. One female vocalist was featured and she looked to be around the same age as the guys. The Harrington and Chamberlain offspring had grown up on the music from that era. Their parents still listened to seventies music.

While the group waited for the waitress to return, they began rehashing all the wonderful times they had had so far. Roman thought it was a good time to make a decision about where to spend the next holiday, Easter. Several suggestions were thrown out, but a trip to the Caribbean was the most appealing. Although Weston and Jessica weren't able to fully commit, they promised to check their calendars. Weston had been mentally making plans to visit L.A. as soon as possible.

"Well," Jennifer voiced softly, "Sam and I can't commit, either. If we're assessing things right, I'll be too far along to travel long distances." Then Samuel leaned in to his wife and gave her a very passionate kiss.

Roman looked puzzled. "Too far along? What does that mean?"

As they smiled brightly at each other, Jennifer's and Samuel's eyes connected soulfully. "We're pregnant," they said in unison.

Roman, Sahara and Jessica appeared to be in a state of shock, but the others were already shouting out their heart-felt congratulations.

Tears ran down Sahara's face and Roman was also an emotional mess. Jessica was the first to hug her sister and brother-in-law, blubbering out her tearful congrats. Jessica couldn't wait to become an aunt. Throwing Jennifer a baby shower had already crossed her mind.

The swelling-with-pride grandparents were next in line to embrace the happily expecting couple. Roman and Sahara thanked Jennifer and Samuel for making them the happiest grandparents ever. They had often prayed for Jennifer and Samuel to have babies before they them-selves were too old and feeble to enjoy grandkids.

After much probing by Roman, he learned that Jennifer was only a couple of months pregnant, her abdomen still as flat as a pancake. Jennifer and Samuel had purposely waited for the trip to reveal the surprise.

The couple had actually planned to wait until New Year's Day to break the news, but Jennifer had gotten antsy about sharing the joy with her family. Once they returned to California, Samuel and Jennifer planned to tell Bob and Devera, Samuel's parents, over a special dinner. It hadn't been easy for Jennifer or Samuel to keep the secret under wraps.

The waitress hadn't returned a minute too soon. With all the hoopla that had taken place earlier, it would've been hard to get everyone's attention. Once the desserts were passed out, the waitress quickly moved on.

On behalf of the group, Weston proposed a special toast to Jennifer and Samuel.

* * *

Back at the town house Sahara brewed up both coffee and tea. Jacque had taken care of selecting the holiday music and Roman was busy fixing nightcaps. For all the activities the group had indulged in, from the start of the day, it was still only a few minutes after ten.

Once coffee and tea were served, the families planned to open a couple of presents and continue with the good times. The Christmas Day dinner wasn't scheduled until 3:00 p.m., but breakfast was to be served at 8:00 a.m. After the morning fanfare was out of the way, everyone would help prepare the special holiday meal, a family affair in every sense of the word.

As Jessica helped out her mother in the kitchen, Sahara suddenly spotted the platinum ring on her daughter's left hand.

Jessica instantly recognized the look of surprise on her mother's face. She had zeroed in on the ring. Earlier she'd thought of hiding it away inside her purse, but she didn't want to hurt Weston's feelings. She should've talked it over with him. It might've helped her prepare for what was occurring right now.

"Gorgeous ring! Christmas present for yourself?"

Smiling halfheartedly, Jessica tried to still her jumpy nerves. "What do you think, Mom? Really?"

Sahara shrugged. "No clue. Your comments have me wondering. A gift from Wes?"

"Could we not make a big deal of it?"

"Wasn't aware I was doing that. Why do you insist on being so secretive? You both told us about your romantic liaison. No one is pressuring you."

"It's a gift from Wes, Mom. A friendship token he calls a promise ring."

"Can I take a closer look?"

"Are you asking me to take it off?"

"If you don't mind."

Jessica reluctantly took off the ring and handed it to Sahara. She didn't see the point, though. Just to get it over and done with she indulged her loving but nosy mom.

Sahara examined the ring closely, impressed by the exquisite, ornate workmanship. As she handed it back to Jessica, she saw the inscription. Instead of reading it, which would've been rude, she handed it over. "Very beautiful. Looks like he had it specially made."

Jessica leveled a questioning eye on her mother. "Why do you say that?"

"It doesn't look like it came from a jewelry store chain. Not to me."

"You saw the inscription, didn't you?"

Sahara shrugged with nonchalance. "I didn't read it. I'm not that insensitive, though you probably think otherwise."

"No big deal, Mom. Can we just let it go?"

"Of course, Jess. The evening has been wonderful so far, don't you think?"

"Couldn't ask for a better time." After a moment's silence, Jessica sighed hard. "It *is* a big deal! I need to stop pretending otherwise. Mind if I ask for some motherly advice?"

"I'd be hurt if you sought it elsewhere. What's on your mind?"

"This relationship with Wes. I'm in love with him. He

says he's in love with me. We are so into each other. I'm scared. No. I'm terrified."

"Of what?"

"Of what's going to happen when we leave here." Jessica moaned. "We only live on opposite ends of the world!"

Jessica went on to explain to Sahara how apprehensive she felt about a long-distance relationship. The travel alone would eventually wear their patience thin. Phone calls and e-mails would grow tedious sooner rather than later. "I couldn't bear it if he ends up getting tired of traveling—and tired of me."

"You just said he loves you. True love never grows weary. I don't think you're giving yourself or Wes enough credit for being strong. Don't sabotage your happiness, Jessica. Give it a chance before stamping a moratorium on it."

Jessica nodded. "I'll try to keep a positive outlook, but I'm still scared. I guess we'd better join the others before they think we passed out in here."

Sahara laughed. "We *have* been in here a while." Sahara brought Jessica into her warm embrace. "You'll be fine, honey. Trust in your feelings for Wes. I'm sure he plans to trust in his."

"Thanks, Mom. Glad I stopped being secretive long enough to share my fears. Jen and I are so blessed to have you for our mom."

"Our family is blessed to have each other. Dad and I are so proud of our girls. And just think. You'll soon be a sweet auntie and Dad and I'll be doting grandparents. How awesome is that?"

"Extremely awesome," Roman said from the doorway. "Are my two girls doing okay in here? Jen and I were getting worried."

"Girl talk, Dad. We're on our way out. Want to help carry some of this stuff?"

Roman gave both his ladies a warm hug before leaping into action.

Weston couldn't quite figure out if Jessica was avoiding him purposely or not. She hadn't said a thing to him since she'd come out of the kitchen nearly thirty minutes ago. What was up with that? She actually had him second-guessing his purchase and then presentation of the promise ring. She had seemed thrilled about it earlier. Now he wasn't so sure. Something had put a damper on her effervescent mood. If it wasn't the ring, he just didn't know.

Jessica hadn't come to him, but Weston had to ask himself what stopped him from going to her. Rejection was a pretty good reason for staying put. But there was no reason for her to reject him. He didn't think it was healthy to start speculating. The only way to know for sure was to ask her. With that settled in his mind, he got up and walked over to where she was seated on the floor close to Jennifer.

As Jessica reached up and took hold of Weston's hand, he sighed with relief and dropped down next to her.

"I missed you," she whispered. "We've been selfish all evening so I thought I should spend a little time with the others. Hope you don't mind."

Jessica had no idea how much Weston didn't mind. He was just relieved to learn why she'd put a bit of distance

Chapter 8

Curled up in front of the cabin fireplace, Jessica and Weston rehashed the evening's enjoyable activities. She was pleased with the gorgeous cashmere sweater, a CD collection and the monetary gift her parents had given her. The Harringtons always gave their daughters the same gifts, but clothing items were normally purchased in different colors. Jessica's sweater was white and Jennifer's was blue. Samuel had also gotten a Shaker-knit sweater, along with the same amount of money as the daughters.

Weston had received from the Harrington family an oldie CD collection by Stevie Wonder, his favorite recording artist. The Chamberlains had presented Jessica with a beautiful bathrobe, one to keep her warm and cuddly in the coldest temperature, especially if she dared to brave NYC in the winter. The hint had been anything

but subtle. Weston's parents always gave him a large sum
of money. This year was no exception.

The gift that pleased Weston the most was the beautiful navy-blue wool sports coat and navy-and-white dotted
tie from Jessica. He planned to wear it to Christmas dinner.
Jessica was thrilled by Weston's other present to her, a gift
set of perfume. She loved the alluring scent, but she loved
the platinum ring most of all.

Jessica stretched her arms high over her head. "Guess
I'd better get back to the town house. Early-morning
wake-up call."

Weston frowned. "We just got here. Relax. It's not
that late."

Jessica laughed. "Try telling that to my body."

Taking Jessica up on her suggestion, Weston whispered
into her ear. His lips found a tender spot on her neck and he
whispered against it. "You are *not* tired, body. You can hang
in there with Wes." Tenderly massaging her neck came next.
"Relax, sweetheart. Let me lay you on a cloud and take you
far, far away."

Weston's hands continue to thrill Jessica, making her
want him to touch her more and more. He was so good at
seducing her, making her body feel wonderful inside and
out. She was like putty in his hands, yet she felt anything
but silly. He made her feel like a desirable woman in every
sense of the word. Weston had her feeling hot all over.

Jessica believed that their first physical union would be
sweet, wildly passionate and loving. Never would it be just
sex. Deep feelings were involved. Theirs was a spiritual
and emotional connection. He'd continue to respect her afterward, just as she'd always honor him. It didn't surprise

Jessica that she actually looked forward to him making sweet love to her.

As Weston lifted Jessica's sweater and pulled it over her head, she offered no resistance. She still had a blouse on, but she wasn't sure for how long. He had just popped open the first button. She bit down on her lower lip to keep from moaning. His hands felt so good on her body. "Right there," she whispered.

"Right here?" he asked, tenderly pressing his hands into her shoulders.

"Yes, right there," she said, moaning softly.

The heat from Weston's hands penetrated Jessica's soft skin. She loved every second of it. She could tell he was using extreme caution in exploring her trembling anatomy. She hoped he knew where to draw the line. She wasn't sure she had the strength or the willpower to put a stop to what felt so delicious to her. His hands came to rest on the top button of her wool slacks; she tensed up. He must've felt her tension, because he quickly moved away his hand.

Jessica's blouse was halfway open as Weston massaged her shoulders and abdomen. When he suddenly landed a moist kiss inside her belly button, she had to grip the rug to keep from losing it. Her body language said she enjoyed his sensual touch, prompting him to continue. As his teeth nipped and teased her stomach, she verbally encouraged him to carry on. Her body had turned to jelly.

Looking down on Jessica was like looking down at an angel. She was intelligent, compassionate and beautiful, everything he had ever wanted in a soul mate. He had never come this close to wanting to make a lifetime commitment to anyone. It was still all about timing. Though he had known Jessica all their lives, he hadn't known her like this. They had many more days to go. Considering it all, they didn't have lots of time to work everything out, but they had a good start. They were in love.

Weston leaned down and kissed Jessica. Slowly, he buttoned her shirt back up. His willpower had kicked in where hers would have failed. She felt both disappointed and relieved that he had called a halt to the seduction.

In no doubt that Weston wanted her like crazy, the same way she wanted him, Jessica ran her fingernail across his bottom lip.

"Think it'll ever happen for us?"

"What is *it?*"

Laughter bubbled in Jessica's throat. Weston knew exactly what she meant by *it*. If he really didn't, she wasn't going to spell it out for him. "What are your favorite things to do in your downtime?" She thought it best to change the subject.

Weston shrugged. "Just sit quietly and listen to music. Long drives outside the city are relaxing, especially when I can put the top down. I like to read. Unfortunately, I don't get to do much of it. Need to do more things I love. I work too hard. What are your hobbies?"

"Reading's my favorite pastime. I read for hours on end. Nothing like curling up with a good book. I like to plant things. Living in a town house only allows me to do window-box planting, but I tend to Mom and Dad's flowers and plants from time to time. They've offered space for my own garden, but I haven't done any planting yet."

"Why not?"

"Not enough time. I work late so my weekends are normally spent doing laundry and grocery shopping. I love to window-shop. My friends go with me, but I tire long before they do."

"What's your favorite department store?"

"Hmm, good question. Let me think. Macy's. I love their quality. My all-time favorite store was called Broadway, but they were closed and sold to another chain. Their clothing was the absolute best."

"NYC has a great Macy's. Maybe we can go there one day."

"I'd love that. Are you a good cook? If so, what's your favorite dish?"

"I'm a great cook, but I mainly eat out or order in. My hours are long so I rarely feel like cooking. Soups are my specialty. I make a mean pot of oxtail soup."

As if Jessica and Weston had suddenly run out of things to say, they lapsed into silence. There were a lot of things they wanted to ask each other, but neither seemed comfortable posing certain questions.

Jessica realized she and Weston hadn't talked about their past relationships. Had he been dating someone prior to coming to Aspen or had it been a while for him? His work seemed to take precedence over his social life.

"Are you involved with anyone back home, Jess?"

Jessica had to laugh. "You *are* a mind reader. I was wondering the same thing about you. We've fallen in love but we haven't discussed past relationships. I haven't dated anyone exclusively in over a year. My work schedule gets in the way. I use it as an excuse not to get bowled over. Dating now and then works best for me, but I do get lonely."

"Have you been hurt by someone?"

"Not really. Severely disappointed, though. I've thought someone was one way only to find out he was the exact opposite. I don't do disappointment very well. I've got plenty of time to get it right. I'm choosy about who I spend time with. And I'm in no hurry to get married."

"You should be choosy. I date off and on, but I avoid getting into a committed relationship. Never felt ready. Not until now."

"Why now? What changed your mind?"

"You. Falling in love with you, the moment I laid eyes on you here in Aspen. It feels good. A long-distance relationship won't be easy, but I think our love will see us through. We can't allow doubts in or have fears take us over. We can and will make this work."

"For *how long* is the question I have to ask. Will talking on the phone and e-mailing be enough to keep us happy and in love? They say absence makes the heart grow fonder, but I'm not convinced. Guess we'll have to wait and see."

"We'll be fine. As I said, I don't mind traveling cross-country. My parents will be living in L.A. soon. At least, that's the way it's panning out."

"I'm looking forward to your visit to L.A. Give me enough notice so I can plan a nice time. There's so much to do in the City of Angels."

"I'd love to see the Lakers play. Dad's a Lakers fanatic."

"The season doesn't end until June so I'm sure I can get my hands on a couple of tickets. If I can't, Dad can. He might have season tickets. I'll find out for sure."

"Thanks. How's the skiing up at Big Bear?"

"Really good, I hear. I'm not in the know on skiing. But I do know there are several ski resorts east and north of L.A. I'll check that out, too, if you come before winter is over."

"Don't know exactly when I'll get there, but it won't hurt to check on it."

The beautiful Christmas carol playing gripped both Jessica's and Wes's attention. "Silent Night" was always a favorite with most. Johnny Mathis had a heartwarming way of crooning it. Weston nestled Jessica tenderly into his arms. As he stroked her hair, the couple got lost in the music, wrapped up in the spirit of Christmas.

A short while later Weston looked down at Jessica. She had her eyes closed. He didn't know if she was asleep or not. Perhaps she was resting her eyes. Whatever the case, he decided just to remain quiet. Curling up behind her, he pulled her back into the curve of his body, where she fitted perfectly.

Weston realized that Jessica *was* asleep and he reached back and pulled a patchwork quilt from the metal rack. After covering them up, he set the alarm on his watch to go off in thirty minutes. Intent on taking a short nap, he closed his eyes. Soon after positioning his leg across Jessica's hip, Weston also fell asleep.

The town house kitchen wasn't big enough for all the people crowded into it. When it seemed impossible to get everything done in an orderly manner, Sahara took firm control of the situation. She first gave the guys instructions and then shooed them out of the kitchen. She also assigned specific duties to the women.

The turkey and prime rib slowly roasted in the double ovens. Jessica was assigned potato-peeling duties, both sweet and white ones, which she would later mash. Jennifer was in charge of tossing a salad and tending the green beans. Samuel would prepare the rice.

Sandra had a large casserole of macaroni and cheese baking in her oven and Jacque was cooking collard greens. Weston was preparing candied yams and was also in charge of warming a variety of breads. The senior Chamberlains normally spent the holidays with Sandra's parents in New York City, but this year the elderly couple had decided on a Caribbean cruise.

Besides having prepared the meats for roasting and making the dressing she had already stuffed into the turkey, Sahara was handling the relish dishes and cranberry sauces. Roman had fixed an extra pan of corn-bread stuffing and was also in charge of making the giblet gravy. The majority of the holiday desserts had been picked up from a local bakery, but a few homemade desserts were left over from earlier in the week.

Everyone had been assigned something to do in preparation of the meal, grateful for the number of ovens and burners at their disposal. All cabins, condos and town houses came equipped with double ovens and four burners.

By late afternoon everyone was gathered around the beautifully dressed table, holding hands as Roman passed the blessing. Dressed in their Sunday best, the group looked happy to share in this special holiday festivity. Once Roman gave thanks to the Almighty, amen simultaneously rang out as everyone took their assigned seat.

As the family of diners devoured the delicious meal, there was near complete silence, with the exception of a few moans and groans of pleasurable delight. There wasn't a single complaint about anything. Fifteen minutes or so had passed when the place suddenly came alive with the animated buzz of dinner chatter.

Dessert was served forty minutes later.

Jessica still felt stuffed from all the food she had eaten earlier…and all she wanted to do was curl up in bed and fall asleep. She had come back to the cabin with Weston but wasn't planning on staying long. She was worn out from going nonstop every day since she'd arrived in Aspen. It was time to start winding down.

The past few days had been a whirlwind of activity. Thinking about the coming week of vacation only heightened Jessica's fatigue. Her parents probably wouldn't mind if she took it easy. She and Weston had made plans to take in a movie and hang out, but she wasn't interested in anything requiring a lot of energy. She had to work the day after she got home so she needed some rest before returning to the daily grind.

Weston came into the room and sat down next to Jessica. He was tired, too, but he planned to get in a few days more of skiing. He wished he could talk Jessica into it, but he didn't want to push her into something she wasn't ready for. She had done well just to get up to the resort. Her fears were real and should be respected.

Jessica looked over at Weston and smiled. "Are you as tired as I am?"

Weston nodded. "Everyone's tired. We barely got the

dishes done after dinner. Our parents are even taking naps, a rarity for them. We've been so busy."

"Once I get back to our place, I'm taking a long soak in the tub. Then I'll curl up in bed and read, if I can manage to stay awake."

"Wish I could join you. What're you reading?"

"Barack Obama's *The Audacity of Hope*. An interesting read. I'm enjoying it."

"I read the first one, *Dreams from My Father*. Extremely good. Maybe I can borrow yours when you're through."

"I can mail it to you. I doubt I'll finish it before we leave."

"No rush, baby. I can read it when I come to L.A."

Jessica gave him a skeptical look. "I doubt you'll have time for reading. I'll want your undivided attention."

"And you'll have it. I love spending every waking moment with you."

"Same here." Jessica stifled a yawn. "Wow, I *am* tired. I should go back before I fall asleep on you again."

"I won't mind. Just stretch out on the sofa awhile. Or go back and lie down in bed. I'll lie down out here. I don't want you to leave yet. Is that selfish?"

Jessica looped her arm through his. "Nothing selfish about you. We can lie down together. We can trust ourselves, can't we?"

"You can trust me. Go ahead. I'll put some music on for us."

Jessica scowled. "Maybe we should forgo the music. It might get a little too romantic for us to handle," she joked, laughing gently.

Weston laughed, too. "Maybe you *don't* trust yourself. You think?"

"If we're asleep, we won't hear the music, anyway. Right?"

"Right." Weston put on the music anyway.

Stopping at the doorway of Weston's bedroom, Jessica took a minute to look around. The bed was neatly made-up. He was very clean and orderly. Nothing appeared out of place. She liked neatness and cleanliness. She also kept her place spotless. Everything in her home had a place and she kept it there. When she took something out to use, she always put it back.

Stepping farther into the bedroom, Jessica took the few steps to the king-sized bed. Sitting on the edge of the mattress, she leaned over and removed her boots. With every intention of remaining fully clothed, she didn't want to send Weston mixed messages. After pulling one of the four pillows into her arms, she laid her head back on another. Stretching out completely on the bed, moving around until she got comfortable, she hugged the pillow to her abdomen.

Minutes later Weston slid onto the bed with Jessica. After making himself comfortable, he lifted her head and tenderly placed it in the well of his arm. He kissed her softly on the lips. "Close your eyes. I'll wake you up before it gets too late."

"Not going to sleep?"

"Eventually. Right now I just want to watch you sleep. It'll be sensual. Think of me as your guardian angel."

"You *are* my angel and I love you." Without further ado, Jessica closed her eyes. She trusted Weston with all her heart and soul. He was a good man.

As Weston watched the even rise and fall of Jessica's chest, he smiled. It hadn't taken her long to fall off to sleep. His heart filled with pride. She trusted him enough to fall asleep in his presence, in his bed. He reached down and stroked the length of her silky hair. She didn't move a muscle. He could see that she was tired. The delicate skin beneath her eyes looked a bit puffy, yet it did nothing to mar her natural beauty. A wrapped bag of ice would take care of it.

There was something erotic about Jessica's breath gently fanning his neck. Holding her close to him was a beautiful thing. It was hard to believe how quickly deep feelings had developed between them. He'd never dreamed he could fall in love with a woman so easily, or like a ton of bricks. Weston still felt bad over how he had once treated Jessica, but she had forgiven him. He had been young and stupid back then, hadn't known a thing about crushes or girls. What he felt for Jessica was more than any silly schoolboy crush. This woman was in his blood to stay.

Jessica rolled over, turning her back to Weston. He drew up behind her and laid his face against hers. "You okay?"

Jessica moaned softly. "Just fine. Your bed is so comfortable." She turned slightly and looked up at him. "Is it time for me to go?"

"Not yet. Go back to sleep."

Now that Jessica was awake, Weston retrieved her boots from off the floor. Taking hold of her right foot, he slid on her boot with ease. He then took care of the other. Weston helped Jessica to her feet. "I'll walk you back."

Taking hold of his hand, Jessica look up at Weston adoringly. "I'm ready. I wish we could spend the night together." Still holding his hand, she moved toward the door.

The doorbell awakened Jessica out of a sound sleep, causing her to mumble and grumble. The clock revealed it was after 9:00 a.m. As the doorbell sounded again, she leaped out of bed and grabbed her robe, wondering where her parents were. Once her body was fully covered, she headed up front. A look through the peephole revealed an older couple with a lovely, green-eyed teenage girl in tow.

Jessica opened the door, smiling brightly. "Hi. Can I help you?"

The stunning woman extended her hand. "I'm Vanessa Carlisle." She pointed at the man and teenager. "This is Thomas and Millicent, my husband and daughter. We're friends of the Chamberlains. They're not in." Vanessa went on to tell Jessica that Sandra had told them where to go if they weren't in. "Are your parents here?"

Jessica shook her head. "But you guys can come in and wait. They're probably off somewhere with the Chamberlains. Please come in."

Thanking Jessica for allowing them to wait there, the Carlisle family stepped inside. According to Vanessa, the Chamberlains had already checked them into the resort and had taken possession of the keys.

Before Jessica offered to call her parents, they walked in the door. The Chamberlains were with them, along with another striking middle-aged couple and a very cute, curly-haired, teenage boy. Jessica assumed they were the other family the couples had been expecting. The teenagers reminded her of her and Weston at that age. She couldn't help wondering if they would also develop a steamy crush on each other.

Sandra introduced the other couple as Bonita and Gorge Holloway. Their son's name was Sean Paul, and he was extremely tall, with a great athletic build.

Jessica wondered if Sean Paul was a high school basketball player. He was built like one. The high school team basketball jersey she glimpsed under his jacket seemed to confirm her suspicions. Jessica thought it would be interesting to see if a romantic liaison developed between the cute teenagers. Sean Paul Holloway and Millicent Carlisle were both sweet sixteen.

Excusing herself to the others, Jessica went back to her room and climbed into bed. She wondered if Weston was already awake. Probably so. Like her, he was a morning person. He didn't believe in burning daylight, either. *What a man, what a man.* She smiled broadly.

Weston *was* something else. He anticipated her every need and desire. She still found it hard to believe he'd put her boots on. How sweet was that? Other than her father and Samuel, there was no other man to compare Weston to, not in the romantic sense. Although he was in the same class of men as Roman and Samuel, Weston was a one-of-a-kind man for her.

As though Weston had received the energy Jessica had been putting out, he picked up his cell phone and called her. Several rings produced no response, not even her voice mail. Just as he was about to hang up, she answered. "Hey, I was about to hang up. Everything cool?"

"All's well over here. What about there?"

"Other than missing you, it's all good. How long you been up?"

"Since about six-thirty. I worked on my laptop and I surfed the Internet for a while. What time did you get up?"

Jessica giggled. "Not up yet. Well, I did get up long enough to answer the door."

"Who was it?"

Jessica told Weston about the new arrivals. She also told him about how much Millicent and Sean Paul reminded her of them. She bet him the teenagers would develop a serious crush on each other before the week was out.

"How do you know they don't already know each other? Their parents might get together like ours do."

Jessica struck her temple with the tip of her finger. "Hadn't thought of that. I'll have to find out. You can bet on it. I'm really curious about them."

"Let me know what you find out. Want to do dinner before a movie tonight? If so, we'll need to leave early."

"With all the leftovers over here! Why don't we eat here first?"

"That's cool. What time?"

"There's no set time."

"I'll be over shortly. Are you getting up?"

"I'll be showered and dressed in about thirty minutes."

"I'm glad we have a little more time to hang out. The New Year's Eve gala is right around the corner. See you in a few."

With Weston's comments resonating in her brain, Jessica clicked off.

More time indeed.

It really wasn't a lot of time, not when it signaled the end of their time together. Three days after the gala they'd be leaving Aspen. As a sharp pang struck her heart, she moaned. The thought of them separating was always a painful one, one that she had better get used to. No matter how many times she told herself they'd be okay distance-wise, doubt set in.

Jessica then prayed that their time left in Aspen would go by at a snail's pace.

After Weston had called to delay his arrival, Jessica had gone into the kitchen to eat. For the better part of an hour she covertly watched Millicent and Sean Paul interact with each other, their body language fascinating to her. Observance had come to an abrupt halt when Sean Paul had been suddenly called away by his father. It seemed that all the men were gathering in town.

When Sahara had come into Jessica's bedroom earlier, she had asked her mother specific questions about the teenagers. According to Sahara, the youngsters had known each other ever since they were small kids. Just as it had happened for her and Weston, the youngsters hadn't seen each other in a long time.

Over a bowl of cold cereal and milk, Millicent, who had a steady boyfriend, had just finished sharing with Jessica her and Sean Paul's history. The likenesses between the two situations were uncanny. The one big difference was the crushes they'd had on each other for years; Jessica had been the only one with a crush. The long separation had cooled the teenagers' heels. Both families lived in New York, but on different ends of the state.

Millicent and her parents had recently moved from upstate to NYC, where the Holloway family also resided. The teenagers now lived close enough to see each other frequently. Millicent didn't know how to break it off with her current boyfriend to go out with Sean Paul, whom she really liked.

Jessica had listened intently to the very interesting conversation. "Has Sean Paul asked you out, Millicent?"

"Not really. He's hinted at it a time or two. He wants us to hang out together when we get back home."

Jessica smiled sweetly at Millicent. "Your response?"

Millicent giggled. "I told him I'd like that. Was I too easy?"

Jessica looked curious. "Why do you say that?"

"I have this girlfriend, Cookie Bayer, who thinks girls should play hard to get. She says the first thing guys want to know is if a girl is easy. Do you agree?"

Jessica felt the eggshells beneath her feet. Giving advice to the lovelorn wasn't something she had ever tried. "It depends on the situation. We want to be cautious, but I don't know about playing hard to get. Let the guy know if you're interested or not. And most guys *do* want to know if a girl is easy. That's their nature. Never be easy in that regard." Jessica frowned. "Get my drift?"

"I think so." Millicent laughed nervously. "You *are* talking about sex, aren't you?"

"Yeah, I am, something you might want to talk over with your mother. She can better direct you in that. I'm not a parent yet."

"We talk about sex pretty regularly. She trusts me to do the right thing."

"You're so fortunate, young lady. Some parents still find it difficult to discuss sex with their kids. Our parents talked to my sister and me when each of us turned fourteen."

"It happened when I got my cycle. I want to go out with Sean Paul, but I don't want to hurt Antoine's feelings. Antoine is my boyfriend. He's so nice."

"I don't envy you. Feelings are delicate. Antoine could get hurt, but I bet he wouldn't want you to stay out of pity. If you'd rather date Sean Paul, you have to be honest with Antoine."

The way some kids were these days, Jessica wasn't too sure about her statements. Nowadays they were killing each other. Young boys were physically abusing girls and vice versa. The crazy world teenagers lived in was rather scary.

"You're probably right. I've got to tell Antoine I like someone else. My parents don't want me in an exclusive relationship, period. They want me to enjoy my social life. Sean Paul talked about dancing with me at the New Year's gala. I'm not sure my parents are letting me go. I want to, though. It'll be fun. I brought a dressy outfit along, not a formal. If you had kids, would you let them go?"

"My parents took me to my first formal when I was sixteen. Jennifer was the same age on her first one. So I'd have to say yes to your question. I don't see any harm, especially if teenagers are chaperoned."

"I really hope Mom and Dad let me go. Do you have a date for New Year's Eve?"

Glad that Millicent had asked the question, Jessica took great pleasure in telling her all about the wonderful Weston Roman Chamberlain, her handsome date for New Year's Eve.

Chapter 9

The full-length swing coat completely hid Jessica's stunning gown from Weston's adoring eyes. She could hardly wait for him to see it. He was beside himself with the desire to see what stylish creation the coat helped to camouflage. He figured he was in for a real surprise since Jessica had been so secretive about what she planned to wear to the New Year's Eve Gala.

Weston had chosen a traditional black tuxedo, his accessories fashioned in a fine African print. He'd been confident enough that his attire and Jessica's would be complementary since they both had a flair for elegance in style and high fashion. He actually viewed them as a perfect couple, perfect for each other, perfect in every way.

Jennifer wore a cool blue gown made of shimmering

stretch silk. The silver shoes on her slender feet had one-and-a-half-inch heels and peek-a-boo toes. Samuel looked handsome and debonair in his winter-white dinner jacket, the shirt and cummerbund fashioned in the same cool blue as his wife's dress.

The older couples' attire reeked of class and sophistication. All four mature women had dressed in stylish gowns. Their husbands had gone with traditional black tuxedos. Sahara's gown had sheer long sleeves and a sheer bodice, its formal length swirling dramatically at her feet.

Sandra also wore a provocative black creation, in simple but elegant lines, fashioned with an intricate spider-web back and sheer sleeves. Her hair was up and pinned in place with jeweled combs. Gold shoes sparkled on her feet.

Vanessa looked youthful and wondrous in a highly fashionable off-one-shoulder red gown, complemented by elbow-length red gloves and stunning gold accessories.

Bonita's high-fashion gown, in gold lamé, was a head-turner, cut low in the back and front. She appeared to glow from head to toe, her shoes and bag also in gold, a much lighter shade than the gown. Dark-topaz jewelry made a very nice contrast.

Sean Paul and Millicent *had* been allowed to attend the gala. Sean Paul wore a tuxedo with a white dinner jacket. Millicent's parents had purchased her very first formal only two days ago. She also wore white, proclaiming her youth and innocence.

The four families had arrived at the resort ballroom early enough to get situated though they had reserved seating close to the bandstand. The room was festive and elegantly decorated, perfectly befitting the occasion. The banquet tables were draped in linen finery and lit by glowing candelabras.

Prime rib or baked chicken, rice pilaf and vegetables were the specially arranged dining choices, along with only a couple of dessert choices. The bar was no-host.

Weston's heart nearly stopped the moment Jessica was out of her coat. He positively loved her dress, excited by how perfect it was for her. The white sequined stunner fitted her figure and personality to a tee. Jessica looked like royalty, every bit his beautiful African queen.

Weston wasted no time telling Jessica how gorgeous she looked. Sliding his hand snugly around her waist, he led her out onto the dance floor. He wanted them to enjoy every second of their evening, from beginning to end. As he took her into his arms, he couldn't resist kissing her shimmering mouth. "Not usually at a loss for words, but I can't seem to find the right ones to express how fabulous you look. Your dress is magnificent. So are you, sweetheart."

Smiling beautifully, Jessica blushed. "Thank you. You're looking quite hot yourself. The tux is elegant on you. I'm enchanted."

"That makes two of us. I see why you were so secretive about your dress. You made an excellent choice. I'm proud to be seen with you."

Jessica kissed him softly on the mouth. "Same here."

Jessica closed her eyes and rested her head against his broad chest. He smelled good. His body felt even better, so close to hers. She was happy the evening was under way. She had something very special planned for Weston and looked forward to being alone with him later. There were only two more days of vacation left.

The great array of songs kept Jessica and Weston out on the dance floor for the first hour. Once dinner was announced, they returned to their seats, looking forward to dancing the night away.

Dinner was served promptly at eight, starting with a crisp Caesar salad. Members of the staff were also formally dressed: black tuxedo short-waist jackets, black skirts or pants, white shirts and black bow ties.

There were no long speeches, but each male in the small group, the head of a household, had spoken on behalf of their family, expressing what a great time had been had by all. Once the brief comments were passed, conversation was kept at a minimum as the group enjoyed their delicious salads.

The dinner portion of the gala was uneventful. Everyone enjoyed their meal, evidenced by the drowsy droop of their eyes. It looked as if everyone could use a short nap. The music had played soft and low all through dinner, but the volume had now been turned up a few notches, bringing everyone back to life.

Jessica closely observed Millicent and Sean Paul, laughing and giggling. The teenagers seemed to be having a good time. Millicent had a confused look on her face. Then Sean Paul leaned over and whispered something into her ear, causing her face to light up brighter than a string of high-wattage bulbs. Sean Paul got to his feet, then extended his hand to Millicent. He had asked her to dance.

Jessica no longer had to wonder what Sean Paul had said to Millicent.

Weston followed Sean Paul's lead by getting to his feet and then extending his hand to Jessica. Smiling softly, she got up from her chair and eagerly followed him out to the dance floor. His arms around her always felt good. She loved how perfectly she fitted into him. His tenderness and warmth were something she had come to live for. The only other arms Jessica felt this safe and secure in belonged to her family members.

As Weston normally did, once Jessica was nestled into him, he tenderly kissed her forehead. "Looks like the teenagers have made a love connection. They like each other."

"As I said before, they remind me of us."

Weston looked down at Jessica. "If I hadn't been so mean to you, you might've enjoyed our vacations. Sorry I was such an idiot."

"Me, too, especially knowing what we missed out on. But we're together now. That's all that counts."

"They're a cute couple, but not as cute as us," Weston joked, laughing.

"*Striking* is a better word for us. We're too old to be cute."

"We're never too old to be anything we want. It's not age that counts. The precious moments we share are what make life worth living. What time do you think we can blow this joint?"

Jessica beamed at her handsome date. "Listen to you. You seem to want to be alone with me an awful lot."

"As much as possible. I love the family stuff, but I also love being alone with you. We're more relaxed out from under the microscope."

"I second that. Leaving a little after midnight is okay

with me. We should stay long enough to ring in the new year with our families."

"I agree." Weston held up his arm and looked at his wrist-watch. "Ugh, two more hours. I can hardly wait for the witching hour."

Jessica smiled softly. "I promise to make the two hours until then very interesting," she cooed. "Time always seems to fly when you and I are together."

"That's for sure." Weston guided Jessica's head to his chest, holding it firmly in place, "You're so special to me. I love you, Jess."

"I love you, too." Feeling a floating sensation coming on again, Jessica closed her eyes, savoring the wonderful moments. She felt so much peace tonight.

As the countdown began, Jessica felt giddy inside. Bringing in the new year with Weston had her ecstatic. So much had gone right for them that she couldn't imagine anything going wrong.

"Happy New Year" rang out all over the ballroom.

"Happy New Year, sweetheart," Weston whispered to Jessica. She returned the same enthusiastic wish to him, smiling brilliantly.

As Jessica's and Weston's lips came together in a fanfare of unbridled passion, his arms holding her tightly, she felt weak at the knees. His tongue instantly searched for hers, uniting in a sweet collision. The couple couldn't seem to get enough of each other as the kiss grew intense. Shrill whistles from their families finally brought the stag-gering kiss to an end.

Jessica looked embarrassed, but that didn't stop her

from enthusiastically embracing everyone and wishing
them a happy new year. Weston followed suit, greeting his
parents in the same way. The four families kissed, hugged
and wished each other a very prosperous new year until
everyone had been covered. The teenagers seemed reluc-
tant to embrace at first, but after a bit of prompting from
the others, Sean Paul gave Millicent a warm hug and a
light kiss on the cheek.

Weston's dark eyes widened with disbelief as Jessica
stepped into the room wearing the kind of silky intimate
items he conjured up in his mind on a regular basis. He
was completely stunned by how seductive she looked.
His heart had already gone off on a wild excursion.

It was crystal clear to him what Jessica had packed
away in the large leather bag she had left in the van. When
he had asked her about it, she had silenced him with a kiss,
telling him he'd find out in due time. It looked as if she
had decided to throw caution out the window. Although
they had discussed making love numerous times, no action
had been taken. He still wasn't sure it would happen, but
whatever occurred he was sure it would be spine-tingling.

With Jessica's hair looking windswept, she resembled
a wild tigress, but the silk robe she wore was done in a
leopard print. Weston's mind was already wondering what
she wore beneath the sexy kimono-style robe.

Slowly, methodically, Jessica moved farther into the
room, keeping her eyes hotly trained on Weston. Her
fingers inched loose the belt and let it fall open. In a seductive show created just for him, she allowed the silky
attire to fall off one shoulder and then the other. In the next

calculated move she slithered the robe down her body until it fell away to the floor. The shimmering black stockings beneath a leopard-print teddy were more than just provocative, causing his manhood to stiffen and throb.

One clear-painted fingernail went up to Jessica's mouth, where she laid it against her pouting, glossy, apple-red lips, looking at him in a sexy, come-hither kind of way.

Weston quickly obeyed the commands of her demanding eyes. He licked his lips provocatively as he came to a halt in the center of the room, right where Jessica stood, looking ready to devour him. His eyes thirstily drank in her head-to-toe beauty. She was a sexy stunner, yet delicately seductive, a stimulating combination to reckon with.

Weston hoped to soon be nestled deep inside Jessica's molten treasure trove, making her sweat and moan sweetly. Either way, he would be fulfilled. If they did make love, would she call out his name? *Most definitely.* If he had his way, she would call out his name again and again, forever.

How could Jessica look that innocent and so downright sexy, all at the same time? He loved the way her eyelashes fluttered. Were her wildly fluttering lashes a sign of nervousness? It was a real turn-on for him.

After Weston took Jessica into his arms, his body burning with passionate desire, he kissed her with wild abandonment, moaning softly at the aching in his loins. He burned to be inside her, ached to make her his own. His manhood continued to expand at an alarming rate, something he hadn't experienced before.

Weston lowered the straps on Jessica's silk teddy, continuing to kiss her deeply. As his lips caressed her bare shoulders, his itching fingers squeezed and manipulated her already erect nipples. His hungry mouth quickly found its way back to hers, deepening the kiss even more.

As Weston's mouth moved from Jessica's mouth to the base of her throat, his tongue teased and tantalized her delicate flesh. Feeling her body reacting wildly to his touch excited him more and more. Every part of him craved her, craved to touch and kiss every inch of her. Hearing her softly whispering his name had him coming apart at the seams. She whispered his name so breathlessly.

As though things between them couldn't get any more fiery and passionate, Jessica took Weston's hand and placed it at the core of her heat. The silk covering of the teddy was the only thing keeping his fingers from tenderly probing her moist flesh. His nimble fingers itched to work loose the snaps, so he was surprised and pleased to find no snaps, but a Velcro strip on Jessica's teddy, which afforded him much easier access to her treasure trove. He had to smile about all the newfangled lingerie. It had been quite some time since he had disrobed a beautiful woman—and never a woman he loved manically.

Weston hoped Jessica loved foreplay as much as he did. He preferred taking his time to cuddle, coddle, caress, kiss and lovingly seduce the woman he was in love with. Jessica definitely wanted the same kind of coming together as he did, seeming to love that Weston's hand was an extremely slow one.

Weston suddenly held Jessica at arm's length, looking deeply into her eyes. "Am I moving too fast for you, sweetheart? I only want what you want."

"Not fast enough," she cooed sweetly. "We both want the same thing. I want you desperately and I can feel how much you want me." She tenderly squeezed his manhood.

Weston moaned. "Oh, baby, I'm not so sure about that. You don't have a clue." Weston wanted her, all of her, more than he had ever thought possible.

Weston kissed Jessica long and hard, probing his tongue deeper and deeper, so ready to take her where they both longed to be. Seventh heaven was their imminent destination, somewhere over the rainbow. There wasn't another person in the world that could give them what they so desperately needed. Jessica was very much ready for Weston to make love to her.

Weston was more than ready to comply.

Jessica squirmed beneath Weston's expert touch. His scorching mouth and sizzling hands were all over her, giving her unadulterated pleasure. Barely able to wait for his manhood to be deep inside her, filling her up, she purred softly, egging him on. Although she was ready for the main event, she loved his patient hands. There was nothing hurried about this seduction and she loved every second of it.

Weston was still dressed, making it impossible to take it to the ultimate level. In the next instant she was unbuttoning his shirt and then unzipping his pants. Just as eager to get on with it as she was, he helped her disrobe himself.

Before Weston was completely nude, wanting to save the best for last, he lifted Jessica and carried her into the bedroom. After rolling back the comforter, he got into bed first and then pulled her in next to him. He kissed her over and over again, making her want him more and more.

Slowly, keeping his eyes locked with Jessica's, Weston removed his silk boxers.

The moment Weston's majestic tool came into full view, Jessica's hands flew up to her mouth. Furling and unfurling her hands was all she could do to keep from screaming out loud. How magnificent his arousal was.

Then fear suddenly set in on Jessica, causing her to grow very nervous, looking as if she didn't know what to do next.

Seeing how nervous Jessica had gotten, Weston realized he might have to go back to square one. There was no reason to rush this. He loved her too much not to consider that she might be having a change of heart. If that were the case, Weston would definitely understand.

Weston looked into Jessica's eyes. "What's going on, baby? What's wrong?"

The only response Jessica was capable of giving Weston came in the form of a deeply probing kiss. She had only been fearful of what he might think of her afterward, but that was over now. Because she didn't know what would happen beyond Aspen, she wanted all of him. Jessica wanted the memories of their lovemaking to remain in her mind and heart forever. All the time they were guaranteed was right now.

Jessica rolled over and prompted Weston to take the lead. He looked at her questioningly, trying to make sure he understood her perfectly. There was no room for mistakes here, none whatsoever.

Jessica smiled, nodding at the same time. "I'm so ready for you," she whispered.

Weston knew that it was now up to him to make the

final determination. It wasn't hard for him to make a choice based on wanting her as much as she desired him. As his tongue traced her breast, she arched into him, thus the decision. Turning their bodies into a raging firestorm was his last coherent thought.

More lathered up than he'd ever been in his life, Weston knew it was time for him to take them to heaven. The abundance of moistness between Jessica's legs allowed him to make his entry, slowly, surely, completely. As she cried out his name, he buried his manhood deep inside her, tenderly rocking back and forth.

Weston wanted the ride to ecstasy to be perfect for Jessica in every way, as he teased and gently manipulated her body, nipping her with his teeth, kissing her in the most intimate places on her body. She struggled to remain in control, tugging hard at his hair every time he made contact with a supersensitive spot.

As this incredible sensation took them both over, the lovemaking intensified. As nude bodies thrashed about in the bed, gyrating together in wild abandonment, they were totally in sync with the rhythm of their tantalizing movements. Jessica was thrilled that she had surrendered all to the man she loved. Weston had submitted his all to her.

As Jessica and Weston's overwhelming climax seemed to rock the floor beneath the bed violently, they breathlessly called out each other's names. Panting and gasping for breath, Weston rolled off Jessica and immediately brought her into his arms. As he wiped the tears from the corners of her eyes, he kissed her thoroughly. "I love you. That was incredible!" He rolled his eyes to the back of his head. "*You* are incredible!"

Before Jessica could respond to Weston, her cell phone rang, irritating them both. The decision to ignore it came easily. She was in heavenly bliss and she wanted to remain there. As a special ring tone sounded seconds later, she knew an urgent message had been left. She looked at Weston and shrugged. "Sorry, but I *have* to get that."

"I understand." He reached over to the nightstand and retrieved her purse.

"I think you'd better get over here in a hurry," said her mother's voice. "Don't call. Just get here. Right away."

Jessica looked puzzled and scared. "I have to go, Wes."

"What! What do you mean? Right now?" He looked at his manhood, doing his best to will it back down. Jessica had him wanting her all over again.

"I don't know. Mom just left a message saying I needed to get over there right away. I hope there's nothing seriously wrong. She sounded so strange."

"I'll walk you back to the town house."

"You don't have to do that."

"Yes, I do. There's no way I'd let you walk back there alone, period. Let's hurry and get dressed."

It was extremely cold outside. With Jessica dressed the way she was, the wind could easily penetrate her skin. She never dreamed she'd be walking through the forest dressed in formal attire. Although she had brought along the sexy change of clothes to the cabin, the teddy and matching robe weren't appropriate for the outdoors. Besides, there was no way she'd wear something so sexy in front of her parents.

The sky appeared low to Jessica, as if she could reach

up and grab a piece of it. The tall pines swayed in the breeze, dancing to the rhythm of the slow-moving wind. The breathtaking sounds of nightfall fell all about them. This was the time of morning when animals came out of the forest to forage for food. Jessica wondered if she would see any wildlife. She sure hoped so.

No sooner had Jessica's thought left her mind than she and Weston saw a family of deer. Her breath caught at the sight of them. The doe, her eyes shining like a beacon, her white markings distinctive, seemed to be very protective of her two babies. Jessica couldn't tell if the other large deer was male or female until she saw the antlers. She wasn't sure if all male deer had antlers or not, but she thought so.

Once Jessica's eyes adjusted better to the darkness, she saw dozens and dozens of wild rabbits scurrying about. She was so excited, yet mindful not to disturb the animals in their natural habitat. All she could do was look at them in wondrous awe.

Jessica was absolutely stunned to see Jarred standing inside the front hallway of the town house. He had his arms open wide to her. For the first time in their long-term friendship she was hesitant with him. Part of her was happy to see him, but the other part was a bit perturbed by his unexpected appearance. That he would show up here in Aspen without giving her any kind of notice wasn't sitting very well.

Instead of Jarred waiting for Jessica to come to him, he rushed over to her and took her into his arms, crushing her to him. He then kissed her fully on the mouth, shocking her senseless. This was not the type of friendly kiss they shared upon greeting and departing. It was the kind of kiss only lovers indulged in.

Jessica was already thoroughly embarrassed by Jarred being there, but the passionate display of affection had turned her face red. As she thought of Weston, she wondered what he must think about all this. When she turned to look at him, the shocked expression on his face had her wishing this wasn't happening.

Weston easily figured out that this was more than likely the guy Jessica had had numerous phone conversations with. For someone who was just a friend, the kiss Jarred had whipped on Jessica had been far more than friendly.

Jessica appeared downright nervous about the entire situation. She could hardly believe this was happening. All the others present looked quite surprised and nervous, too. Three of the four families had come back to the town house once the gala was over. The Carlisle family were the only ones who had gone back to their place.

Jarred held Jessica at arm's length. "You don't look too happy to see me. Sorry I didn't call first. I wanted to surprise you."

"Well, you did that, for sure. I *am* surprised. What made you decide to come to Aspen?" She regretted that question as soon as it slipped off her tongue. She was more concerned with his response than anything. That Jarred had showed up in the middle of the night was puzzling to her. It was after 3:00 a.m.

"Loneliness, I guess. I missed you something awful. The holidays haven't been the same without you. My flight was delayed out of L.A. for several hours. I should have been here at nine-thirty, in time to bring in the new year with you and the family."

Now that Jessica's concerns had been realized, she groaned inwardly. She couldn't believe what Jarred was putting down. What was he hoping to accomplish by this asinine move? He acted as though they were lovers when they were anything but. For him to fly all the way to Aspen on a whim was insane, on New Year's Eve, no less.

Jarred was there now, so Jessica had to deal with it, but that didn't mean she had to like it. When she got him alone, she planned to tell him exactly what she thought of his not-so-brilliant idea. With that settled, she introduced him to the other guests. Everyone in her family was very familiar with Jessica's best friend, but none of them seemed pleased by his surprise visit. Roman looked really upset about it.

Weston couldn't hide his dismay over what was right before his eyes, but he knew he had to remain cool and calm. He was sure Jessica wasn't playing games with him, but he couldn't say the same thing for Jarred. He was adversely affected by what was happening, but there was nothing he could do about it. This was Jessica's showdown.

As much as Jessica wanted to explain things to Weston, this wasn't the appropriate time or place for it. It had to be done, though. However, it was hard for her to explain something she didn't quite understand herself. She wasn't even sure Jarred knew what he had done. Why all of a sudden was he showing a romantic interest in her? When had he decided to make her the target of his unwanted affection?

Samuel stepped in to rescue Jessica. He took Jarred's coat and hat from his hand, offering him something hot or cold to drink. Jarred asked for a cup of hot tea, which Jennifer offered to make.

When Jarred told everyone there were no vacant rooms at the resort, another serious problem was presented. Samuel looked to Weston at that point, since he had leased the last two-bedroom cabin. Weston knew it was selfish of him, but he wasn't about to house the guy rivaling him for Jessica. There was no way he wanted to share any space with Jarred, period. Standing in the same room with him wasn't at all pleasant for Weston, especially since he and Jessica had just finished making love.

As far as Weston was concerned, Jarred wasn't acting like just a friend to Jessica. Somewhere between L.A. and Aspen, Jarred seemed to have decided that he wanted a different type of relationship with her. Weston was almost sure of that. Jessica had looked very surprised to see him there, but beyond that he couldn't tell a thing. It looked like he might have to fight for her after all, even though he didn't think she expected such.

All things considered, Weston thought it was time for him to say his farewells. He was tired and more than a bit upset. Jessica's friend turning up out of the blue wasn't something he had figured on. It was especially hard on him because he didn't know what it all meant, nor did he know how he felt about it.

Jessica wasn't an easy one to figure out, Weston deliberated. Nothing in her demeanor gave her true feelings away. Whether she was happy to see the guy or not was anyone's guess. He was sure Jarred was also trying to figure that out.

Weston held his hand up in a farewell gesture. "Good morning, everyone. Hope to see you all at breakfast." His eyes zeroed in on Jessica after that remark, but he only held her in his gaze for a moment. Weston then turned and headed for the exit.

Looking totally perplexed, Jessica didn't seem to know what to do. Was running after Weston an appropriate response in light of what was happening? But how could she let him go without saying anything? They had just made heart-stopping love. He deserved more than a wall of silence from her. "Excuse me," she said to Jarred. "I'll be right back."

Jessica grabbed hold of the knob before the door shut completely. After stepping out into the hallway, she called out to Weston.

Weston stopped dead in his tracks, keeping his back to Jessica for several seconds before turning around to face her. Seeing her standing there, looking so unsure, caused his heart to ache. The look of uncertainty disturbed him. He quickly walked back to her, taking both her hands into his. "Are you okay?"

Jessica nervously shuffled her feet. "I wanted to tell you goodbye. I also want to thank you for a beautiful evening, every part of it, especially our after midnight rendezvous. You *are* beautiful to me. I love you." She wrapped her arms around his neck. Then her lips met up with his in a searing kiss. "See you at breakfast. Pleasant dreams."

Weston lifted her hair at the nape of her neck and brought her back in close to him. "They'll be pleasant, as long as you show up. Promise me you'll be there."

"I promise."

Weston smiled. "I love you. If you need me, I'm just a phone call away. Good night, sweetheart." As he walked away, he turned around and blew her a kiss.

Chapter 10

Jessica loved Jarred, but it was really hard for her to understand why he was acting as though he had a personal interest in her. He had been going out of his way since he had first arrived, to make Weston think they had more than a solid friendship. Now that he had left her with no choice, she planned to confront Jarred about his disingenuous behavior. He had been staying in the spare bedroom at the town house. Roman wasn't too happy about it, but Sahara had convinced him that they couldn't leave Jarred stranded.

So much for her and Weston spending their last days just hanging out together, taking things slow, Jessica thought. They both had been looking forward to the time they could devote to each other now that the family-oriented festivities were out of the way. All that had changed with Jarred's unexpected arrival. He had been an absolute butt at breakfast. Weston had left long before the meal was over, obviously upset by the things Jarred had been doing and saying. However, he was coming by later.

Jarred came into the living room and set down on the coffee table two mugs of hot cider. "You should probably let it cool first. It's really hot."

"Thanks." Jessica turned sideways and looked Jarred right in the eye. "What is *really* up with you? Why are you acting so strange all of a sudden?"

As Jarred took a seat, he shrugged. "Isn't it obvious? Are you really missing the point of what's going on? If so, do you want me to spell it out for you?"

Jessica looked annoyed. "Spell it out for me. I don't play guessing games."

"I'd like us to be more than friends—"

"Impossible." Jessica felt bad for cutting Jarred off before he had finished his sentence, but she hadn't been able to curb her matter-of-fact response.

"How come?"

"Because we're friends."

"Is that the only reason?"

"No."

"Maybe you should go ahead and spell things out for me since I don't get it."

"I'm romantically involved with Wes."

"And?"

"And what?"

"You're returning to L.A. and he's going home to New York. That should pretty much end things between you two. Don't you think?"

"No, I don't think. We're going to have a long-distance relationship."

Not believing a word of it, Jarred sucked his teeth. He couldn't understand how Jessica thought such a thing could ever work out. "How long do you suppose that'll last?"

Jessica didn't like all the negativity Jarred projected. "For as long as we want our relationship to last. We *are* serious about each other."

Jarred looked skeptical. "The intentions may be good, but Wes is a hot-blooded brother. Do you actually think he's going to remain faithful to you during the long absences? If so, you're more naive than I've suspected."

"I'm not the least bit naive." Jessica sounded exasperated. "Some people *can* be in a committed relationship, you know. Everyone is not like you."

Jarred narrowed his eyes. "That was a low blow. What are you trying to say?"

"I believe I said it. You haven't been able to commit to a single soul since I've known you. Wes and I *will* work out our long-distance issues. We are committed to doing just that. I wish you weren't so negative about this."

Jarred's eyes softened. "I'd be able to commit to you. It's that way for me because I've never been with the right person before. You *are* right for me. Why do you want to involve yourself in a long-distance relationship when we can be together every day? Flying back and forth between two cities will get old. Trust me on that."

Wishing she had the nerve to tell Jarred exactly what she thought of his comments, Jessica got up from the sofa and paced the floor. If she dared to speak her mind, she could lose his friendship. She didn't want that to happen, nor did she want to offend him, despite the fact he had insulted her plenty.

"Could you be romantically interested in me?"

Oh, how she wished Jarred hadn't asked that question. She couldn't beat around the bush on it. She hadn't had one romantic thought about him. He wasn't her type. Although handsome and charming, he owned numerous character defects. Above all, he lacked the ability to commit to another human being. Even when he was in a supposedly exclusive relationship, his eyes wandered. That wasn't all that roamed, either. He had dated more than one woman during most of his so-called serious relationships. Jarred was a big cheater, the one character defect in a man that she could definitely live without.

"You see me as that bad, huh?"

Sparing Jarred's feelings was important to Jessica. She didn't have to be mean-spirited about this because he didn't agree with her and Weston's plans for the future. "I just don't see an *us,* you and me romantically linked, period."

"Why not?"

"Please, let's not go there. Just accept that I'm in love with Weston."

"In love with him? When did that happen?"

"Probably many, many years ago, back when I couldn't even define love. I've always had a thing for Wes. It's much more than just a thing or a fling. I do love him." She had no desire to hurt Jarred, but she had no stomach for leading him on, either.

"You *don't* love him. You can't possibly. You don't even know him."

"This issue is not up for debate. Let it go. Okay?"

"I'll leave it alone. For now. But we *will* revisit the issue. Count on it."

"Not if I have a say in the matter. And I do."

"You only think you have a say. And I'm sure you think you have a say in what Wes does when he's not with you. You won't—and he won't."

"He won't what?"

"Honor you. Not at all."

"You know a lot about that, don't you? Who have you ever honored?"

The excruciating pain of Jessica's statement to Jarred was visible. "I honor you. In spades. I know I haven't been the righteous lover to the women I've been involved with, but there are reasons for that. I never dreamed you'd be so judgmental. You *are* judging me, you know. Critically."

"No more than you're judging Weston and me. Sorry if what I've said hurts you. I don't understand why it's okay for you to say what you want yet I can't. We've always spoken our minds with each other."

"But never so cruelly. You've been downright cruel."

"And you haven't?"

Jarred raised an eyebrow. "You obviously think so. Not my intent."

"Exactly what *is* your intent? I'd really like to know."

"I intend to win your heart for myself. Put Weston on alert for me."

"Put him on alert yourself. He'll be here in a few minutes."

"I'll do that. If you'll excuse me, I'm going to the little boys' room."

Jarred had Jessica really worried. He wouldn't hesitate to tell Weston that he intended to win her heart, and in no uncertain terms. Jarred was pretty bold that way—another thing she didn't particularly like about his character.

It wasn't that Jessica didn't think Jarred had a lot going for him—he did. He was a good person and a great friend, extremely supportive of his family and friends. He just wasn't good with romantic relationships. He was very sensitive to others, just not the women he was intimately involved with. Jarred was also well-known for giving to others less fortunate than himself. All in all, Jarred was a fairly decent guy, with faults.

The doorbell caused Jessica to jump. The bell had scared her only because she had been lost in her thoughts, concerned about what might happen next. It was probably Weston. She hurried to the entry. As she had eagerly anticipated, he pulled her into his arms and gave her a staggering kiss. His genuine affection let her know he wasn't holding her accountable for Jarred's bad behavior.

As Jessica turned to usher Weston into the living room, she saw Jarred standing there, staring hard at them, looking very formidable. Deciding not to let her best friend intimidate her, she shot him a warning glance. Once in the living room, Jessica and Weston sat down on the sofa. Much to Jessica's surprise and utter dismay, Jarred squeezed in between them, ignoring her silent warning.

Weston gave Jessica a questioning glance.

All Jessica could do was shrug. Jarred had her on edge. She had no idea what he would do or say next—and that scared her.

"So," Jarred said in a surly tone, "Jessica tells me you

two are in love. I won't pull any punches about my response. I don't believe it. You two don't know each other. How can you possibly be in love?"

With another unpleasant ordeal facing him, Weston sat up straight. "We've only known each other most of our lives. It's possible for us to be in love because we are. I get the feeling that you strongly disapprove of our feelings. Am I right?"

"Your intuition is definitely working for you, bro. I *don't* approve. I disapprove of long-distance relationships even more. In short, they just don't work for most people."

"I like your use of the word *most*. Jessica and I aren't most people. We are two exceptional people who happen to be madly in love. We can also accomplish anything we put our minds to."

"I can agree with the *mad* part. You two have to be mad, as in insane, to think your relationship has a fighting chance with the distances you'll have to combat. You live on opposite coasts, for Pete's sake."

Jessica started to fidget in her seat. Feeling her angst, Weston reached around Jarred to put a calming hand on her back. His eyes let her know he was in control, that he could handle anything Jarred brought on. Weston didn't fully understand what Jarred was trying to prove, but he was curious enough to stay the course. Jarred had a personal interest in Jessica—an interest that went beyond friendship, an uneasy theory for Weston to swallow.

"Just before you got here, I asked Jessica to give you a message. She said I should give it to you myself. So I will. I have every intention of winning Jessica's heart for myself. I'm in love with her, as much as you say you are, if not more."

Weston hid how much Jarred's statement shocked him. As stunned as he was, things had also been made clear to him. Jarred's statement about not pulling any punches rang resoundingly in Weston's ears. He had surely kept his word.

Weston had to be very careful how he handled things. He had to be sure not to make the huge mistake of underestimating a worthy opponent. Jarred *was* a clever man. He had to give him that much.

For all Jarred's confident talk, Weston had to wonder if he'd considered where Jessica stood in all this. It was really up to her. They could love her more than life itself; it was only about whom she chose to love back. Jessica had confessed her love for Weston. He wouldn't boast about that. It wouldn't be too bright of him.

Weston stroked his chin. "I commend your candor. But I'm not sure we should look at loving Jessica as a contest. She's not a prize."

"Oh, I beg to differ. She's the perfect prize. I place a high value on her friendship, and an even higher value on her love. Maybe it isn't a contest, but we both want to win Jessica's heart. Am I wrong?"

Weston couldn't argue with that. Still, he didn't see Jessica as some prize. Instead of getting into a discussion about it, he decided to say nothing. Jarred was spoiling for a fight. That much was clear.

"Let me ask you this, Wes. How can you say you love someone you terribly mistreated in the past? I know how badly you treated Jess because she told me."

Looking thoughtful, Weston pursed his lips. "The past should remain in the past. We were just kids. I've apologized to Jessica. She accepted. We've moved on."

"Enough of this, Jarred," Jessica yelled, jumping to her feet. "You are so out of line...and I want it stopped right now!"

Jarred raised both hands in a conceding manner. "I'll back off. I'll go back to my room and take a short snooze. See you later?"

Jessica didn't respond, fearful of only making matters worse. She didn't want anything to delay Jarred's departure. The air had grown rather foul.

Jarred got up and extended his hand to Weston. "No disrespect intended."

Knowing Jarred was lying, Weston laughed inwardly. "None taken."

Jarred gave Jessica a peck on the cheek, then left the room. She thought of following him to the bedroom to give him another piece of her mind but decided against it. She didn't want to hear anything else her best friend had to say in defense of his actions. There was no justification. He really had Jessica riled.

Jessica reseated herself. "Sorry about that, Wes. Really sorry."

Weston hunched his shoulders. "There's nothing to be sorry for. But I'd like to know if you're considering Jarred in a romantic way?"

Jessica gritted her teeth. "How can you ask me that? Suddenly doubting my love for you?"

"My question was a reasonable one. Especially when Jarred seems to think he has a real chance with you."

"He doesn't. Not even a ghost of a chance."

Jessica was hurt by the pointed question Weston had posed. How did he think she could consider Jarred as anything but a friend? She had made wild, passionate love to him. If he doubted her now, maybe he'd doubt her when they were miles apart, a very unsettling thought for her to entertain.

Sensing that he should also leave, Weston got to his feet. "I'm going now. Don't want to make things worse. You have a lot to think about. Must feel great to have two men falling all over the place for you. Make that one. I'm not into female-worshipping."

Looking horrified, Jessica leaped to her feet again. "You've got to be kidding! Is that what you think I'm all about? If so, you don't know me. Period."

Weston grinned menacingly. "By golly, you took the words right out of my mouth. Maybe I *don't* know you. *Not at all.*" Disgusted for losing control and saying things he hadn't meant to, Weston practically ran for the door. He wanted to be alone, needed time to think about what had happened. Feeling sick inside, he wished he could take back the unfair statements he'd made. He couldn't.

The thought to try and stop Weston from leaving came to Jessica's mind, but she decided not to act upon it. It would be stupid of her. God forbid he should think she was begging him to stay. His words had cut into her like a serrated dagger, tearing her tender heart to shreds. *He still has that mean streak in him.*

As much as Jessica wanted to regret making love to Weston, she couldn't. The wonderful experience had been too awesome for her to have an ounce of remorse.

Weston knew he had to apologize to Jessica for his earlier behavior. He owed her that much. This was all just one big misunderstanding. Everyone had said thoughtless things, things that never should've been said. Ever since Jarred had arrived they'd been at each other's throats. *So much for a happy ending to a merry holiday season.*

Weston would take the high road on this one. The more he thought it over, the more he understood an apology from him was a must.

After Weston grabbed his heavy jacket, he put it on and then left his cabin, securing the door behind him. "Brr," he chirped, gritting his teeth, shivering from the cold blast of air. He broke into a full run, anxious to get himself in out of the cold. He loved winter, but there were many times he had prayed for an early spring, hoping the groundhog wouldn't see his shadow.

As Weston neared the Harrington town house, his eyes were drawn upward to the balcony. Snow flurries began to fall hard, blurring his vision. As his sight cleared, what he saw caused him to stop dead in his tracks. His heart pounded against his rib cage with force, making him feel slightly nauseated. This just wasn't happening. It couldn't be. His eyes were deceiving him. They had to be. There was no other plausible explanation.

Jessica's and Jarred's lips were locked in a very passionate kiss. That was how it appeared to Weston. But that just couldn't be. Jessica and Jarred were only friends. At least that's what she had convinced him of. Even though he knew Jarred had a romantic interest in her, the feelings simply weren't mutual. There wasn't any reciprocation on her part. Jessica was madly in love with him.

Weston had been pretty darn sure of Jessica's love for him—up until now, before this crazy intimacy between her and Jarred had happened. There was no way he could face her right now. If she lied to him, tried to make him believe he hadn't seen her kissing Jarred, her credibility would be shot. He couldn't stand it if she tried to make a fool of him, tried to make him feel foolish.

With Weston's fears planted deeply in his mind, he turned around and headed back toward the cabin. He needed to leave Aspen right away. It was the only feasible thing to do. Getting out of this city was all he could think about. He had found the love of his life in Aspen and now he was losing it in the very same place. He'd call his parents once he was on his way to the airport. Perhaps he'd call them after he was already seated on the plane. That way, neither his mom nor dad could talk him out of leaving.

No doubt Sandra and Jacque would think their only son was acting rashly.

A single tear escaped Weston's eye.

Weston wanted to kick himself for going off the deep end. Feeling like a pouting juvenile, he was uncomfortably seated on an airplane. The decision to leave Aspen had been made in the heat of anger, in the midst of excruciating pain. Although he deeply regretted the stupid move, there was no turning back now. The plane was about to push back from the gate. Despite all the romantic movies, where the plane came to a screeching halt to reunite feuding lovers, that wasn't happening here. Not in this lifetime.

Since the plane was still at the gate, Weston thought he could at least get in a call to Jessica. He felt apprehensive, especially about her reaction to him bailing out on her like a lovesick kid. In spite of what had happened earlier, he pulled out his cell phone.

Not only had the kissing scene been shocking to Weston's entire system, it had nearly killed his spirit to witness it. Even if it had been the other way around, that Jarred was kissing her, there hadn't seemed to be any resistance on her part. Still, he should've at least given her a chance to defend it. After dialing her number, he held his breath in nervous anticipation.

"Hello." The male voice was easy to recognize.

Even though Weston knew it was Jarred's, he decided to bite the bullet and ask for her anyway. "Jessica, please."

"Sorry. She's unavailable." Derisive laughter came next. "She's busy, busy taking care of me. When you snooze, bro, you lose."

Jarred had recognized Weston's voice and had taken advantage of the awkward situation he had single-handedly created. Without responding to the churlish remarks of his rival, Weston hung up, fearful for his relationship with Jessica. He'd try to call her later, once he settled down back at home.

That Weston had run away rather than confronting the situation head-on wouldn't help matters any. All he could do was pray she'd understand why he hadn't stayed to fight for their love. It wasn't that he didn't want her, because he did, desperately. He just wasn't interested in playing right into Jarred's unscrupulous hands.

If Jessica *had* been kissing Jarred back, Weston felt that he wasn't meant to be with her. That hurt a lot. Wanting to give Jessica the benefit of the doubt, he still hoped his eyes had deceived him, yet...

To take his mind off all the unpleasantness, Weston closed his eyes, embracing the sweetest, most intimate moments he had shared with Jessica. The girl had set his entire anatomy on fire. As he truly realized how much was at stake, he grimaced.

Jessica had given all of herself to him. Had he been unfair to her in return?

Weston hadn't slept a wink the entire night. As he sat up on the side of the bed, he couldn't believe how intense his thoughts of Jessica were. He had made a grave mistake leaving Aspen like that; it had been a very rash decision. He should've gone to her and talked about what he had seen go down. Maybe it hadn't been as bad as it had looked. *Who are you trying to kid?* The kiss he had witnessed had looked very passionate.

Weston could still kick himself for his reaction. How could they build a solid future together if he ran away from her whenever a serious issue arose? He looked over at the phone for the hundredth time. He had started to call her so many times but had repeatedly backed out at the last second.

What to say to Jessica was Weston's biggest dilemma. She had to know by now that he had skipped out on her. He hadn't even said anything to his parents until after he'd headed to the airport. All the while he'd been heading down the mountain, he had prayed that the sudden snowfall would worsen, and send him back up to the top, back into Jessica's comforting arms.

There had to be a reasonable explanation why Jessica had been intimately involved with Jarred like that; he hadn't trusted her enough to find out. He had called his parents to find out if she had contacted them, but he hadn't been able to deal with their comments, either. Just as he'd figured, his dad tried to talk him out of leaving Aspen, telling him it was a terrible mistake to run out at the first sign of trouble.

Love doesn't bolt like that, Jacque had said to his son, the distinct sound of disappointment in his voice. Love stays and faces the issues, stays until problems are resolved, remains until a decision is made by both to end the relationship.

Weston's mother had also been surprised and dismayed by his course of action. He couldn't forget the anguish in her voice when she'd learned he was leaving Aspen, leaving on a note of anger and distrust.

The phone rang just as Weston reached for it. He had finally decided to call the woman he loved. It might already be too late. A lot of time had passed. Hearing his mother's voice on the other end caused a tinge of joy to rise, but it only lasted a second. "Mom, have you spoken with Jess?"

Sandra cleared her throat. "I spoke with her mother before calling you. Sahara talked to Jessica, but she already knew you were gone. She doesn't know why you left. Jess went to the cabin to see what was up when you didn't show up or bother to call. The cabin was empty, of course. She's a very hurt young lady."

Weston punched at his thigh. "This is messed up. I need to call her. I was about to do that when you called. I'll call back once I talk to her."

"Okay, son, we'll wait."

After Weston dialed Jessica's number, he only let it ring once. Cradling the phone, he stared off into space. The right words hadn't come to him yet. Were there any right words in this instance? So many wrong things had been said. He had acted out of character, hadn't used an ounce of the common sense God had given him. Tired of beating himself up with words, Weston stormed into the bedroom to shower.

Chapter 11

Devastated was an understatement for what Jessica felt when she'd first learned that Weston had already flown back to New York. The pain had sent her reeling. Still, she hadn't regretted the deep intimacy she had shared with him. It was impossible to regret the most beautiful moments in her life.

Stretched out on her king-sized bed, Jessica wiped the sleep and the tears from her eyes. She massaged her breaking heart with the heel of her hand. It was still early in her neck of the woods, but she was sure she couldn't fall back to sleep. With so much vacation time on the books, she thought of taking off another week; staying busy won out. She had already spent too much time thinking about Weston.

It was hard trying to figure out what had made Weston

jump ship. Had there been a change of heart about seeing each other beyond the holidays? Why hadn't he just told her that? Not knowing was tough. She couldn't possibly deal with the unknown. With her emotions ready to erupt, she moaned in agony. Plumping her pillows, she laid her head down, praying that Weston would call soon.

Just as Jessica had thought, she couldn't go back to sleep. A hot shower would help get the day started. Before entering the bathroom, she picked out fresh undergarments and a casual outfit, jeans and a sweater. The temperature had fallen during the night, leaving behind winter-cool air. Dressing warmly wouldn't hurt.

The bathroom colors brightened Jessica's mood. She liked lavender and yellow together, calming yet effervescent. The yellow flower appliqués on the walls lent the room a nice gardenlike appearance. The glass-block window adjacent to the hot tub and the overhead skylight let in ample natural sunlight. The shutters could be opened a little or a lot to allow in more sun.

As the sun's rays beamed off the clear glass shower door, the light reflected on the wall-to-wall mirrors. The dressing-table mirror was sun-streaked, too. The bathroom was a cheerful place to hang out. Too bad she didn't spend more time there.

As hot water pelted down over Jessica, she thought about sitting down on the ceramic tile, right in the middle of the shower floor. Instead, she increased the flow of water, stepping out a couple of minutes later.

Sadness had overwhelmed Jessica, causing her tears to fall. She didn't want to entertain unhappiness. Eating her favorite foods would help out. The pantry and refrigerator were bare; replenishing her food stock was necessary. She usually purchased enough food to last a week, but she had only picked up a few things before leaving for Aspen. It hadn't made sense to buy groceries when she'd be away on vacation.

The local grocery store was crowded with patrons as Jessica pushed the metal cart around the store, up and down the aisles. Two cases of bottled water were the first items written down on her grocery list; the last to be retrieved from the bottom of the cart. A quart carton of two-percent milk was needed to go along with the cereal and bananas.

Rice Krispies weren't her favorite, but she'd chosen them anyway. They were Weston's favorite; it was as if she were expecting him.

She selected several types of fresh fruits: white grapes, apples, citrus, pears and red and black plums. She tossed a loaf of wheat bread for toast in the upper portion of the buggy, along with a tub of soft margarine. Turkey breakfast sausages and a dozen eggs were also needed.

Nearly out of many household items, Jessica stocked up on tile and tub cleansers, furniture polish, air fresheners and dishwashing liquid, laundry liquids and fabric softeners. Then Jessica moved into her favorite aisle, the comfort foods. She needed comforting, lots of it. These were the items she'd come for in the first place. After loading up the cart with a variety of chips, pretzels and nuts, she moved farther down to where the red licorice and other gummy-type candies were shelved.

* * *

Ringing Jessica's doorbell for the fifth time, Weston had to accept that she wasn't in. For good measure, he rang it twice more. Calling her over the phone hadn't been the right solution. Seeing her face-to-face was the only way for him to right this wrong. He would've paid an exorbitant amount for his airline ticket if he hadn't logged so many frequent-flyer miles. The cost wouldn't have mattered to him. All he truly cared about was getting back together with Jessica. She was the only woman for him.

Was he still the only man for her?

Knowing he had to locate a nearby hotel, Weston made his way back to the rental car, glad it came equipped with a navigation system, which he'd used to get to Jessica's place. Both his own cars had the same electronic equipment.

Weston had actually gained time flying east to west, thanks to the three-hour time difference. There were a few hours of daylight left. Driving around in a city he didn't know too much about wasn't an easy task. The navigation system would make it a lot easier.

Just as Weston opened the door of the black SUV, a late model, pearl-white Thunderbird convertible pulled into the driveway. As the garage door went up, he raced toward the opening, hoping to get to Jessica before it closed. He wasn't sure if she'd seen him or not, but Weston had to make his presence known.

The minute Jessica stepped out of the car Weston pulled her into his arms.

"Oh God," he cried, planting his lips into her hair, "please forgive me for being so stupid. Can I please come in so we can talk?"

Jessica looked both stunned and frightened. She hadn't known who had grabbed her until after she had heard Weston's voice. She sighed, relieved that she hadn't been accosted by some stranger. She should feel relief over Weston coming to see her, but her anger had already taken control. "We don't have anything to say to each other. Your actions have made things very clear."

"*My* actions? I'm not the one who was kissing someone else. How would you react if you saw me kissing another woman, the way you were lip-locking Jarred? I saw the whole thing." Weston wished he had a sock to stuff in his mouth. He hadn't intended to go off like this. To sit down and talk calmly with her had been his goal.

As the memories of that day on the balcony flooded Jessica's mind, she felt horrified. That Weston had been a witness to the kiss hadn't crossed her mind, not for a moment. He more than likely hadn't seen how she had resisted. Jarred had overwhelmed her with his strength. He'd never do that again. The hard slap across his face had sent him a message he wouldn't soon forget. Too bad Weston hadn't stayed around to witness that. Too, too bad about all of it.

Jessica gripped Weston's hand, squeezing it tightly. "So sorry you saw that. It's not what you probably think. Trust me, I didn't invite Jarred's kiss—"

Weston silenced Jessica by kissing her deeply. He didn't need to hear anything more. The details of what had happened could go to the wind for all he cared. He only wanted them back where they'd been before Jarred had shown up in Aspen. Pulling his head back slightly, he looked into her eyes. "I didn't come all this way to fight with you. I came to fight *for* you. Can we please go inside?"

"Since you flew way out here to see me, I don't have a choice."

"You have a choice. If you don't want to talk with me, just say so. I won't force my affections on you."

"Sorry for being flippant. I'm stunned by all this. Looks like I'm the one who messed up everything between us. I had no idea I was to blame. We can go in, but I need to get the groceries out of the car first."

"I'll help you."

Jessica pressed a button on the car remote and the trunk popped open. Since she lived alone, Weston was surprised by the number of grocery bags she had.

Jessica read Weston's expression perfectly. "An eating binge. That's how miserable I felt about not hearing from you. Most of the bags are full of junk food. I would've overdone it. Made the mistake of hitting the store on an empty stomach."

Weston grinned. "I'll help you eat this stuff. If it's okay, I can stay for two or three days. I planned to get a hotel."

"I have a lovely guest room. No hotel room, unless you want it that way."

Weston winked. "Let's see how things go. We can sort it out later."

In the kitchen of Jessica's three-bedroom town house Weston carried several bags over to the granite counter and set them down. As he headed out the door leading to the garage, Jessica came up and threw her arms around his neck, kissing him passionately. Looking down at her, he clearly saw the tears swimming in her eyes. The last thing he wanted was to see her cry. "It's okay, sweetheart. We're together now. Do you want *us* as much as I do?"

"Desperately. I've missed you something awful. Sure I can't explain what happened with Jarred? It'd make me feel better."

Weston kissed Jessica's forehead. "It's not necessary, but if it'll help, go for it.

"Let's get the groceries inside first. Then we can sit and talk."

"Thank you. If you can manage the rest of the stuff, I'll get the teapot going."

"Good enough."

Jessica's tears fell quicker than she could wipe them away. Weston here in her private space was more than she'd hoped for. A phone call would've sufficed, but he had seen fit to fly here to straighten out the mess. Something she was solely responsible for. He had certainly been redeemed. Had she?

What Jessica had thought Weston had done was unconscionable in her opinion. He had hurt her deeply by not bothering at least to give her a call. It had been excruciatingly painful for her to deal with Weston's failure to contact her, but she hadn't been willing to compromise herself by calling him.

Jessica's dignity would have been severely at stake had she done otherwise. She had made sweet love to him, had given him the most valued parts of herself: her heart and her precious body. Jessica couldn't have given him any more in this instance.

As mad as Jessica had been with Jarred for forcing his

affections on her, she hadn't held him totally responsible for what she had initially thought was Weston's infantile behavior. He should've had more faith in her, unyielding faith in their love.

Jarred had been there to comfort her. He was a sensitive soul, but he'd gone a bit overboard since their return to L.A. Jessica finally had to tell him to back off and give her room to breathe.

The two friends had been constantly hanging out together over the past couple of days, but she was careful not to send mixed messages; she still had no interest in him on a romantic level. He'd been on his best behavior. Not once had he brought up his sudden romantic feelings for her. Since neither was dating, they planned to continue hitting the social scene together, along with their other friends.

Jessica was still in love with Weston. She'd never get over him. She wasn't into kidding or lying to herself. Not once had she tried to hide her love for him, nor had she pretended he was out of her system. He was a part of her, inside her heart to stay. Her pride had definitely gotten in the way—and she'd have no problem admitting it to him.

After unloading the rest of the bags, Weston emptied the contents. He didn't know where the items went, other than the refrigerated products; all he had to do was ask. He suddenly felt nervous. He'd stay busy until they had a chance to talk. Once he'd unpacked the canned items and snack foods, he asked Jessica where to put them.

Jessica opened the cherrywood cabinet doors to show Weston where to store everything. "The tea's just about ready. Want to stay in here or hit the living room?"

"It's up to you, wherever you're comfortable. I'm just glad I'm here with you."

Jessica smiled to show she was glad, too.

Jessica's kitchen was a cozy type of comfortable, decorated in cheerful colors of sky blue and apple red and crisp vegetable greens. The round cherrywood table had six matching chairs. A wraparound breakfast bar accommodated four metal-backed bar stools. The appliances looked barely used. She wasn't big on cooking so that could explain the great condition. The side-by-side refrigerator doors held all sorts of colorful magnets. A blue, red and green ceramic bowl of fresh fruit was in the center of the table.

Weston was eager to see the rest of the place, loving the warmth it gave off.

Jessica steered Weston through the double doors and walked the short distance to the formal living/dining room combination. The upscale decor was in creamy beiges and warm taupe. Splashes of gold accents warmed the living and dining spaces. Striking hardwood glass coffee and end tables complemented the spacious room.

On one living room wall, above the fireplace mantel, hung a lifelike oil painting of the Harrington family. Apparently it was a pretty recent picture. Smiles were bright and the love between them was apparent.

Jessica directed Weston to a seat on the creamy beige sectional sofa. She then went back to the kitchen for the tea. Unable to stay seated, feeling pretty nervous, he followed right behind her. Trying to make himself right at home, he gathered up a cheese ball and a box of crackers and placed them on a serving tray. Once he riffled through a utility drawer, he came up with a cheese knife.

Weston leaned against the counter just to watch Jessica pour the hot tea into a ceramic, Oriental-style teapot. Dressed in casual jeans and a winter-white sweater, she looked pretty as ever. His heart thumped like crazy. It was hard to believe he stood here in her kitchen. It wasn't so long ago he hadn't been sure they'd see each other again. The highest hurdle had already been jumped, but he wasn't taking anything for granted.

Jarred was still a force to be reckoned with.

Once Jessica and Weston returned to the living room, he set the tray down on the coffee table. He took a seat and Jessica sashayed across the room to turn on the CD player, loaded with the latest in love ballads and upbeat tunes. There was also one jazz vocal CD and a gospel one included in the mix of eight CDs.

Before anything else could transpire, Weston took Jessica into his arms and kissed her with all the passion inside him. He wanted there to be no mistake about what he felt for her. Nothing had changed. If anything, he loved her more. He hated that Jarred had forced himself on her like that, but he didn't want her to relive that moment. Perhaps it had been a fearful one. He'd let her talk, but wouldn't press her for details. Everything she shared had to come on her own accord.

Jessica poured both her and Weston a cup of tea. She sat back and rested her head on the sofa's back. The pillow she pulled toward her served as a security blanket, her fingers stroking and rubbing against it. "I wish I could turn back the hands of time. I can't. Sorry you had to witness the woman you love sharing a passionate kiss with another man. It wasn't what it looked like. Jarred paid the price for forcing his affection on me. I'm not proud of slapping him so hard, but he deserved it."

"You're damn right he did. Glad I didn't know it was by force. I'm just happy it's over...and he's out of your life."

Jessica's heart fluttered. How was she to tell Weston that Jarred wasn't out of her life, that they were still best friends? She hoped he didn't expect her to end the friendship. It'd only cause more problems for them if he did. She didn't want that. "Jarred and I are still friends. We worked out our issues. He knows I only feel friendship for him, nothing more. Can you accept it for what it is?"

Trying to contain his displeasure, Weston blew out a shaky breath. How did Jessica continue a friendship with someone who'd violated her personal space? He had to get a grip on his anger. Otherwise things might go badly. She wouldn't allow anyone to dictate to her. He wasn't a dictator or demanding.

Moving over closer to Weston, Jessica took his hand and laid her head upon his shoulder. "Can we get past this? Or is it too much to ask?"

Weston gently pressed his hand against the side of Jessica's face. "There's nothing you can ask that I won't try to do. I don't like your being friends with Jarred. But I will live with it. I just hope you know what you're doing."

"Please trust that. We're still hanging out together, but the boundaries are etched in stone. He won't try anything with me again, not like that. He *does* value our friendship."

"I'll try to accept that." Weston felt as if he'd been punched in the stomach. Still, he wanted to get through this with their relationship intact. It wouldn't be easy to

see or know that she was around Jarred. He had to consider
her wants. Opposition wouldn't help matters. With love
came sacrifices—and sacrifice his feelings on this one, he
would.

Jarred had better watch himself, should be ever mindful
of how he treated Jessica. Weston would take matters into
his own hands if he dared to disrespect her again.

The hours had passed by too quickly. Jessica felt comfortable nestled in Weston's arms. The couple had moved
from the sofa to the floor, after finishing the tea and
snacks. Stretched out on the carpet, they'd been kissing
and hugging each other silly. He felt good to her; she was
his medieval fairy-tale heroine. Things were back to
normal. They were still madly in love. Prayers had been
answered.

Weston gently lifted Jessica's head from the well of his
arm. "It's really late. I need to find a hotel room. What's
close by that you'd recommend?"

"Up the stairs and to the right. Or to the left. That's if
you want to sleep in the same room with me. I've got a
pretty big bed."

"Are you suggesting we sleep on opposite sides?"

Jessica lowered her lashes. "I want to sleep in your
arms, all night long."

How could Weston deny her that? He wanted nothing
more than to sleep next to her all night long, an eternity
of all night longs. "I want to sleep in your bed."

Jessica smiled warmly. "Ready to go up? I am."

Weston nodded. "I'm bushed. Let's do it."

"That, too. I want us to do that, too."

Weston had to chuckle at Jessica's little minx routine. This trip was turning out so much better than Weston had expected. He had halfway thought Jessica might tell him that she had discovered she was really in love with Jarred, that she had been sadly mistaken about loving him.

While Weston showered in the master bathroom, he wondered if Jessica was eagerly awaiting him. He couldn't wait to lie down next to her, holding her all through the night, making wild, passionate love to her. All the cues had to come from her. She was the author of their story. All he dared to pray for was a happily-ever-after ending.

Dressed in a sexy white silk chemise, Jessica had propped up herself in bed. Bare beneath the gown, purposely, she wanted Weston to know she wanted all of him. She had already made up her mind to take off from work while he was in town, wanting to show him her beloved city. Just maybe he'd fall in love with L.A., too. There were a lot of exciting places to explore. Most of the night spots she had in mind were cozy and intimate. They could pack a lot of excitement into two or three days in the City of Angels, but she'd relish the time they'd spend home, alone, in each other's arms.

Standing in the doorway wearing only a bath towel, Weston looked over at Jessica. Had she already fallen asleep on him? While his heart was at it again, thumping harder and harder, his manhood throbbed, too. Maybe he should go down the hall and fall into bed in the guest room. He wouldn't sleep a wink. How could he fall asleep when she was only a few yards away?

"Wes," she whispered into the silence of the candlelit room, "aren't you coming to bed? I've been waiting for you."

That was all Weston needed to hear. She had convinced him to spend the night in her bed. He didn't need to hear another word. Allowing the towel to drop to the floor, he climbed into bed, and immediately brought Jessica to him, caressing her bare arms, showering moist kisses onto her sweet neck and ears.

"Being with you feels so right," she whispered. "What made you decide to come to L.A. without saying anything?"

"My love for you. Nothing more. I love you that much, sweetheart."

Jessica's lips softly grazed Weston's. She then united her tongue with his. As the kiss deepened, she could hardly keep still. Her intimate zone was beyond heated, more like blazing hot. Having him inside her would eventually put out the raging inferno. She was in no hurry, too much passion left to enjoy. "I feel so good."

Lifting Jessica on top of him, Weston closed his eyes, his mouth hungry for the taste of her bare flesh. Close to losing control, he stroked and coddled her nakedness. *Take it slow. No rush. We have all night long.* His last thoughts blew right out the window when Jessica's soft hands tenderly curved around his manhood. She had the warmest, softest hands, her touch fiery. He couldn't get enough of the tenderness.

Weston's hands locked into Jessica's hair. In the next moment he rolled her off him and onto her back. His lips roved every inch of her anatomy, his tongue teasing her belly button. As he slowly entered her, she rose, eagerly meeting his throbbing sex.

Jessica intently watched their shadows on the wall as Weston slowly moved around inside her, taking her so sweetly, so tenderly. Lying with him was exactly where she wanted to be, moving harmoniously beneath him. Sweating palms followed shallow breathing as she surrendered all. This was her utopia. Peace was all around her.

Jessica's calm would soon be swept away in the crescendo of their fulfilling lovemaking. A tumultuous climax was sure to come and push her over the precipice of sanity. "Love me, Wes. Yes, yes," she moaned softly, basking in the climactic buildup. "Take me there," she cried out, "right now, before I die from the anticipation."

Weston increased the force of his deep thrusts, desiring to give Jessica what she'd asked of him, taking from her all he needed. Deeper and deeper he plunged, burying himself in her moisture-filled canal. As the skies opened up and showered a myriad of colors downward, they found glory in the powerful, earth-shattering release.

Trembling from Weston's skyrocketing lovemaking, Jessica reached up and wiped the sweat from his brow. "That was good!"

Leveling a skeptical eye on Jessica, he smirked. "Just good, huh?"

Grinning, Jessica purred softly. "Marvelous! I have no complaints."

"I'll settle for that." He pulled her close to him, as close as he could get without being inside her. "Thanks for letting me stay. I can only imagine how restless I would've been in a hotel room."

"Know what you mean. I hope you'll stay here the whole time. By the way, I'm taking off while you're here. We'll just hang out around L.A., Hollywood and a few other famous and infamous hot spots."

"Heard a lot about Venice Beach. Is it on the tour route?"

"It can be. It'll be a little chilly, but the folks will be out in force."

Weston feathered his finger across Jessica's brow. "You know something?"

"What?"

"You've worked up quite an appetite in this old guy. The snacks are long gone. Let's raid the fridge."

"Go ahead. I'll lie here and bask in our precious memories."

"Sure you don't mind me prowling around in your kitchen?"

"Positive. Bring me something good. I'm hungry, too."

After dragging himself out of bed, Weston headed straight for the bathroom for a quick shower. It suddenly dawned on him he needed to bring in his bags. He'd do that while he was downstairs. Then he'd come back to Jessica, sweet, sweet Jessica.

Unable to believe her good fortune, Jessica fought back her tears. Things had just fallen back into place for her and Weston so easily, as if they'd never been out of order. This man had everything she wanted and needed in a mate. She felt his dismay over her decision to remain friends with Jarred, yet he had set his feelings aside to meet her needs. She wouldn't make him regret it. One huge mistake was enough on her part.

Jarred knew right where Jessica was coming from. She had made sure of that. If he ever dared to overstep the set boundaries, he could consider himself history. He was a good friend, but not the man of her dreams.

Stopping by the bed, only towel-wrapped again, Weston leaned over and planted a juicy kiss on Jessica's mouth. Once he had mentioned his bags, she gave him the security code to the alarm, suggesting he pull his car into the garage before unloading it.

Jessica calmly watched Weston as he strode out the door. He walked with confidence. She liked a confident man, loved the kind of man he was, both confident and sensitive. Deciding she should also freshen up a bit, she slipped out of bed and rushed into the bathroom. With enough moonlight streaming in from the domed skylight to provide ample lighting, she stepped in the shower and turned on the hot water.

Back in the bedroom, Jessica removed from the chest of drawers another sexy nightgown, soft, silky and slinky in baby-pink. As she slid back into bed, she felt so grateful for Weston's love. She felt secure in it, as she hoped he was in her love for him. They each truly deserved the best. They truly deserved each other.

Chapter 12

As far as Jessica was concerned, the smoked turkey on rye was just the right combination to hit the hunger spot. Spicy brown mustard topped off the flavor, making her moan softly with each bite.

Instead of a lettuce salad Weston had put together a small fresh-vegetable platter consisting of carrot and celery sticks, cherry tomatoes and several slices of jicama. A creamy ranch dip filled the center of the platter.

The small round table in the corner of the bedroom was the perfect place for a midnight snack. The melon-scented ball candle was aflame, making it an intimate affair. The two bottles of ice-cold mountain water were right there to quench their thirsts.

Weston awakened to find Jessica's side of the bed empty. Wondering where she had wandered off to, he sat up straight in the bed. He rubbed the sleep from his eyes, surprised to see one of the candles still burning brightly. Maybe she had lit another before she left the room, he thought, getting out of bed.

It didn't take Weston long to find Jessica. Wrapped in only a thin blanket, she was seated in the living room, staring into the flame of a single votive. The candlelight flickered across her lovely face, softening her features even more. It disturbed him that he couldn't read her facial expression; her eyes appeared dull and blank.

Weston knelt down before Jessica. "Are you okay, sweetheart?"

Jessica looked up at him for the first time since he entered the room. "Just couldn't sleep. I got up because I didn't want to disturb you."

"I wouldn't have minded."

"I know. But you're tired, traveling all that distance. I was feeling selfish before I left the room, wanting to make love to you again and again."

Weston couldn't stop the grin from spreading across his face. "I would have been happy to oblige you."

"I know that, but not at the risk of your fatigue. I couldn't do that."

"I feel pretty rested right now. Want to give it another whirl?"

Jessica gave a slight giggle. "Hmm, sounds tempting." She gestured for him to sit down. He sat at her feet. She reached for his hand. "I've been thinking about us, this long-distance stuff. You really think we can handle it?"

"I do, honey. I'm more than willing to put in the flyer miles. Don't fret."

"I'm trying not to. There's also the matter of my friendship with Jarred."

"We've already settled it. Come on. Let's go back to bed."

"You go ahead. Be there in a few minutes. I want to sit here and enjoy the candlelight a bit longer." She began to stare into the flickering light again.

"There's a candle still burning in the bedroom...."

The look Jessica gave Weston let him know he was way too insistent. For whatever reason, she needed her space. He didn't necessarily see it as a bad thing, but he didn't see it as a good one, either. He felt as if she had already shut him out. He wanted to spend every moment with her; she obviously had other ideas.

Instead of fighting Jessica on this, Weston got on his knees again and kissed her forehead. "See you soon." He got up and started out of the room.

Jessica watched as Weston walked away, his shoulders slightly slumped. Had she hurt him again? She hoped not. Would he get used to her need for solitude from time to time? She was a deep thinker, one who needed time alone with her thoughts.

In the back of her mind Jessica had been wondering how Jarred would take the news of her reunion with Weston. He was convinced that Weston had taken what he wanted from her and had purposely left her high and dry. She hadn't believed that for a second, not even before he had showed up. Jarred had made every character-maligning statement in the book about Weston. There would definitely be another showdown between her and her best friend. That was a bet she could bank on.

* * *

Breakfast was another very quiet affair. Weston wasn't too keen on Jessica's apparently sullen mood. Maybe she was just tired. They *had* made love when she had come back to bed and also again at the crack of dawn.

Jessica looked up and flashed Weston a quick smile. "Dinner in or out?"

"In, if that's okay with you. We have such a short time together."

"My sentiments, too. It saddens me. Is shrimp pasta okay?"

"Whatever is easy and quick. I'll help out in the kitchen."

"We can make dinner together, then." She blew him a kiss, surprising to him but also pleasing.

Weston's eyes drank in Jessica's loveliness, following every move she made. The white silk robe she wore made her look so seductive yet sweet. "Breakfast was good."

"*Just* good?" she asked.

"Okay. I deserved that one. Marvelously good," he mocked.

"Thanks."

They both laughed.

The small talk was driving Weston to distraction. Why was she so reserved all of a sudden, a far cry from the wild, very vocal seductress of last evening? Instead of trying to guess at her mood, he'd just inquire about it. "What's up with you this morning? You're not exactly talkative."

Jessica shrugged. "I'm always like this in the mornings. I guess we haven't spent enough mornings together for you to know that. Nothing to do with you. I promise."

Weston wanted to believe Jessica, yet he still had a niggling doubt. He decided to dismiss it, though. Letting it go was easier.

"I'd like to take you by my office this morning. Up to meeting the staff?"

"All the way, kid. What about seeing the Staples Center? Can we get that in, too?"

"Sounds like you're not coming back to L.A. We can only do so much."

"I *am* coming back, as often as humanly possible. Are you ever coming to New York City to visit me?"

"Yep. Sooner than you might think. Don't know if I can be away from you too long. I'm so addicted to you." She went on to say how she'd look at her calendar when she got to the office. Although she had just taken a vacation, and was taking a couple of days off now, she told him no one at the office minded her taking off again because she worked so hard and rarely took long vacations.

Jessica failed to mention to Weston that she wanted to fly back to New York with him when he left, but only if he asked her to.

Now Jessica was really talking and Weston loved what she had to say. This was good, really good conversation, something he wanted to hear more of. Anything to do with her visiting New York held his keen interest.

"Why don't you fly home with me this time? I have plenty of frequent-flier miles we can use. What do you think?"

Jessica swallowed hard. It was as if she had spoken her thoughts aloud. "Are you serious?"

"I don't say anything I don't mean."

Pushing her hand through her hair, Jessica blew out a

steady stream of air. "This is kind of eerie. I've been thinking of going back to New York with you. If you want me to, I will, but I still have to check the calendar."

"Now I have to ask if *you're* serious."

"If my schedule permits, I'd love to try and swing it."

"Girl, we are definitely on. Let's get the kitchen cleaned up so we can get over to the office and check out that calendar. I may have to work some while you're there, but it won't be all day, just a few hours in the morning. Is that cool?"

"With the time change, it'll be just fine. I'll still be asleep that early. I can stay at your place, right? No hotel."

"I think you know that answer, but I wouldn't have it any other way." Weston got up from his chair and pulled her up from hers. "I hope this works." He kissed her thoroughly, still totally surprised by her desire to fly home with him. This unscheduled visit was getting better and better. Each time he'd thought things were going badly, she ended up proving him wrong.

Both Jessica and Weston felt totally relaxed, dressed in dark jeans and casual oxford-style shirts as they popped into the San Fernando Valley real-estate office. His black shirt carried a red designer logo. Her pink-and-white striped shirt had a logo also, but it was a popular department store brand. She also wore a navy blazer that nicely accented her dark-blue denims.

In a matter of minutes Jessica had introduced Weston to all of her coworkers. Welcomes and niceties were exchanged. All the staffers were open and friendly to him, which Jessica appreciated. She worked with a great group of people, anyway. It didn't take her long to bring up the possibility of taking more time off to fly back to New York with Weston.

Hank Rodman and Tony Anderson told Weston it was okay with them to keep Jessica on vacation. Then they'd get more of a chance to shine. She was often the top-selling agent each month.

Jessica's personal assistant, Melissa Wright, said she'd also like to see her boss take more time off simply because Jessica was all work and very little play.

Weston noticed that everyone in the office seemed genuinely fond of Jessica.

Jessica wished her coworkers a wonderful, productive day before she whisked Weston off to her private office in the very back of the six-office suite.

After seeing Weston comfortably seated, Jessica picked up her calendar to peruse the entire week. The date circled in red ink caught her attention quickly, an annual real-estate luncheon. Though she shouldn't miss it, she had already made up her mind not to go. At least no one from their office was being honored this year. No one would miss her at such a large function.

As the private line on Jessica's desk phone rang, she sat down in the high-backed leather chair before answering it. It was her mother, Sahara, and Jessica immediately told her that Weston had arrived in L.A.

It was unlike Jessica not to have called her parents with the news by now, but she'd been so overwhelmed with his presence. It had been more important for them to get their relationship straightened out than it was to call her parents about what would or wouldn't transpire between her and Weston.

Sahara had already known Weston had flown into L.A., from her conversation with his mother, Sandra, but she hadn't said anything to her daughter. Now that Jessica had mentioned it, Sahara insisted they have dinner with the Harrington family this evening. Sahara mentioned inviting Jennifer and Samuel over, too.

"I don't know, Mom. Let me check with Weston first. We planned to stay in and have a quiet evening. Can I get back to you?"

"Isn't Wes there with you?"

"Well, yeah, he is."

"Then go ahead and ask him about dinner, Jess."

Jessica scowled hard. Covering the phone with her palm, she told Weston what her mother wanted.

"It's up to you, sweetheart. You know how I am about family obligations."

"Mom, we'll come for dessert. And we won't stay that long. Okay?"

"Sure, honey. I understand. See you around seven."

The old myth about it never raining in Southern California was blown to smithereens yet again. As Jessica and Weston made a mad dash for her car, trying to dodge the heavy downpour, their screeches rent the air.

While Jessica fumbled around in her purse for the keys, Weston spun her around and kissed her tenderly. "Are you a brave soul?"

"I'd like to think so."

"Good. Let's walk. We're already soaked." Taking her

purse, he popped the trunk and dropped it inside. "I love walking in the rain."

The statement astounded Jessica since she also loved strolling in the rain. After putting her arm through his, she looked up at the office windows, wondering if the others were watching. Her coworkers were probably curious about her relationship with Weston. She hadn't shared any information about him since they hadn't had any contact post-Aspen. Only their families knew they had fallen in love. Well, she *had* called her girlfriends, but she'd only given them minor details. It had appeared to be already over.

Weston offered his jacket to Jessica, but she declined. His jacket was as wet as hers, but she was happy her fairly new Coach bag wasn't out in the rain.

The park where Jessica walked during the lunch hour was right across the street from her office. She loved to sit and look out the window to see the children playing there in the afternoons. As Weston guided her in that direction, he stopped every few steps to kiss the rain from her nose and steal a kiss from her luscious lips.

Was this the craziest thing they had done so far? No, it wasn't, Jessica mused. They had fallen madly in love after all these years.

Weston kept his arm around Jessica's shoulder as they strolled into the park. The rain came much harder. She thought they should turn back. A brave soul didn't act in a cowardly manner. Rain never hurt anyone, at least not by falling down on them. It just left a body a bit chilled and wet.

At any other time Jessica would've been horrified

that her hair would frizz up. Funny, but it didn't bother her to look and feel like a wet rat. She would have to wash and blow-dry her hair. In the interest of time she'd flat-iron her long tresses and let them flow about her shoulders, the layers falling smoothly.

A lightning strike caused Weston to turn Jessica back in the direction of the office parking lot. He also worried about her getting sick. They couldn't have that. She was returning to New York with him and he wanted her in tip-top physical condition.

The moment the couple entered Jessica's town house she quickly excused herself. Badly in need of a hot shower, she hightailed it upstairs, ran into the bathroom and turned on the water. Wishing she hadn't committed them to dessert at her parents', she stripped hurriedly out of her wet, smelly attire, tossing it into the wicker hamper.

Following right behind Jessica, already butt-naked, Weston guided her inside the shower, behind the glass doors. As they settled beneath the steamy, pulsating mist, he pulled her back fully against his body. Taking the plastic bottle of shampoo from the metal caddy, he commenced washing her hair.

Weston's fingers moving all about in her hair excited Jessica to no end. As he began to massage her scalp deeply, she dropped down on the built-in seat and let him do his thing. If it were possible to fall asleep in the shower, she could with ease. The hot water and his soothing hands had her completely relaxed, ready to succumb.

Before rinsing the shampoo from Jessica's hair, Weston lathered up his own curly locks. Minutes later, after he'd thoroughly rinsed out the coconut-scented suds, he applied a generous amount of rich conditioner to both their heads. Since the conditioner had to stay in for a while, he used the wait time to seduce her.

As Weston lifted Jessica into his arms, she wrapped her legs around his waist. He sat down with her and positioned her snugly on his lap, kissing her all the while. The water wasn't the only hot thing. As always, she burned white-hot for him. Allowing him carte blanche, she closed her eyes. This was her idea of heaven. His hands caressed and explored her nudity, his kiss warm, wet, wild yet tender.

Lifting Jessica a second time, Weston slowly and gently slid her down onto his granite-hard, aching-with-need manhood, condom-protected. She purred softly. As her body shivered with pure delight, he filled her up. While she moved herself up and down and around on him, her trembling hands entwined in his wet hair.

Tossing her head back, her eyes fiery with lust and passion, Jessica rode the rapturous waves. This kind of delicious lovemaking should never end. She felt his ardor all the way down to her toenails. Her body had started out humming sweetly. The song it belted out now thrilled her senseless.

If only Weston knew... He did know.... He had to know.... Her body revealed her intimate secrets, every single one of them, every time he made sweet love to her. At the same moment their shuddering climax detonated, shaking their inner cores, the shower ran out of hot water. Jessica didn't freak out, nor could she barely catch her breath. She laughed along with Weston, the cold water freezing off their tails.

As they stepped out onto the plush bathroom rug, he wrapped her up in one of the thick bath sheets she'd laid out. Once he'd towel-dried her body, she eagerly returned the favor. Massaging lotion and oil into each other's bodies followed.

A quick nap was decided on once the call to Sahara and Roman was made with deep regret. The Harringtons were a bit disappointed, but Jessica and Weston didn't want to drive around in the rain. More time alone was also desired. The walk in the rain had been fun, exhilarating and romantic. The day had already been full of sensuality. He had made more than her scalp tingle. Everything was beautiful, running smooth as silk.

Jarred's number was on the home-phone caller ID. Jessica decided not to respond. The timing was all wrong. He'd find out Weston was in L.A. in due time, and she was grateful that her lover hadn't questioned her about not picking up. Growing closer and closer to the man she loved was the most important order for this first visit.

By candlelight, naked as the day they were born, Jessica and Weston prepared dinner side by side. He drained the pasta in the sink while she stirred the plump shrimp into the marinara sauce. After dipping a wooden spoon into the sauce, she brought it up to her mouth to sample. She rinsed off the spoon and stirred the tomato concoction some more.

Weston pulled out two place settings and hurried to set the table. The fresh salad mixture she'd cleaned and stored in a plastic bag was removed from the refrigerator. He then poured Italian and blue cheese dressings into a glass server and blended them together well. Jessica liked the two sauces mixed. In the mood for red wine, he retrieved crystal wine stems and half filled each one. Wine made Jessica sleepy so he didn't want to ply her. Awake and fully alert for the rest of the evening was how he wanted her.

Instead of setting the food out on the table, the couple filled their plates straight from the pots. Before sitting down and digging in, Weston held Jessica's hand and said a blessing of thanks.

The pasta tasted wonderful and both were proud of how it had turned out. The lightly toasted French bread and tossed garden salad were also delicious.

Weston held a forkful of pasta up to Jessica's mouth. "Was your mom upset?"

"Disappointed, I'd say, but understanding. She'll get over it. We talked about lunch tomorrow. No plans were made."

"Lunch is good. Their place or out somewhere?"

"Probably a nice restaurant somewhere. Ports o' Call was mentioned, a sleepy, colorful little fishing village. Lots of quaint shops and tourist traps."

"Sounds like an idyllic spot. What about Venice?"

"That's an alternative. Several restaurants are right on the boardwalk."

"If you don't mind, I'd prefer Venice Beach."

"Not a bit. We'll call my parents in the morning."

"What's up for the rest of the evening?"

Wiggling her eyebrows, Jessica giggled. "Play house or doctor?"

Weston cracked up. "Either one works for me, as long as I'm the doctor."

The kitchen was cleaned in minimal time, as they worked together. The doorbell rang just as they curled up on the sofa. Jessica sucked in a deep breath, wondering who was at the door. She wasn't expecting anyone. Her parents wouldn't come by without calling, especially knowing she had company.

She opened the door to find Jarred standing there, looking pitiful, making her nervous. "What's wrong?"

"Nothing. Just needed a little company. Inconvenient time?"

Jessica nodded. "I'm entertaining."

"Who's here?" He rudely pushed past Jessica before she could respond.

Weston braced himself the moment he laid eyes on Jarred, his rival's surly words ringing in his ear. *She's busy, taking care of me.* He grimaced. Hoping there'd be no encore of their previous meetings, Weston swallowed the huge lump.

Jarred gave Jessica an intense, questioning look. "Haven't had enough, huh? Still a glutton for punishment, I see." Jarred had his back turned to Weston so his comments weren't heard. Not that Jarred cared. "You want me to leave?"

Jessica pressed her lips together, a stressful moment for her. Why did Jarred like to complicate things for her? He seemed to enjoy making her uncomfortable. Sighing hard, she threw up her hand. "Can we call a truce here?"

Ignoring the question, Weston got up from the sofa and went directly upstairs.

"So much for a truce." She looked exasperated. "This is impossible."

"You're impossible," Jarred shot back. "You can't have your cake and eat it, too."

"What's that supposed to mean?"

"Figure it out. You're a big girl."

As Jessica thought about Jarred's comment, his arrogant tone bothered her. Then a light suddenly came on in her eyes. "For your information, I *can* have my cake and eat it, too. Weston is my cake, the only sweet I desire. We've settled this. No revisiting."

"Yeah, unless sweetie pie breaks your fragile little heart again. You women never learn. I'm out of here. Eat all the cake you want. Don't be surprised if you choke on it. Or worse, end up eating humble pie."

Jessica struck her forehead with an open palm. Biting down on her tongue, she watched him storm through the house to get to the front door. Once the door slammed shut, she rushed up the stairs to have it out with Weston.

"Don't give me that look, Jess. He's your friend. Not mine."

"You could've been civil."

"Civil!" He stretched out on the mattress and propped his head up with a pillow. "Do you know how many phone calls he intercepted, telling me you were busy taking care of him? And you want me to be civil." Weston snorted.

"He did what?"

"Don't act so shocked. You know exactly what your best friend's capable of."

Jessica sighed in a conciliatory manner. "You said you came here to fight for me, not with me. Is that still true?"

Weston licked his lips. Attempting to temper his anger, he took in a couple of deep breaths. "Already told you why I was here. It still holds true."

"That's a relief." She walked over to the bed and pushed her fingers through his hair. "I love you. But that shouldn't mean I give up my friends for you."

"It doesn't. But neither does it mean I have to be friends with someone just because he's your friend. Does it?"

"Damn it, Wes. I'm not asking you to be buddy-buddy with Jarred. Just cordial."

"Are you asking him to mind the manners he doesn't seem to have?"

"You *are* the bigger person."

"Thanks a lot. I think."

Jessica kissed him full on the mouth. "I love you. Don't want to fight."

"Then we won't." He kissed her back. "Please don't try to sell me on your best friend. I'm not buying his act. I don't like him, period. The reasons are obvious."

"The feeling is mutual. He doesn't like you, either. But I wish it was different."

"It's not, nor will it ever be. Stop trying to push the envelope. If he and I never see each other again it will be too soon."

This issue was definitely a lost cause, with no chance of them becoming friends, Jessica conceded, glad the guys hadn't come to blows. Keeping the two men apart wouldn't be a difficult task. Although she felt saddened by what had transpired, the clock was ticking away. She had new memories to make with Weston, wonderful memories.

Climbing onto the bed with him, Jessica stretched out and nestled into his arms.

Determined not to let Jarred come between them again, Weston kissed Jessica long and hard. He wasn't normally this adamant or stubborn about things, but Jarred wasn't as good a friend as she thought. He was capable of even more mischief. They hadn't seen or heard the last of him.

Loving the perfumed scent of her skin, Weston held on tightly to her. Her hair was squeaky clean and coconut fresh. He took pride in how he'd taken such good care of her hair. Just the sound of her voice made his day. A smile from her lifted his spirits. She was a stylish woman, choosing just the right clothing combinations. Everything suited her so well. How had he existed without her all this time? He hoped they'd never let anything or anyone get in between them ever again.

Weston lowered his head and kissed Jessica. "You make my heart beat with such hope. Don't know how I've lived my life without you."

"You haven't, not if I'm the woman of your dreams. I've always been there. You just didn't know it."

"Have you always loved me?"

Jessica cocked an eyebrow. "Why do you ask?"

"Because I think you have."

"Then I have. Have you loved me?"

"Yes, the very idea of you. You're the woman who has

thus far escaped my grasp. That's why I'm holding on to you so tight."

"Don't worry. I won't go. I belong here. I believe that."

"Me, too." He kissed each of her eyelids. "I love watching you sleep. Did you know that?"

"Not really, but I've awakened to you looking down on me. I get a warm rush when that happens."

"That's 'cause you're feeling the sunshine streaming from my heart."

"What a nice thought, warm and tenderly spoken." She laughed softly. "You're right. I do feel the sunshine."

Jessica loved her space, yet she didn't feel the least bit crowded with Weston there. It was as though he had always slept right next to her, as if he belonged there. She imagined the sun streaming through the shutters to capture the warm golden highlights in his hair. His skin was smooth, looking as though it had never been introduced to a razor. She hadn't seen a five o'clock shadow on him in Aspen.

The music in Weston's head was soft and seductive. He recalled dancing with her to the tune his brain hummed in the private dining room in Aspen, "Tonight" by Kem. A couple of hot dance spots in New York came to his mind. She would love their coziness. As he was, Jessica was a romantic at heart.

Rolling up on his side, he touched two fingers to her lips. "We're powerful together. Do you feel what I do? An amazing sense of fulfillment?"

She nodded. "Utterly. The right words are hard to find. I love feeling loved."

"You are loved. Lots. Me—never been in love before now. What about you?"

"A few serious infatuations, back when I couldn't define love as anything but a warm, fuzzy feeling. It's more than that, you know. Way more—a state of being, wanting and needing, sharing, giving and taking, sacrificing, compromising, surrendering."

"Every bit of what you've put so nicely."

"It is what it is. You say you love me, but do you believe in the four-letter word?"

"Wholeheartedly. Just as important, I believe in us, in you and me."

"I feel so good about us, Wes."

"You're not alone. We're good together."

"Is there such a thing as a happy ending?"

"I hope we'll find out."

Chapter 13

As Sahara talked about the baby shower she was to attend next weekend, she had a look of empathy on her face. One of her closest friends, Carol Baxter, was in her late forties and pregnant, a totally unexpected, late-in-life first-time pregnancy.

Roman sighed. "Glad it's not us. I can't imagine having kids at our age. Can hardly wait for grandkids, but I don't want more children."

"Oh, I think it'd be fun," Sahara said calmly. "We should try for another one."

"No, *we* shouldn't." Uncomfortable with her remark, Roman looked petrified.

Weston and Jessica laughed at the look on Roman's face.

"Let's order," Roman said, clearly unnerved.

Roman gestured for the waitress, who hurried right over to their window booth inside IHOP. The couples had decided on breakfast so Jessica could take Weston on his sightseeing tour without the worry of getting back in time for lunch.

Roman looked up at the attractive waitress and smiled. "First off, young lady, I'd like to order a *change in topics* for my appetizer."

"Beg your pardon?" The waitress looked totally perplexed.

The others laughed at Roman's comical remarks.

"Don't mind him," Sahara instructed the young woman, waving off her husband's comments. "He's just being facetious. Kids, go ahead and order. I need another minute."

Their minds already made up, Weston and Jessica gave the orders to the waitress: a short stack of pancakes for each, scrambled eggs and turkey sausage. Sahara had settled on oatmeal, over-medium eggs, bran muffin and turkey sausage. Super-hungry Roman requested a combination meal of steak, pancakes, eggs and hash browns.

Orange juice and coffee were ordered all around.

Jessica looked across the booth at her mother. "Were you serious earlier?"

Sahara laughed gently. "Hardly! I love ruffling my dear hubby's feathers." She playfully nudged Roman with her shoulder. "You and Jen were a handful. I don't wish a second of your childhood away, but no more babies for me. Grandkids, I'm ready for."

Jessica also felt a little uncomfortable with the topic, but she didn't think her parents were hinting for her to hurry up and have children. Marriage normally came first, at least it used to. Jessica hadn't given the idea of children a lot of thought. She liked babies and older kids, loved to play with them, but she wasn't sure about motherhood as a full-time gig. There was a lot of life to live yet. So many things she still wanted to do. World travel was at the top of her list. Kids too soon would hinder that.

In tune with Jessica's nervous vibes, Weston covered her hand with his. He figured the topic had probably jangled her nerves a bit. "I'm loving L.A. so far and eager to see more. As you know, the rain kept us inside last night."

That wasn't all that kept us indoors, Jessica thought warmly, remembering how sensually romantic their entire evening had been. *Love and food and sex by candlelight.* Laughing inwardly, she hoped her parents didn't ask what they'd done for fun.

"I'm sure you're pleased by Jessica flying back to New York with you," Sahara mentioned. "She'll love your city as much as we do."

"I hope so. We'll take in a Broadway play or two and see a few famous attractions. Your fear of heights will keep us away from some landmarks."

Dismayed, Jessica wrinkled her nose. "I can look from the ground up. Can't I?"

Weston smiled sheepishly. "Of course you can."

Weston thought the waitress had arrived at just the right time. He had to be more careful. His feet didn't belong in his mouth. He'd rather have food there instead.

Venice Beach was as lively as Weston had heard. People were milling about everywhere. He loved all the boardwalk shops. Displays of artwork and sidewalk artists were amazing. Street vendors and entertainers were nothing less than colorful. The clothing some folks wore was rather interesting. This very popular area didn't have the exact flavoring of his fabulous New York City, but it was more than spicy. He also liked the warm feel he got from the people, though he had expected L.A. residents to be cold. He had heard that folks in L.A. weren't very friendly, but the same was said about New Yorkers.

As Weston and Jessica strolled along the beach, he was saddened by the community of homeless folks nearby. New York was no different in that regard.

The "girlfriends" had all gathered at Jessica's to give Weston their strict version of the litmus test, having dragged their protesting love interests along with them. The group of eight had invaded Jessica's home without prior warning. A private, girls-only powwow had convened in the kitchen while tea and snacks were being prepared for everyone.

General consensus: Weston was everything Jessica had said, nothing at all like Jarred had presented him.

Megan Thomas, cute, bright and witty, thought he was hot, equally as hot as her man, Rodney Jefferson, whom she thought *People* magazine should seriously consider as the next sexiest man alive.

Brandy Wilcox, a stunning redhead, laid-back and colorfully charming, said his fascinating looks and sexy body gave her goose bumps, warm ones. Crazy about Ethan Wise, her exclusive date for over two years, she felt Weston was a lot like him, the same type of man who turned her on. Jessica thought it interesting that Brandy had made such a determination after a mere fifteen minutes in Weston's presence.

Shauna Fields, pretty, fashionable, reserved, yet highly opinionated, simply gave the thumbs-up sign. She was so deep into Beau Liston, legally named Beauregard Romeo Liston III, that she paid little attention to other males. Beau was a pretty big guy, very muscular, so his name was only the brunt of the guys' jokes behind his back.

Jarred was there also. Interestingly enough, he'd brought along a date, a woman no one had heard him mention before he'd introduced her. Lori Clark, very pretty, but unusually quiet, hadn't made any comments about Weston.

Jessica could only imagine the picture Jarred had painted of Weston for Lori. Not a very flattering portrait, she guessed. While the women planned to ask their guys later what they each had thought of Weston, Jessica really didn't care to know; only her opinion about him counted.

It bothered Jessica to see how Weston and Jarred avoided each other. She was sure it was obvious to the others, but it was better than an ugly scene. She didn't try to get them to engage. That would have to happen without her, but she had her doubts.

"That was fun. And interesting," Weston said. "Your friends are impressive."

"Who're you telling? Bleeding anywhere?"

Weston chuckled. "No blood, but it was kind of painful. The sisters are good at dissecting a body. They must've enjoyed biology class."

"No doubt, yet they think they're subtle." She looked at her watch. "It's later than I thought. The one place I really wanted to take you closed at five, the African American Museum. We'll drop by before the Staples Center tomorrow. It's on the way there."

"It's cool. We can't get everything in. And I'll be back."

"Glad you feel that way, glad you'll be back."

"Started packing for New York yet?"

"Not a stitch. I'm not taking that much. Just enough for three to four days."

Since Jessica hadn't said exactly how long she'd stay in New York, Weston felt a twinge of disappointment. He'd hoped for a week. Three to four days was a start, a good one. He didn't want to be without her, period. Separation was inevitable, unless one or the other made the move. At any rate, that couldn't happen anytime soon. A lot was involved in a move. Permanently didn't occur overnight.

"We had snacks a short while ago, but I'm hungry again. What about you?"

Weston nodded. "I'd like a big steak, grilled with onions. You have a grill?"

"Out on the patio. Steaks in the freezer have to thaw first."

"That's no good. We can run to the store and back quicker than that."

"A fresh-meat market is right up the street. Want to get the grill going while I go to the store?"

"We'll do it all together. No rush."

Weston had been right. It had taken less time to shop for steaks than to thaw them. While Jessica seasoned the meat, he was outdoors tending to the gas grill. She had a barbecue grill, too, but firing up charcoal also took lots of time.

After placing the meat on a large platter for Weston to carry outdoors, Jessica began husking the fresh corn to cook it in the microwave. She would also microwave the sweet potatoes.

Weston smiled at Jessica as he lifted the platter of prepared meat from the counter. "How'd you want your steak cooked?"

"Medium-well. I like my meat dead as a doorknob."

Weston laughed. "I'll make sure it's no longer alive."

Tossing a green salad was Jessica's next kitchen chore, the easiest one yet. As she thought about dessert, she was sure there wasn't any. Another trip to the store wasn't a pleasant prospect. Then she remembered the frozen cherry pie she'd stored in the freezer a week or so before the trip to Aspen. Passing by the oven, she turned it on and set the temperature to 450°. A cookie sheet to place the pie on was pulled out from a lower shelf.

Weston popped into the kitchen to get the long-handled barbecue tongs, leaving just as quickly. Meat needed constant tending to when grilling since it could burn easily. She walked over to the French doors and peered out at him. He seemed right at home. That made her smile. His feeling comfortable in her home was important.

The man was certainly deft at grilling steaks, Jessica noted. He enjoyed showing off his cooking skills. His willingness to help out around her place was a check mark in the plus column. He loved to cook and she was happy since she didn't. Suddenly, she had a vivid image of them seated on her cozy patio during weather-permitting months. She envisioned them sharing the same chaise, his arms wrapped snugly around her. While sipping on cool drinks by the light of the moon, or candlelight, when the moon wasn't available, they'd help each other chase away the stresses of the busy days. Chatting nonstop would be one of their favorite pastimes. They'd make each other smile and laugh. Time spent with him would be filled with all sorts of surprises.

Before helping Jessica bring in the meal from the kitchen, Weston lit the candles on the table. She came into the dining room just as he headed out, and they bumped hard into each other. Laughing, he spun her around a few times, then kissed her until she trembled.

"Everything's ready. We can eat now, sweetheart. Let's get the food out."

Standing on tiptoes, she requested another kiss from him. "Make it hot and wet."

"I'm yours to command. Don't hesitate." He made the kiss hot and wet.

Jessica said the blessing this time around. She also voiced her thanks for Weston's company. Before digging into the delicious-looking food, they both slathered lots of butter on the sweet potatoes. The steak had been seasoned to perfection. He smiled as he told her just that. She raved about how tasty and tender the meat was, giving him his props. His expression told her how much he enjoyed the sincere compliment to the chef.

Filling his fork with sweet potato, he leaned over and

put it up to Jessica's mouth. "My food always tastes better after your lips touch my fork."

Flattered by Weston's nonsense, Jessica wrapped her lips around his fork in a provocative manner. She then picked up from her plate a piece of steak. After she popped the meat into his mouth, he drew her finger in as well, sucking on it gently. He closed his eyes in dramatic fashion. "Now, that's the tastiest morsel yet, so sweet."

Jessica cracked up. "Not as sweet as you." She took a sip of wine and shared it with him from her mouth.

Savoring the intimate moment, Weston entwined his tongue with hers, showing his appreciation for her with a staggering kiss. "Does it get any better than this?"

"If we want it to, but only time will tell."

Just what we don't have a lot of. Weston dismissed his dreadful thought. They could have the rest of their lives if they wanted that, too.

Jessica dug into her salad, keeping her eyes hotly on him. She suddenly felt warm all over, her feminine treasures red-hot for him. She couldn't wait for them to curl up in bed later. She had chosen a couple of romantic DVDs to watch, but she wasn't sure how much actual viewing time they'd get in. Instant combustion occurred every time they touched each other in an intimate way.

"Dessert now or later?" she asked.

"Both. The cherry pie first. You, later, my very favorite dessert. You have ice cream to go with the pie?"

"As a matter of fact, I do. I initially thought I didn't have any dessert. A thorough check of the freezer revealed a lot of sinful delights."

"I'm looking at the most sinful one of all. How many

calories are in one of your kisses? They *are* loaded with sugar."

"You don't want to know. However, there's no way to reduce the calorie content. My kisses aren't served with artificial sweeteners. Only pure sugar doled out here."

Weston loved her witty charm. "Bring the calories on, babe! None are wasted calories. I'm sure of that."

The couple had fun feeding each other the pie. Drizzling ice cream on upper body parts and licking it off had them laughing so hard. They were getting into so many habits they'd miss when apart. Learning more and more personal stuff was a treat also. Weston was surprised that Jessica loved to play video games. His surprise was his love for taping soap operas to watch late at night.

Weston was happy they hadn't gone out. Something about being alone with Jessica made everything worthwhile. He loved the quiet intimacy they shared, especially when no one was around. The day had been full, starting at breakfast with Roman and Sahara. The older couple had been invited to sightsee with them, but the offer was declined since the kids didn't have much time left. Both families had completely backed off, allowing Jessica and Weston's relationship to develop pressure free.

Picking up one of the two DVDs Jessica had chosen for viewing, he read the synopsis on the back. Chick flicks. That was okay. He loved romance stories, more so romantic comedies. *The Wedding Date* seemed like a good choice from what he'd read. *Madea's Family Reunion* had a romantic theme, but he'd heard it also dealt with serious issues like domestic violence. Neither movie was a newer release.

In the mood for some good music, Weston got up from the bed and turned on the CD player. Jessica was in the bathroom preparing for bed. No telling how long that might take. She had more lotions and potions that she used daily or nightly. He thought that both women and men alike should make it a priority to take good care of themselves.

Jessica kept her hair and body in good shape, another real turn-on for him. Every part of her body from head to toe received special treatment. Watching her paint her nails had been a blast for him. She'd even let him paint a couple of her toes, promising to let him polish all ten the next time she did a pedicure.

The gown Jessica wore had Weston's eyes bugging, black see-through lace, soft and alluring. She smiled at him, flirting with her lashes…and his heart leaped. "When Love Calls" breezed into the room. He whipped her into his arms and whirled her about the room. Holding her close, he pressed his lips against her forehead. They fitted so well together.

Was this a match made in heaven? Weston didn't have to waste any time wondering. His instincts told him it was.

Blackness slid over the window in her bedroom. A silver half-moon lit the sky. Stars twinkled in unison. Tree branches rustled in the wind, as though dancing to the soft music. A barking dog interrupted the peace momentarily. Serenity was restored.

Weston watched Jessica light the fireplace with a flick of her finger on the remote. She lit several candles before turning out the lights, the candlelight mirroring in the window. An instrumental CD was selected, easy listening, more mood music.

As Weston stared out the window, he saw something adjacent to the patio, a large something he hadn't seen before. He peered closer, hoping to find out what it was. A hot tub, he finally figured out. She owned a hot tub. Why hadn't he seen it before? It was very close to the patio, where he had used the grill earlier. He had missed it completely.

"The hot tub, does it work?"

"Practically brand-new, since I rarely use it."

"Why'd you buy it?"

"I didn't. Housewarming gift from Mom and Dad."

"Nice. Mind if I turn it on? I'd love to take a relaxing soak."

"Suit yourself. Just don't expect me to join you."

"Why not?"

"It's cold outside. Duh?"

"News flash, babe. *Hot* tubs, mega heat, duh? Think about joining me while I go outside and fire it up."

"Don't think I'll change my mind."

"Just give it some thought, please."

As Weston ran down the stairs, Jessica shook her head. Dead of winter and he wanted to soak in the hot tub. Well, L.A. winters were mild, but it was chilly outside.

Jessica sat down on the chair by the window after putting on the CD her mother had given her at breakfast. *Let's Go to That Place,* Joe Jordan and Friends. Sahara had gone to high school with Rodney Washington, the song-writer for several cuts on the CD. Her mother had also given her a picture album full of photographs of her and Weston.

From the cradle to Aspen, Jessica thought, admiring the photos. Where had all the time gone?

The first few pages of pictures made her laugh. Two separate shots of her and him made her howl. Why did parents love to photograph their babies in the nude? It seemed a little whacko, but she'd probably do the same thing. Nude pictures were actually very cute. Weston, as a baby, was adorable, with the cutest, chubbiest cheeks. Braided hair, no less; thick and long. Had she seen these as a teenager, no doubt she would've teased him about being pretty as a girl. He was beautiful as a man, a manly man.

Gales of laughter ripped from her throat at the funny picture of her with an orange mustache; tomato sauce. A bowl of SpaghettiOs was on the high chair tray. A shot at the floor showed several little Os there, too. Then she noticed the fistful of Os she clutched.

A sound outside made her look out the window, searching for Weston in the blackness. Why hadn't he turned on the porch light? She then saw that he was okay.

Up until now she hadn't thought about his request to join him in the hot tub, which was suddenly appealing to her. This was one of those compromises she'd spoken of earlier. A sacrifice, too, since she was subjecting her body to the cold night air. God forbid she should get sick.

Not to be deterred by her negative thoughts, Jessica ran over to the chest of drawers and riffled through the lower drawer where she kept her swimwear. She then went to her walk-in closet and pulled out a terry/velour bathrobe. Stripping out of the gown, she put on the one-piece bathing suit. As she thought about her rubber flip-flops, she recalled right where they were in her closet. She'd need the sandals after getting out of the tub.

Weston came back into the bedroom. His eyes widened at what Jessica wore now. He rushed over to her and gave her a big kiss. "Thanks for reconsidering. Ready to go outside?"

"Yeah, as soon as you put on your swimming trunks."

Grinning, Weston winked at her flirtatiously. "Don't have any."

"Then what're you wearing?"

"My birthday suit, baby, what else?"

"Ooh, the hot tub idea is getting hotter by the minute," Jessica cooed, leaping off the bed and landing right into his open arms.

The hot tub jets kicked out a mighty force as the strong currents swirled about them. Jessica was beyond relaxed and Weston's aching back benefited therapeutically. Bending over the grill had left his back tight and his legs a bit stiff. The water force had already loosened his muscles somewhat. He hoped for total relaxation.

Jessica scooped up a handful of water and dripped it over Weston's head. His laughter roared from deep within his stomach. A water fight ensued for several minutes. As body parts grew languid, Jessica got quiet. As she leaned into him, she wrapped her arms around his waist. Keeping her eyes open was hard since she felt relaxed enough to fall asleep. Seeing the droop of her eyes, Weston tenderly brought her head to his chest.

After their shower, Jessica had immediately succumbed to fatigue. As he watched her sleep yet again, he fought the urge to smooth back her hair. She looked so at peace. He didn't have the heart to disturb her, yet he wanted to bring her into his arms where she'd sleep the entire night. He wondered if she was having a dream. If so, did she dream of him? He laid his head as close to hers as he could without disturbing her. The urge to touch her hadn't gone away. Unable to stave off his desire any longer, he lifted her head and laid it on his chest. When she didn't stir in the least, he was pleased. His thoughts turned to the hours that lay ahead, the hours that would eventually lead them to the airport where they'd board a plane bound for New York City.

He could hardly wait to get her home. There were so many places he wanted to take her. NYC never slept. They could go out any hour of the day or night. Nightlife was plentiful and shopping sprees were right at the fingertips 24/7. If there was enough time, they'd drive up through the New England states. It wouldn't happen on this trip, but they'd get it done on one of her later visits, assuming there'd be more.

All of a sudden Jessica felt nervous. Their flight had just been called. Flying off like this was so unlike her. She had recently become somewhat of a risk-taker. Hanging out with Weston had rubbed off on her. He was the big adventurer. He'd told her that he had lost count of the number of trips he had taken on the spur of the moment.

Impromptu social activities suited Weston best. His work schedule was pretty regimented, but he tried to be as flexible as possible. Getting his work out of the way first meant that he didn't have to worry about it come time to play. Until his vacation to Aspen, he'd severely neglected the social stuff.

Jessica looked behind her as she started toward the Jetway, as if someone were there to bid her farewell. Of course no one was. Family-and-friend send-offs were a thing of the past. Her parents and Jennifer had called before she'd left the house to wish her safe travels and an enjoyable time. She gripped Weston's hand, squeezing it tightly.

Weston looked at Jessica with concern. She had acrophobia, but no fear of flying. At least that's what he'd been told. He gently squeezed her hand in a reassuring manner. He could ask if she was scared, but he dismissed that. She'd probably tell him if she was.

Jessica didn't surprise Weston when she offered him the window seat. She might fear looking out the window even if she wasn't scared to fly. The plane was designed with two seats on both sides and a row of seats in the middle. Before sliding over to the window seat, he stored their bags overhead. She slid her laptop case under the seat after he sat down. Weston kept his DVD player with him. He had brought along several movies to watch if they didn't like the airline's movie offering.

The flight had been very eventful, inasmuch as Weston and Jessica had enjoyed themselves tremendously. He had made sure she was totally relaxed the entire time. What with eating, watching a couple of movies and talking up a storm, the hours had flown by rather quickly. Jessica had planned to take a nap at some point, but Weston had kept her engaged in one activity or another.

In Jessica's opinion Weston's large one-story flat was beautiful, the space so well-appointed. Each room spoke to her, making her feel warm and welcome. As she walked around, she saw his personality everywhere. The home's warm decor fit him to a T.

The furnishings were elegant, the grand antiques rare finds. He preferred mahogany hardwoods, ornamental glass tabletops and lots of plush leather in the recreational areas and in his private office. Both formal rooms had Oriental-style furnishings, created from grossly expensive silk fabrics and the finest in hardwood.

Smoky black and stainless steel appliances graced the country-style kitchen. A mixture of plush carpeting and marble and ceramic tiles were laid throughout. The navy blues, grays and reds, with numerous brass accents, gave the large rooms a masculine feel.

The fabulous bedroom, with a fireplace and private sitting room, his favorite spot in the house, looked like something out of a home fashion magazine. This area also had an Oriental flair, the red, black and gold bedding done in Far East patterns. Colorful Asian fans in different sizes and prints hung on the walls.

The big brass bed, shining like new money, was set on a walk-up, hardwood dais. This was his favorite piece of furniture. Thick throw rugs were on each side of the bed, with one large one at the bottom. The low wood table, with a lazy Susan, sat in the center of the sitting room, surrounded by large pillows. It was also used for private dining.

Weston cleared one of his dresser drawers for Jessica to store her personal belongings. He had moved his few items into a drawer in the guest room dresser. She hadn't brought along a lot of clothes, completely emptying her suitcase in a matter of minutes. He hadn't asked her where she wanted to sleep, with him or the guest room.

Apparently Weston wanted her in the same room with him, Jessica guessed. She had no objections. Sleeping in the same bed with him hadn't taken much getting used to. They both enjoyed the intimate arrangement.

"You can hang your clothes in here." He stepped into the vast walk-in closet. "What kind of hangers do you like?"

"I've never been asked that," she said on a chuckle. Jessica could see that he had all types of hangers, plastic, wooden and metal, but no wire. "Plastic works for my tops. Metal will do for my jeans and dress pants. I see you have plenty of both." She backed out of the closet and grabbed a couple pairs of jeans to hang up. Jessica didn't like packing but she despised unpacking.

"I'll be in the kitchen. See you when you finish. Holler if you need anything."

Jessica blew him a kiss, watching after him as he left. She loved his cute butt, so round and firm. She hung up the rest of her things, then took a seat on the plush chaise in the sitting room. She felt fatigued. Cramped up in a narrow seat for over five hours wasn't an ideal sitting position.

As Jessica looked around at his intimate space, she liked what she saw. The bed was comfortable-looking and she couldn't wait to lie down on it. The African-American framed artworks displayed on identical antique easels were beautiful treasures, positioned on either side of the mantel. Along with two oversized chairs and a sofa and love seat, the sitting room housed a full wood and glass entertainment system. A CD/DVD player and a DVR accompanied the large plasma television.

Thinking a quick shower wouldn't hurt, Jessica got up and wandered into the master bathroom, another huge area with every possible creature comfort. Everything was sparklingly spotless. He also had a hot tub, walk-in shower and dual sinks. The cultured-marble counter ran the length of the room. Many candles were on display, some brand-new, others partially burned.

Walking back into the bedroom, she retrieved clean undergarments from the dresser. Instead of fully dressing so late in the evening, she removed her robe from the plastic hanger. As the food scents reached her nose, she closed her eyes to try and identify the delicious smells. Several seconds later, she gave up, unable to tell what Weston was cooking.

Weston heard the shower water running as soon as he entered the bedroom. His heart lurched. It made him feel good to know she felt comfortable enough to shower without feeling the need to ask first. As he stepped into the bathroom, he saw her clothes neatly folded and stacked on the dressing-table chair. The clear glass allowed him to see inside, where she stood under the water. Her naked body caused an instant expansion below his waist. His desire to make love to her hit him hard.

Instead of acting on his desire he turned around and headed back to the kitchen, where he had lasagna baking in the oven. Although frozen, the pasta dish was amazingly good. He'd eaten it numerous times and had also served it to guests, who'd given it rave reviews. The salad had already been tossed and the table set. Champagne chilled in the refrigerator for a toast welcoming her to NYC.

Chapter 14

Jessica had lain awake the better part of the night, her eyes bright as drops of crystal. New surroundings had kept her from sleeping, she supposed. Watching Weston sleep was just as thrilling for her as watching her sleep was for him. He didn't snore. She had thought most men did, although her father was a quiet sleeper, too.

Lying in the big brass bed reminded her of a song her parents had played to death, "Lay, Lady, Lay." The mattress was as comfortable as her own, if not more so. She was still amazed by the size of his bedroom and cozy sitting area. His reference to his place as a house wasn't an adequate description; it wasn't a single dwelling. The residences were linked by two-car garages and patios, more of a town house effect, but with only one story. New Yorkers often referred to their apartments and townhomes as flats.

The fireplace was on, waving an array of brilliant colors, mesmerizing Jessica. She carefully crept out of bed and planted herself on the grayish microfiber chaise lounge situated right in front of the fireplace. As she put her feet up, Weston stirred. She caught and held her breath, as if her breathing might disturb him.

Weston's arm stretched over to where she should've been. He appeared to reach for her, but the only object there was a pillow. He pulled it to him and wrapped his arms around it. He couldn't possibly think the inanimate object was her. She muffled her soft laughter. No life was in the pillow, but the scent of her hair was on it, along with the alluring fragrance of the perfume he'd given her for Christmas.

Jessica turned her attention back to the roaring fire, the smell of cedar filling her nostrils. On the mantel above the fireplace was a picture of his parents. Her eyes widened as she spotted a good-sized picture of herself taken in Aspen. He was also in the picture, both dressed formally. A photographer had been commissioned that night. She had a copy of the photo, too, but it wasn't on display in her home. Nor was it that large. She'd remedy its absence as soon as she got back home. She would proudly display the photo.

Weston silently crossed the room. She didn't see him until he towered over her. As he lowered himself onto the chaise, she scooted over to make room for him. His lips instantly took possession of hers. His breath still tasted and smelled of mint toothpaste though he'd been asleep a long while. Jessica's body began to tingle as her heart flipped.

Their tongues linked. His hand tenderly cupped her breasts, his manhood ready for her, ready to make love to her in every room just to preserve the memories. The sofa in the kitchen came to mind, one of many perfect spots for taking her to heights yet unattained. Right now they'd take each other in the chaise.

His thumbs hooked the edge of her bikinis and she rose to make the removal easier. His fingers found their way to her inner core, already slick with moisture. She writhed in response to his gentle touch, her body heating right up. With her fully stretched out along the chaise, he turned over and laid himself on top of her. The first thrust had her rising again, this time to meet his hardened flesh.

Jessica suddenly panicked. "A condom. We aren't protected," she whispered in his ear.

"It's okay. We're fine." Weston guided her hand down to his erection so she could feel the latex for herself. He had put it on before he'd come to her.

"Sorry. I didn't know. Should've felt it."

"Save the regrets. Apologize later, for wearing me completely out."

As Weston thrust deeper into her molten heat, her body trembled and she bit down on her lower lip, opening wide to receive the next one. The moment of interruption hadn't quelled his desire. He was still hard as granite. The next thrust was met with the same fiery response and the next deeper one had her moaning sweetly.

"Let me on top," she rasped. "I feel like taking a wild, hot ride. You make me feel so sexy and desirable."

With relative ease Weston swapped places with Jessica. Their lovemaking hadn't been awkward since the first few minutes of the first time. As she moved her hips over him with reckless abandon, he moaned with pleasure, wishing this moment could last forever. Passions continued to flare as she rode him wild and hard. As his eyes glazed over with love and lust, she worked him over, her strokes frenzied. As his fulfillment broke free, he screamed out his love for her.

Spent, fully satiated, happy he'd climaxed along with her, Jessica fell forward and laid her head on his chest. Too tired to move, they both fell asleep minutes later.

Jessica didn't awaken until Weston picked her up and carried her into the bathroom, where he'd already drawn them a hot bath. How he'd gotten out from under her without disturbing her intrigued her enough to ask him about it.

"I'm the man, girl. You were completely knocked out, dead to the world. I'd thought you'd wear me out."

She chuckled at his response.

Music drifted from speakers mounted in the ceiling. Several candles had been lit to create a romantic ambience. Closed shutters blocked out natural light. Before Weston lowered himself into the tub, he retrieved two new bath sponges from the linen closet, dropping them in the water.

Settled in the tub, Weston picked up a sponge and loaded it with shower gel to lather up Jessica's sexy body. She washed him at the same time, their sponges clashing a time or two. They stayed, played, splashed and thrashed around in the tub until the water grew too cold.

Weston had fun creating a sensual art form of towel-drying Jessica's body. He made a mental note to pick up a dozen or so bath sheets, the thick towels she used back home.

"What're your taste buds craving?" Weston inquired.

"You," Jessica sang out, "sweet-tasting you."

Fulfilling her request, he stretched himself out right there on the bathroom floor, telling her to feast off him any way she desired, thus initiating another possible bathing session.

Seated at the kitchen table, her legs propped up on another chair, Jessica perused the *New York Times* while sipping on hot coffee. The coffee brew station was on a timer. It had already perked by the time the couple entered the room.

Weston was busy preparing scrambled eggs, thick slices of grilled smoked turkey and toast. He looked over at her. "Where do you want to go first?"

"Wherever you take me. This is your beloved city. And I'm easy to please."

He raised an eyebrow. "Don't know about all that. You *have* been a bit insatiable since you got here."

"A bit? What an understatement!"

He laughed at her indignant expression. "Interested in Ground Zero?"

"Very much so. I imagine it's a sad affair."

"A real tear-jerker. We won't linger. We'll do local transportation. Driving around the city can be a little tricky."

"So I've heard."

"Dress warmly and comfortably, especially your foot-wear."

"I plan to. It's really cold. Your place is so lovely and warm. I hate to leave it so soon. Getting acquainted with your personal space has been fun."

"Glad to hear it, since you'll be spending lots of time here, as I will in L.A."

Jessica narrowed her eyes at that statement, but made no comment, hoping he'd be in L.A. more than she'd be in NYC. While she really didn't expect him to do all the traveling, he'd promised to do the majority of it.

The couple sort of mapped out their day over the delicious breakfast Weston had prepared. Jessica gave him an idea of some of the things she'd really like to see. The Metropolitan Museum, fondly referred to as the Met, was on her list. She also mentioned Central Park and Greenwich Village. He, in turn, made a few suggestions of New York's must-see attractions, such as the Statue of Liberty, Empire State Building and Times Square.

Once things were pretty much settled on, they took care of the kitchen duties.

As Jessica pulled on wool-lined leather boots over warm socks, she wondered where Weston was. She hadn't seen him since they'd come back to the bedroom to get dressed, over thirty minutes ago. He'd grabbed some clothes from the closet and had disappeared, but she hadn't expected him to be gone so long. He hadn't once taken this long to get dressed at her place.

Taking a survey of how she looked, Jessica peered into the full-length mirror. Her jeans were a bit wrinkled even though she'd hung them overnight. On the other hand, her heavy raspberry-colored wool sweater was wrinkle free. Since it'd be windy outside, she had brushed her hair back in a ponytail to wear under a sports cap. Her makeup, foundation and blush appeared flawless. She had yet to put on lip gloss. Jessica thought ChapStick might be a better choice for protecting her lips against the cold weather.

Weston came up behind her and wrapped his arms around her. "You're beautiful. Love the color of your sweater, the way it brightens your complexion."

Checking out his funky, trendy attire, she smiled at him in the mirror. "How hot are you? You're rocking those gray jeans, boyfriend." She leaned back and pressed her head against his chest. "You think I'm dressed warm enough?"

"It's all good. Your heavy jacket will help handle it."

She turned to face him. "Where were you? I missed you."

"Just handling some business. Are we good to go?"

Jessica didn't like his elusive response. Instead of commenting on it, she struck a seductive pose. "I'm so ready for New York City. Bring it to me."

Weston was glad Jessica hadn't pressed him on his whereabouts. He'd been busy on the phone making plans for the evening, wanting to surprise her with a special outing.

The couple had taken a break from touring the museums to eat in one of the popular eateries. Lucky for them, they were seated right away in a cozy pizzeria. The table for two looked out onto the street, where New Yorkers bustled by.

Jessica picked up the menu, though she had already decided on a vegetarian pizza. She asked that the onions be held. Her toothbrush and mouthwash were back at Weston's place. Giving him lots of kisses was definitely on her agenda.

"What do you think so far?"

"Everything's wonderful, so much history in this city. I love that. I've already learned plenty. Thanks for an exciting morning."

"We've covered a lot. Had enough for one day? Or do you want to continue?"

"Let's eat first. Then we'll see."

Jessica had fallen hard for Weston's city. To let him know or not was the question in her mind. She hadn't expected to fall in love like this, hadn't expected to be bowled completely over. The color and flavor of New York City had slipped into her spirit with ease. She had been claimed by a place she'd never thought she'd fit into, a world she'd only seen a fraction of. What else was in store for her? Lots more excitement, she hoped.

The city was so alive and it made Jessica feel just as vibrant. The sounds of lots of action had come at her from every corner. She had a keen ear and had picked up on many different vibes, mellow to funky. Tangible, soulful vibrations had reached out to touch her deep down inside. New York was a melting pot, with so many cultural offerings, endless attractions. Jessica couldn't wait for the next wildly awakening experience.

After hanging out in the city for another two hours, once they'd finished their meals, Jessica had experienced a lot of incredible things. Times Square had been a most amazing venture for her. She couldn't wait to see it lit up at night. After all the sightseeing, her feet hurt. Weston had massaged them for over twenty minutes, but they were still sore and tender. Her shoes had been comfortable, but she wasn't used to walking for hours on end. Weston had way more stamina than she did.

Stretched out on the bed in leopard-print lounging attire and fighting hard against the fatigue, Jessica felt sexy. Sexy with no man to share it with wasn't very hot. Weston had gone out, but he hadn't said where he was off to. He'd been acting so strange, making her feel he was hiding something. She hoped it wasn't a woman. *How awful would that be?* Just the thought of him with another female was unsettling.

No sooner had that last thought cleared her mind than Weston popped into the bedroom. Her eyes immediately went to the gift-wrapped package under his arm. He came around the side of the bed and leaned over to kiss her.

Weston handed Jessica the box. "For my sweetheart. I hope you like it."

Her hands trembled as she carefully dismantled the package. The paper was too beautiful to rip off and she was into recycling. She lifted out of the box the most beautiful purple dress she had ever seen. Getting onto her knees, she held the dress up to herself. "I love it. I probably shouldn't ask, but what's the occasion?"

As Jessica was about to put the dress back in the box, she spotted a long white envelope lying inside. Her name and his were written on it. She ripped open the envelope, with no thought of recycling it. She couldn't believe her eyes.

Weston had secured tickets for the Broadway play *The Color Purple*. The show was for tonight at eight. No use pinching herself. She was dead, already in heaven. Wonderful things like this didn't happen down there on earth. Not for her, not with a handsome, sexy man, a sensitive, caring man. This was a man who loved her—one who continuously proved it.

Tears streaming down her face, Jessica threw her arms around Weston's neck. "How did I get so lucky? Do I really deserve you?"

"You deserve everything you get. Model the dress for me?"

"Absolutely!" She picked up the off-the-shoulder dress, cut low in a V in front and back, and leaped off the bed. Before disappearing into the bathroom, she turned around and blew him a kiss. "I love you…and the dress. Thank you so much."

Jessica figured Weston was wondering why she hadn't put the dress on in front of him. It wasn't as if she hadn't dressed and undressed before him. When he saw it again, she'd be in it. He'd asked her to model it for him; he'd get just what he'd asked for.

Shoes. Jessica racked her brain to recall what shoes she'd brought with her. In basic black, the stylish crisscross pumps would work okay. She didn't have an alternative. If she could choose her footwear, she'd pick a lighter or darker shade of purple. A pair in silver or gold would also be nice. The dress could be dressed up or down. She preferred to gussy up completely for this special occasion. Her trillion-cut diamond pendant and earrings were the perfect accent.

Jessica poked her head out the bathroom door. "You'll have to wait to see the dress. I want to keep it a surprise."

"One good surprise deserves another." Weston was slightly disappointed, yet he knew she and the dress were a winning combination. They were made for each other, just like her and him. "Guess I'll have to wait."

"Guess so," she shouted, closing the door.

Jessica jumped up and down like a giddy little girl, enthusiastically clapping her hands together. She had had so much fun already. Weston kept her in awe. She loved being surprised by him. On the whole, she wasn't big on surprises. She liked to know exactly what was up, be aware of what was going on around her.

As she gave a couple of full turns in front of the mirror, she giggled. The dress looked super on her, a fantastic fit. He obviously knew how to pick women's attire; she hoped she and the dress dazzled him right out of his socks. "The color purple, royalty, majestic," she breathed. "Also the name of the much-heralded play."

Weston hadn't been able to keep his eyes off Jessica all evening long. Seeing the dress on her for the first time made him so proud of his choice. She was a stun gun in purple. And the out-of-this-world scent she wore drove him crazy. This particular fragrance was new to him, making his nose want to nuzzle her neck all night long.

To match Jessica's attire—and in honor of the special event—Weston wore a dark purple silk shirt and lavender tie and handkerchief. His sports coat and dress slacks were heather-gray. He looked debonair and she felt proud to be seen on his arm. Weston had had more than his fair share of intrigued glances from a host of beautiful women.

As she sat in a booth in one of the coziest, most elegant restaurants Jessica had ever patronized, bluesy lyrics had her happy feet tapping to the melodic music. Feeling all sorts of emotions, she stared into Weston's eyes. He was such a dynamic man. His desire to go beyond the norm to pleasure her made her feel so special. She wished she could bottle him for her exclusive use. Sweetness poured from his pure heart.

"How's your burger?"

She licked her lips. "Can't recall having one this good. What about your steak?"

"It's the main reason I eat here. Omaha steaks, some of the best beef money can buy. Wish you had ordered one."

"I just had a taste for a burger. I was surprised to see them on the menu of such a high-caliber restaurant."

"The place is upscale, but the food has that down-home quality. I come here often, too often, in my opinion."

"It's after midnight, yet it feels like early evening. We've had a busy day. I'm tired, but I'm not looking forward to it ending."

"You can say that again. I was glad when you didn't press me about where I'd been earlier. Shopping for your dress and picking up the theater tickets took longer than I thought. All worthwhile, though. The dress had to be perfect and the evening incredible. I believe I've achieved both goals."

"You have. No doubt."

"Want to dance?"

Jessica held out her hand. He got up from his seat and led her out to the small dance floor. The moment she floated into his arms, she felt his arousal. "Jess, my sweet Jess," he whispered into her ear, "you've no idea how much you turn me on."

"I think I do."

Serenity slipped over the couple while Jessica laid her head on Weston's chest. Dancing was the perfect ending to a perfect evening. There was more sightseeing to be done over the next couple of days, but if she didn't see another landmark she'd be satisfied. Just being with Weston was enough exhilaration for her.

Greenwich Village, Empire State Building, the Statue of Liberty, checking out the Apollo Theater in Harlem, a visit to the Bronx Zoo and shopping at Macy's overloaded Jessica and Weston's schedule over the next two days. She had also met all of his coworkers at his real-estate office. She had been treated in the same kind way as her office comrades had responded to him. She was made to feel comfortable and welcome by everyone on board. He had taken her to his favorite haunts for meals in between the tours, quaint restaurants and fun cafés located off the tourist route.

Seated inside the Hot Spot, which more than lived up to its name, Jessica and Weston had so far enjoyed all the karaoke performances. Up until now, everyone who'd dared to brave the ready-to-pounce crowd could sing like a bird. The guy currently onstage was either clowning or he was truly the worst singer in New York City. Surprising to Jessica was that people encouraged him rather than booing him off the stage. His version of Diana Ross's "Touch Me in the Morning" was horrendous.

"Want to give it a try?" Weston asked Jessica.

"Uh, you've got to be joking. I wouldn't even consider getting up there and making an utter fool of myself."

"Then I will." He got to his feet and left a shocked Jessica behind.

As the music to "Distant Lover" drifted into the room, Jessica nearly fell out of her seat. He looked poised and confident up there, arousing hope in her. Maybe he could really sing. Would he dare to get up there if he couldn't? They were all about to find out.

Not only could Weston sing, but he had a powerful onstage presence. With of catcalls and shrill whistles and loud screams, the ladies quickly let him know what they thought of his voice and his sex appeal. Marvin Gaye would be proud of the brother.

Weston was the hottest act in the Hot Spot thus far.

Jessica just sat there in complete awe, listening to her dream man crooning his heart out, his voice strong and smooth as velvet. The lyrics to the classic and their meaning slowly seeped into her mind, demanding she pay close attention.

Distant lovers categorized their situation best. The miles between them were many. She didn't fear the distance as much as she had initially, but deep concern remained. She had fallen hard for New York City and the boy from NYC, but could she actually live here on a permanent basis, if asked to? Jessica wasn't so sure about that. She positively loved Los Angeles. L.A. was home.

Just as Weston left the stage, to a standing ovation, he

blew a flurry of kisses to Jessica. Seeing the glint of her tears, he wondered if she was happy or sad. Had the lyrics to the song made her cry? It certainly hadn't been his intent. Happiness was all he wanted for her. Anything less than that was unacceptable.

Jessica remained standing. She went straight into Weston's outstretched arms the second he reached the table. "Bravo! You were wonderful up there. I had no idea my man could croon like that. You were exciting to listen to and to watch."

His expression was one of humility. "Thank you. I had a good time up there. Your gracious comments make me feel even better. A standing ovation, no less. Can you believe that?"

"I certainly can. You got just what you deserved. The ladies are wild for you."

"Only interested in what I do for one lady. Again, what *do* I do for you?"

She lifted his chin with a closed fist. "Keep me higher than a kite. I don't know if I'm coming or going half the time. You just do it for me. Period."

Weston's heart sighed as he kissed Jessica's mouth, wanting to do so much more to her. He could spend half the night telling her what she did for him. Whisking her out of there and right into his bed would do for starters. "I love doing it for you...and to you. The latter is my favorite."

"Mine, too," she said on a chuckle. "Do me when we get home?"

Did she say *home?* He twisted his finger around in his ear to make sure there wasn't a wax buildup. "We'll do each other. How's that?"

"Love the hot visuals I'm getting. Where'll we do it?" The finger gesture wasn't lost on her. He had heard her right. She *had* called his place home 'cause it felt like her home, bright, warm and cozy. He made her feel right at home. She now had two homes.

"Let's surprise ourselves."

"Let's. Speaking of surprises, here's a big one for you." Jessica got out of her seat and headed for the stage. She looked back. Smiling, she winked at him.

Jessica whispered her request to the guy in charge. The song should verify what Weston thought he'd heard: "A House Is Not a Home."

Jessica knew she was no Dionne Warwick or Luther Vandross, but she could hold her own. As she delivered the song provocatively, her eyes never left Weston's face.

Home, she thought. *Home is wherever my heart lies. My heart lies with Weston's.*

Chapter 15

Why'd it feel so strange to be back at home? Jessica had only been gone a few days, but it already felt as though something vital was missing. The place felt cold and lifeless even though she had turned on the heat to warm things up. She waited for the furnace to kick in, to no avail. It was still cold. She had to wonder why she felt so chilled.

Weston's absence. That was the only explanation for what she felt.

Good grief. You're turning into a lovesick puppy over him. How long have you lived without him? Long enough to not go into a tailspin when he isn't around.

Tell that to your heart. But...don't expect it to listen.

Suddenly feeling weary, Jessica dropped down on the mattress tiredly, her thoughts balled up in him. "Can I get a break?" She didn't want a break. "I want you."

Jessica smiled at the romance novel on the nightstand. She and Weston had a hot romance going, one that pretty much played out like the book. The couple in the novel also lived in separate states and had a problem with the distance between them. She had purchased the book after reading the synopsis, wondering how it turned out for the couple.

Where are you right now? What're you doing? Thinking of me, I hope.

Wondering how far her weary legs would carry her, Jessica looked over at the bathroom door. Maybe she'd just stretch out on the bed and let sleep claim her entire being. Sleep might come a lot quicker after a shower, a real steamy one.

Jessica barely had enough strength to lift the receiver. The hot shower had zapped away what little strength she'd had left. "I know it's you. Please be you. Maybe your sexy voice will snap me out of this."

"Sweetheart, I miss you."

She sighed. "We miss each other. Got in about an hour ago."

"I know. I wanted to let you settle in. I couldn't wait any longer. I need you."

"We need each other."

Weston laughed at her similar responses. "You sound so tired. Your answers are kind of strange and weary."

"I'm really exhausted. Making love to you always wears me out."

"Get used to it. Hey, babe, I'll call you back after you rest up awhile."

"Promise?"

"Promise." What was he to do with her? Love her with all his might. He hung up after telling her he loved her, reassuring her he'd call back. And he would keep his word.

Weston slowly unbuttoned his shirt. As he removed the rest of his clothes, he looked over at the bedside clock. It was 10:00 p.m. for him, 7:00 p.m. for her. A three-hour time difference between California and New York. When he pulled back the comforter, he spotted black lace panties. He didn't have to ask which of his women the panties belonged to. He only had one.

Weston hastily dialed Jessica's number. "Found something that belongs to you."

"I know. Enjoy."

"You left them on purpose?"

"Yeah, but they're clean."

He cracked up. "I know. Still, I'll enjoy them."

She took her turn to laugh. "Love you."

"More than yesterday?"

"More than when this conversation first began."

"That's my girl. You know what a brother needs and right when he needs it." He made a kissing sound into the phone. "I'll try not to call back anytime soon."

"Don't try too hard," she came back at him.

"Point well taken. Rest well. Dream of us making out in the backseat of your car." He couldn't help grinning as he hung up the phone.

Sweet Jessica, the woman he had forsaken all others for.

* * *

Do I even know what I'm doing? Jessica had to wonder. Love could hurt, even when it felt terrifically good. Love evoked tears and anguish and bitterness. And also laughter and joy, she reminded herself, unmitigated joy and uncontrollable laughter.

"Tonight" by Kem was now her favorite song, theirs. Her ears perked up as the tune gently stroked the airwaves. She could almost feel Weston's arms around her. He'd kiss her while they danced if he were there. The song had special meaning for them. It had become their theme song. They'd made love for the first time the first night they'd heard it.

Before climbing back into bed, Jessica made a couple of phone calls. She had called her parents the moment the flight attendant had permitted the use of cell phones. The safe-on-the-ground call had taken place while the pilot taxied to the gate. Her friends would also want to know she was back at home safe and sound.

Weston was puzzled by the doorbell ringing as he ran toward it. Rarely did he have visitors drop by without calling first. Then he thought of Sean Raymond, his best friend, who'd been working out of the country for a year, over in Iraq. Sean was a civilian contractor. It could be him since he was due back in town any day now.

Weston could have been toppled by a feather. "Long time no see, London Reese! What a surprise."

London stepped into the foyer. Her arms wrapped around his neck and then her lips met with his for a brief kiss. "I just moved back to NYC. And I'm free. Divorce is final and I am happily single again. It actually feels damn good."

"No visible wear and tear. Whatever's been going on with you, you look wonderful, London." He thought she was extremely attractive, still a bombshell.

Her dark eyes gave him the concentrated once-over. "So do you. Can we sit?"

Weston silently scolded himself for not minding his manners. However, he wasn't so keen on inviting the vivacious London in. "Sure thing. Come into the living room. Before we catch up on things can I get you something to eat or drink?"

"White wine, please. Pinot grigio if you have it."

"Coming right up." Weston took off, wondering where this visit might lead.

London picked up Weston's vibrating cell phone to take it to him. *Just answer it and take a message,* a clever voice commanded. She obeyed the command because she desperately needed to talk to him, without any distractions or interruptions.

Jessica Harrington. Where had she heard that name before? It sounded familiar, very much so. "Hello." Just in case Jessica was a rival, she had used her sultriest voice.

"Uh…uh, Weston…please," Jessica stammered, wondering what the woman behind the sexy voice looked like—and why she was answering her man's cell phone. She had called the cell only because she'd gotten a fax tone on his landline.

"Sorry, but he's in the shower right now. Can I take a message?"

Jessica was sure her heart had stopped. Breathing was suddenly difficult. The woman's comments as to Weston's whereabouts had given her the absolute chills. "No message. I'll…call back…later. By the…way, may…I ask… who… you are?"

"Perhaps you should ask Weston," she said, her chuckle throaty and wicked.

London smiled devilishly. She loved being a naughty girl. If Jessica was a love interest for Weston, then she had definitely created the beginnings of a romantic rift. If it was a business colleague… Oh well, they'd eventually reconnect. *The nerve of me!* To ensure that there'd be no more interruptions, she turned off his phone and dropped it behind one of the sofa pillows. Then London threw her head back and howled.

Weston came back. "What's so funny? I heard you from way down the hall."

"A private joke of a sort. I love it when I get the last laugh." She patted the sofa cushion next to her. "Let's get this reunion party going."

Raising an eyebrow, Weston handed London the glass of wine. He didn't take the seat next to her. Instead, he sat down on the arm of the sofa, at the opposite end. He had good reason to keep his distance from the sexy, beautiful London Reese.

London understood Weston's reluctance to get close to her. Finding her way back into his life would be difficult at best. He wasn't the type who got burned twice, and definitely not by the same person.

London brought Weston up to date on the past and current events in her life. As a CPA and a tax preparer, she had gone back to work for a large corporation. Her business had failed after two years. She was back at square one and trying to reestablish herself.

As she spoke of her divorce, her tone dropped a couple of decibels. Talking about her husband's countless infidelities was still painful. Weston wasn't the kind of man who'd maliciously point out to her that "what goes around comes around." He would never say she'd gotten exactly what she'd deserved—even if she had.

London had cheated on Weston with one of her ex-boyfriends, right after she and Weston had decided to date exclusively. He had been terribly hurt by it. She was sure he had felt pain and rage, but never had he privately or publicly displayed his emotions.

"Sounds like you've had a rough time. Sorry about that."

"I bounce back hard. You know me."

Weston didn't know London, not a bit, even to this day. He had thought he did. She was a slick one, too. Birds of a feather, he thought. An interesting mess occurred when the two hunters clashed. In the case of London and Dean, it sounded to him like two player-players had been involved.

"Where are you living?"

"A fantastic apartment complex not too far from here. It's nice." She giggled. "Actually, it's quite posh. You know me. Love the luxuries."

Why did she keep saying he knew her when he didn't? He didn't know her and he had no desire to get to know her.

"Hope you'll drop in on me sometime soon," London cooed flirtatiously.

Weston didn't respond to that. He had no intention of

dropping in on her or to have her continue to drop in on him. In fact, he didn't plan to see her beyond this visit.

"Are you romantically involved, Wes?"

"In love is what I am. That sweet, crazy kind of love."

Was Jessica Harrington the someone he loved? How interesting that would be.

"Are you guys living together?"

Weston shook his head. "She's an L.A. girl."

"Is she moving here to New York?"

"I wish. I don't think so, but the distance will get worked out. Rest assured."

"Sounds like you're willing to move to L.A." *Fat chance.*

"I'm actually considering it. My parents are moving back there also."

"I hope it all works out for you and J…your lady." *Oops, my mistake. Watch your mouth,* she told herself, cringing inwardly.

Weston looked curious, wondering about the *J* he'd heard her almost say. He could've sworn she was about to call out Jessica's name. But she didn't know Jessica, nor had he mentioned her by name. Just his imagination, he figured, perhaps the result of missing his lady so much. Or was it really his imagination? One could never be sure when London Reese was involved.

An hour later, when London finally stood, Weston was happy this little reunion was over. His mind was on overload from too much information. The lady had always loved to talk about herself.

Still upset from what had occurred earlier, Jessica totally ignored Weston's call. *Ask Weston indeed.* She'd die before she did that. The woman's voice had been laced with poison when she'd told her to ask him who she was.

It had to be someone close to Weston. Didn't it? A stranger wouldn't answer his cell phone. She had specifically said he was busy "taking a shower." The latter part bothered her the most, made her fearful and angry and jealous and sad and confused.

Jessica dialed the message center and put in her password. "Hey, I promised to call you," Weston said. "Maybe you're still asleep. If so, it's 'cause you need it. If you don't call back tonight, I'll understand. Know that I miss you, fiercely. Love you, Jess."

Jessica was just about to hang up when she heard music. Then Kem's voice came over the line singing "Tonight."

Deciding not to waste another precious second playing silly games, Jessica dialed Weston's home number. After only one ring, the voice mail picked right up, no fax tone. Wondering where he was, she chewed on her lower lip, her stomach queasy.

It was one o'clock in the morning in New York City.

"Wes, where are you?"

Though anxious to call Jessica, since he hadn't heard from her again last night, Weston refrained. It was too early yet. After taking the towel from his waist, he slipped on a pair of boxers. Once he put on his socks, he pulled on a pair of burgundy denim jeans and a gray-and-burgundy sweater. He often wore a sports jacket and an open-collar dress shirt to work, but he wasn't up for it today. Casual worked best for his dark mood.

Realizing his cell phone was missing, he looked around for it, trying to recall where he'd had it last. He searched for it for a couple of minutes before using the house phone to call it. He followed the rings, which led him into the living room. The ring tone was coming from the sofa. Once he moved the sofa pillows around, he spotted it, wondering how it had gotten there.

As Weston checked his cell for missed calls, London came to mind. Had she put his phone behind the pillows? That was a ridiculous notion, he decided. It had probably slipped out of his pocket.

Weston closed the blinds in his office. The sun was shining a little too brightly, threatening to lift his dark mood. Until he heard from Jessica, there'd be no light in his life. He had already lost count of how many times he'd phoned her. He was sick of hearing her cheerful message, wanting to reach through the phone and silence it. The recording of her voice didn't do for him what the real thing did. All he wanted was to hear her sweet voice telling him everything was all right, that she loved and missed him.

If only he could figure it all out.

Chapter 16

The night had been without end for Jessica. Each time she had fallen asleep it had only lasted twenty to thirty minutes. It was highly unusual for her to awaken all through the night. She was normally a sound sleeper. When she had managed to fall asleep a few times, the short naps had been fitful. Bliss was starting to turn to bitterness. The situation with Weston had her feeling bitter and blue even as she tried to rebirth hope.

Once again it appeared that their love affair was over. She had so many warm memories. But memories couldn't keep her heated up as physical contact did. Weston had become so important to her. She'd find herself figuring him into everything she desired to do. Was he still available to her? Or had he already checked out on her?

* * *

Lying across his bed, Weston was both worried about and also angry with Jessica. She wasn't answering her phone by design. Not one response from her to a single e-mail. If she was upset about something, he wished she'd just tell him about it. He wasn't a mind reader. No use continuing to rack his brain for answers that only she possessed.

"Finally, Jess. I've been trying to reach you for a long time." Weston's decision not to call her had lasted less than forty-eight hours.

Even though Jessica had known the caller was Weston, she was temporarily at a loss for words.

"Aren't you going to say anything?"

As if Weston could somehow see her, Jessica hunched her shoulders.

Pushing his hand through his hair, Weston sighed with frustration. "Can you please tell me what's going on? I can't figure this one out on my own. I've tried."

"Who is she?"

Weston figured he could feign ignorance. But he knew exactly whom she'd referred to. Deep down inside he'd been pretty sure London had had something to do with Jessica's odd behavior. "She's an ex-girlfriend."

Jessica was totally surprised by Weston confirming the relationship between him and this woman. His honesty had her groping for something appropriate to say. She swallowed hard, sweat popping out on her brow. "Are…you…or were…you in love with her?"

"I had thought I could love her. It didn't happen,

though." He went on to explain that London's cheating ways had brought their relationship to an abrupt end.

Jessica's heart actually went out to Weston. Then, when she thought of him showering naked in this woman's presence, her heart hardened all over again.

"London recently moved back to the city. She just dropped in to say hello. I can only guess that she answered my cell while I was out of the room."

"Out of the room showering? Her place or yours?"

"What?"

"Don't feign innocence. You know *what!*"

"Afraid I don't. If you're not willing to enlighten me, I don't know what to say."

"How about the truth?"

"The truth about what? I've already told you why she was at my place. I'm no mind reader. And why are you so insecure all of a sudden?"

"Insecure! I don't think so. You hang out with your ex-girlfriend—and I'm suddenly insecure. Is this a joke of some sort or what?"

"Sorry if I offended you, but you are acting so weird. It's ludicrous. You have a best friend who's madly in love with you, yet you begrudge me a few minutes in my ex's company. I didn't invite her here. Can you say the same about your boy, Jarred?"

"This is obviously not getting us anywhere. Call me back when you grow up." Incensed, Jessica slammed the receiver down, causing Weston to wince.

Well, he thought, their conversation certainly hadn't played out like that in his head. First of all, he had been surprised that she'd even answered the phone. Because she had, he had figured she was ready to cut through the silence. He had been wrong on all counts. Flying to L.A. was definitely out of the question now. They had made the phone connection, but it couldn't have gone any worse. He had made a valiant attempt to get through to her. Failure was his to claim.

Had she just sealed her fate with Weston? Jessica wondered, tears streaming down her face. Was he, too, through with her? One minute she had given him praise for his honesty and in the next one she was berating him, telling him to grow up. She could also do a bit of growing up. Her behavior was definitely juvenile and downright silly.

The conditions between them *had* gone badly in an instant, from worse to worst. She had been consciously rude in blurting out the very question she had planned to avoid like the plague.

Who is she?

As badly as Jessica had wanted to know the answer to her one burning question, she believed she could've found a more diplomatic way to inquire about the lady. Then she had had the nerve to shout at Weston to tell the truth, her gentler and roundabout way of calling him a liar.

Jessica shuddered as she recalled the anger in Weston's tone. It seemed that she wasn't the only bitter one. Bliss had gotten away from him, too.

Jessica crossed her legs and began to rehash all the experiences she'd had with Weston. She smiled softly. For the most part, their encounters had been wonderful. They had had a couple of snafus, but none too big for them to overcome.

Could they possibly conquer this one, too?

If Jessica didn't want Weston's ex around, and he did, wouldn't it be unfair of her to keep Jarred in her life? Jarred was only a friend to her, but his interest in her had changed drastically. Weston was well aware of the change. Would he be within his rights to demand that she cut Jarred out?

He would if he didn't have anything to hide, Jessica concluded.

Jessica tried hard to turn off her mind. Just thinking about all this bad stuff was painful. She would have to come to terms with Weston, one way or the other. They shouldn't leave things up in the air. That would only cause more devastation. This should be simple enough to resolve, but it wasn't. Stay together? Or go their separate ways?

Weston felt that Jessica was such a hypocrite. As he paced back and forth across his bedroom floor, he looked ready to explode. She wanted to keep a "friend" in her life, but wanted to dictate to him whom he could or couldn't have in his. He didn't want London in his life any more than Jessica did, but principle was involved here.

As Jarred had once told Jessica, she wanted to have her cake and eat it, too. Well, so did he. He also wanted the freedom to choose his own friends, exes or otherwise, and to spend time with whomever he so desired.

Had he and Jessica reached a stalemate? Possibly so, but only time would tell.

The first guests to arrive at Jessica's town house were Megan and her boyfriend, Rodney. While the two women took care of last-minute items out in the kitchen, he stayed behind in the living room to answer the door and to host the other arrivals. He was also given the job of stacking the CD player with music appropriate for the evening's festivities. The entire group was big on easy-listening music and jazz vocals.

As everyone sat around talking about their fabulous plans for Valentine's Day, Jessica had the strangest look on her face. Rodney and Megan were flying up to San Francisco to celebrate the lovers' holiday. Shauna and Beau had tickets to a Beyoncé Knowles concert, with dinner in an upscale restaurant before the megaentertainment. Melissa and Rich had reservations on a romantic dinner cruise out of Marina del Rey. Brandy and Ethan hadn't finalized their plans yet, but they were considering holing up in a boutique-style Santa Barbara hotel and ordering in room service.

Jessica couldn't help wondering what she and Weston would've planned had they been together. No doubt it would have been a romantic adventure. She fought off her emotions. No use crying over what was obviously never meant to be.

Chapter 17

Seated in front of the computer in her home office, Jessica was at her lowest point emotionally since she had last spoken to Weston. A few weeks had passed since that fateful day, but to her it seemed like an eternity. His handsome image popped into her head so many times in a single day that she couldn't even count them all. Getting him out of her mind was impossible. Getting him out of her heart wasn't something she even wanted to accomplish. True love couldn't be turned off so easily.

As Jessica scrolled down her dozens of personal e-mails, she spotted an e-mail address she'd never seen before. Normally she didn't open mail from unrecognized screen names, but this one aroused her curiosity: California Boy.

Jessica wasn't surprised to find herself wishing the

note was from Weston, but he certainly wasn't a California Boy. Jarred came to mind next, but he'd never e-mailed her under an alias. Besides, he had once again promised to accept her offer of friendship only. She loved Jarred dearly but only as a friend.

Jessica's heart belonged solely to Weston.

Seconds into the interesting read Jessica's heart began to flutter. California Boy was requesting a date with her on February fourteenth, Valentine's Day. The lovers' holiday was only a couple of days away, yet she didn't have a date. She had been asked out; she just hadn't felt romantic enough about anyone to accept.

It took Jessica a couple of minutes to figure out who S.A. was. She didn't know anyone with those initials. Secret Admirer was the only thing that seemed to fit. A night of dinner and dancing was promised, along with a limo ride to a fancy restaurant in L.A. S.A. would be there to meet her.

Feeling she should at least respond to the note, Jessica began composing her reply e-mail. Declining the invitation was the only course of action, since she didn't know the sender. Too many nutcases were running around for her to take a chance that the sender might actually be sane. Once she explained her position to S.A., she hit the Send button. Jessica couldn't help wondering if she would hear back from the mystery person behind the Valentine's Day invitation.

As the three-page letter Jessica had recently written to Weston popped into her mind, she retrieved her journal from the top of her computer desk. Tears formed in her eyes as she reread it. That she deeply regretted her decision to cut off communication with him—and her second thoughts on it—was the gist of the letter.

Jessica desperately wanted another chance with Weston and she hoped he'd give it to her. She ended the note by confessing how much she loved him and saying that she had forgiven him. Both of them had handled things badly.

"You've got mail" suddenly sang out from the computer, startling Jessica momentarily. A quick look at the screen let her know it was from California Boy. She couldn't believe how quickly he had responded. He must've been online already.

Dear Jessica:
Thanks for responding so quickly. I understand where you are coming from. I *am not* a crazy man and I *am not* a stranger to you. You *do* know me. If you will agree to go out with me on Valentine's Day, when the limo driver picks you up, he'll have solid proof of my identity. You *will* know who I am before you get into the limo. I'd never put you in harm's way. I hope you will trust me. If not, my heart will be deeply wounded.

The e-mail was signed S.A.

As Jessica's heart pounded faster than sound, she gave serious thought to what had been asked. If S.A. was willing to reveal his true identity before she got into the limo, she didn't see any harm in considering his proposal. However, she had to know exactly who her secret admirer was. For whatever reason, she believed it might be Weston. Since she couldn't be certain, she had to be careful not to set herself up for more heartache.

Only seconds after Jessica had sent her reply to Cali-

fornia Boy she received his return e-mail. He was happy
with her response and he promised her she wouldn't regret
her consideration. On the morning of February fourteenth
he'd also send her a huge clue about his identity. If she
didn't figure it out, the driver would reveal it.

Deciding not to dwell on this madness for another
second, Jessica got up from the desk and left the office.
After entering the master bedroom, she walked over to the
dresser and pulled out a clean set of underwear to put on
after her hot shower.

As soon as Jessica got out of bed on Valentine's Day,
she grabbed her robe and trudged down the hallway to her
office, where she quickly turned on the computer. This was
D-Day, the moment of truth. She could hardly wait to get
the clue that would finally reveal the identity of California Boy/ S.A.

Before opening the latest e-mail from California Boy,
Jessica sucked in a deep breath. The anticipation of its
content was so high it made her extremely nervous. As she
perused the short note, her hopes were quickly dashed.
There wasn't a single clue as to who he was. The e-mail
only let her know that the driver was to deliver a surprise
package containing information on his true identity.
Waiting a while longer wasn't a bit pleasant for Jessica,
but she was too curious to call it off now.

After viewing the package's content, you can either
make my day or make me feel like an absolute loser.
The decision is all yours, Jessica.
S.A.

In another rare event in her life, Jessica had taken off the entire day from work just to prepare for her date. It darn near took an act of Congress for her to miss work. In celebration of Valentine's Day, even before she knew she'd have a date, she had scheduled a spa appointment to include a facial, a full-body massage, a manicure/pedicure and a wash and set.

Jessica had also purchased a brand-new, sexy, fire-engine-red dress. If Weston turned out to be the mystery man, she had high hopes of setting a four-alarm fire at evening's end. If it turned out not to be him, she'd still love wearing the beautiful red dress that showed off her petite figure quite nicely.

The Pier 1 Imports box, decorated with a huge red bow, contained the first clue, a wooden travel-sized chess set. Jessica had beaten Weston at chess in Aspen. The night after they'd gone out for dinner and a movie, she had worn a custom-made T-shirt purchased from a shopping-mall kiosk. The shirt read I Beat Wes at Chess.

Jessica began to read the handwritten note she'd also removed from the package.

"I've always loved playing games with you, Jess. I hope you enjoy this one."

The handwriting on the parcel was another exceptional clue. Jessica would know that handwriting anywhere. Her breath caught as tears sprang to her eyes.

California Boy/ S.A. and Weston were the very same person. No doubt about it.

The music CD and the calla lilies, her favorite flower, were the final clues. The CD was labeled Made Especially for Jessica. Without hearing it, she was willing to bet it was a collection of the songs they had listened to in Aspen. Another note instructed her to give the CD to the driver to play on the way to the restaurant—and to bring along one change of clothing and her toiletry items.

Standing outside the limo, poised to get inside, Jessica handed the driver the CD and politely asked him to play it for her. He immediately agreed to do so. Once she was comfortably seated in the back of the black stretch, he offered her a glass of wine. When she accepted, he poured red wine into a crystal glass.

Settling into the driver's seat, he said, "Sit back and relax, Miss Jessica. I'll deliver you safely to your destination."

Ten minutes into the ride, the driver's cell phone rang. Upon answering the call, he nodded. "Yes, sir, we're already on the way. Will do, Mr. A."

Mr. A., Jessica mused, wondering what the single initial stood for. "Admirer," she quickly assessed, laughing inwardly. This was so exciting.

The chauffeur peered at Jessica in the rearview mirror. "The gentleman wants to know if you're okay, Miss Jessica."

"I'm just fine."

He reported Jessica's remarks back to Mr. A. After a few more words had passed between the driver and the caller, he hung up the phone. "Mr. A. will call periodically to see if you're okay. He wants to make sure you're comfortable. He also asked me to tell you he can hardly wait to see you."

Jessica smiled softly. "Same here. I guess it'll do me no good to ask for a name."

The driver laughed. "You're right. Besides, I only know him as Mr. A."

As the limo pulled up to the valet lane at the St. Regis Hotel, located in the heart of Los Angeles, Jessica gasped with excitement. Although she hadn't seen him yet, Weston was right there to open the door for her, holding on to a dozen red long-stemmed roses. As he presented the flowers to her, he lightly kissed her forehead.

The very moment Jessica's and Weston's eyes locked, she fell into his arms. Not a single word passed between the couple. Both were crying and laughing, all at the same time. All eyes were on the happy duo. Making a spectacle of herself wasn't an issue for Jessica at the moment. She couldn't care less who witnessed their amazing reunion, an awesome moment in time.

Weston had missed Jessica more than he'd ever thought possible.

The most secluded table in the house had been reserved for Weston and Jessica. Rose petals and tiny red, purple and gold foil hearts were strewn about the fine white linen tablecloth. A trio of red and white candles nestled in a triple crystal holder served as the centerpiece. The setting was absolutely breathtaking.

Weston sat across the table from Jessica and looked into her eyes, something he loved to do. Although he longed to be right next to her on the booth-style seating, inhaling her alluring scent, he thought he should give her some space.

Jessica folded her hands and placed them in her lap.

"I've been trying to date again, but can't get past my feelings for you. I'm only here because of this." She pulled out the letter and handed it to him. She had planned to read it, but she felt too nervous. "What are you *really* up to? Why are you here in L.A.?"

Jessica looked down at her trembling hands. "Maybe you shouldn't answer until after you read the letter. I wrote it shortly before I got the e-mail from you. I hadn't written in my journal since we last saw each other."

"Wow! That's really something else."

Several minutes into the reading Weston broke down emotionally. Jessica was close to losing it, too, but she somehow managed to hold it together. She had written the letter as though she had been talking to God and Weston at the same time. She had known all along that they belonged together, but fear had had her handcuffed. That was why she had asked God to show her some kind of sign. Reading in between the lines was what had nearly killed her. It had to be one way or the other between them, all or nothing.

Weston folded the letter and moved over to sit next to Jessica. After laying the papers on the table, he took her hand in his. "Do you want me to move to L.A.?"

Jessica's eyes widened with disbelief. "Of course I want that. When?"

Weston smoothed back her hair. "I'm flying back to New York tomorrow, on a late-evening flight. But I plan to move to Los Angeles in a month or so, permanently. Does that work for you?"

Jessica found it increasingly hard to hold it together so she let go of her pent-up emotions. Her tears fell furiously, her lower lip trembling uncontrollably. Weston's willingness to move to L.A. had her overwhelmed with joy. This was the stuff fairy tales were made of, yet it was happening to her and for her…and for him and for them.

Jessica kissed Weston softly on the mouth. "I can't believe this. I'd ask you to pinch me if I didn't think it would hurt." They both laughed. "Are you really moving to L.A.? Please tell me I heard you right."

Weston kissed Jessica back, passionately. "I wouldn't kid you about something so serious. I'm moving here just to be with you. Wherever you are is right where I want to be. Spend the night with me in my hotel room?"

Jessica quickly sobered at Weston's request. All she could think about was the last time they'd slept together. The sweet intimacy they had shared should've made it impossible for them to split the way they had, yet they'd done so anyway.

Weston quickly reached into his jacket pocket and pulled out a gift box. "I don't want you to spend just one night with me. I'm asking for a lifetime of nights. Will you marry me, Jessica Nicole Harrington? Please say yes!"

Jessica didn't need to see what was inside the gift box to make up her mind about marrying Weston. She wanted to be his wife more than she wanted anything else in this world. "Yes," she cried, "yes, I'll marry you!"

Since Jessica's hands were still shaking badly, Weston opened the gift box. As he lifted out the glass slipper, she felt breathless. A two-carat brilliant-cut diamond ring nestled inside the slipper on a bed of bright-red silk—the most breathtaking gem she had ever seen. Weston had outdone himself once again.

Weston slipped the ring onto Jessica's finger, kissing her gently. "Happy Valentine's Day, sweetheart! I promise to try and make every day of our marriage just as special as our engagement date, Valentine's Day. I love you, Jessica."

"I love you, too, Wes, with every fiber of my being. As for making our marriage special, that's something we both have to work on. I promise to do my part."

"I want to make you the best husband you could ever want. I already know you'll be the best wife. We can have a great life together."

Jessica cupped Weston's face with her two hands. "We can have it all. Just you and me, together forever, forsaking all others."

As if Weston hadn't already done enough for Jessica to try and make her Valentine's Day the best, he told her to get ready for the massage he had scheduled. It would be administered after she received a chocolate body scrub. He then handed her a basic black, one-piece bathing suit he had purchased for her.

Jessica had not a clue what a chocolate scrub was, but it definitely sounded scrumptious to her. Weston was a serious chocoholic so she was surprised he wasn't receiving a body scrub, too. However, he was joining her later for a fun dip in the hot tub. No sooner had she had changed into the swimwear than a knock came on the door. Since Weston had disappeared, she couldn't thank him for all the amazing surprises. Jessica ran to get the door.

Two extremely well-maintained, statuesque females entered the room after introducing themselves as Ingrid and Ana, from Sweden. The blondes were also rather pretty. Wasting no time at all, the two sexy-looking therapists went right to work on setting up the portable massage table.

In a matter of minutes, the therapists began working Jessica over.

Feeling utterly divine and totally relaxed from the serious work-over administered to her by the very capable Swedish therapists, Jessica plucked off the silver tray one of the chocolate-dipped strawberries. As she held the strawberry up to Weston's mouth, he bit a large chunk out of it. She sank her teeth into the other end, tasting it first and then consuming the remainder of the sweet, juicy fruit.

As Jessica's full, moist lips met with Weston's, she flicked her tongue across his lower one, tasting the sweetness of the chocolate left there. "Mmm," she moaned softly, "your lips taste divine."

Weston picked up another strawberry and held it over the wick of the candle until the chocolate began to melt. As he let the liquid drizzle onto Jessica's breasts, he had fun slowly licking off the sweetness, making her purr softly.

Weston looked deeply into Jessica's eyes. "Do you, Jessica Nicole Harrington, take Weston Roman Chamberlain to be your lawfully wedded husband?"

"I do," she breathed, trying hard not to giggle. Jessica rested her forehead against Weston's. "Do you, Weston Roman Chamberlain, take Jessica Nicole Harrington to be your lawfully wedded wife, to have and to hold, from this day forward?"

"I do," he whispered huskily, "always and forever."

"We now pronounce each other husband and wife," they said, sealing their vows with a staggering kiss.

As the steamy jets swirled and pounded around their nude bodies, Jessica settled herself onto Weston's lap. As if it wasn't hot enough in the hot tub, the heat flaming from their bodies, their skin slick with the expensive massage oils, had caused the water temperature to soar.

Jessica had made sure Weston's manhood was well oiled so the drying heat wouldn't affect their lovemaking. As he entered her molten treasure, their lips came together in a flesh-melting kiss. The sweet tension heightened, as they began riding the waves of their combined passion, not in any real hurry to reach the much sought-after pinnacle. While Jessica and Weston wildly heeded the call of their love-starved bodies, she knew she'd never get enough of the man she loved enough to marry. They could make love all night…and she'd still want more and more of him.

As the couple's world splintered into a million tiny fragments, their earth-shattering climax was more powerful than the first. They breathlessly screamed out each other's name, confessing their undying love.

Jessica and Weston couldn't wait for their magical fairy-tale day to arrive, the day they would finally enter into holy matrimony, into wedded bliss, forsaking all others…until death do they part.